WILDHEATH CRAGS

WILDHEATH CRAGS

DAVID BALDWIN

© David Baldwin, 2022

Published by Davroba Publishing

All rights reserved. No part of this book may be reproduced, adapted, stored in a retrieval system or transmitted by any means, electronic, mechanical, photocopying, or otherwise without the prior written permission of the author.

The rights of David Baldwin to be identified as the author of this work have been asserted in accordance with the Copyright, Designs and Patents Act 1988.

A CIP catalogue record for this book is available from the British Library.

ISBN 978-1-7396404-0-8

Book layout and cover design by Clare Brayshaw

Cover image Photo 54592521 © Solarseven | Dreamstime.com

Prepared and printed by:

York Publishing Services Ltd
64 Hallfield Road
Layerthorpe
York YO31 7ZQ

Tel: 01904 431213

Website: www.yps-publishing.co.uk

Preface

I have thought long and hard about whether I should write down what occurred during that bizarre week in Yorkshire almost a year ago. It is not something that I particularly want to recall, since I do not do so with any affection. Had I not had my unfortunate accident on the first afternoon, none of what follows would have taken place. Nevertheless, someone other than myself should be apprised of what did occur, even if it is merely to understand my current, confused state of mind and to determine how much of what I was told is true and how much is fiction.

What I am about to recount is to a large extent based on a number of anecdotes imparted to me during a series of encounters with four people. Although I made a few notes, I did not keep a journal but it has not been difficult to remember what was said or the order in which events unfolded. I have a very good memory for conversation, and the many interchanges I had could have taken place yesterday. However, I do not find it easy to put pen to paper at any great length. I have deliberated whether simply to present a moderately short, impartial account of what transpired, but this would not do justice to the pernicious atmosphere pervading my surroundings as I maintained a grip on reality. Accordingly I have tried to produce a narrative in the form of a factual novel outlining my muddled thought processes on each day, but my writing style may seem a little cumbersome, principally when I am attempting to reproduce anything other than straightforward dialogue. I am a practical man by nature and, in the fifty years since I left school, I have never had to write anything more thought-provoking than a run-of-the-mill, business performance report.

Finally, those who have expert knowledge of three nineteenth century novelists regarded as prime movers in important social change may take more than a passing interest in what I may have brought out of the shadows into the light of day. In so doing, I fervently hope that I have spared the three sisters an affront to their hitherto stainless reputations.

Douglas Lockwood

June 2016

CHAPTER ONE

Sunday

"Christopher's house had an outside toilet," she began, looking at me out of the corners of her eyes to see if I was really listening. "It was one of the reasons why he started smoking. He was a sensitive lad with a skin as thin as tissue, and he couldn't bear the thought of the humiliating jibes he'd receive from his middle-class, grammar school classmates if they ever found out. 'It's one of those, is it?' one such young buck had sneered tactlessly when he arrived for a sleepover. 'Do you keep coal in the sideboard as well?' Fortunately the toffee-nosed boy was one of Christopher's best friends and he wasn't a blabbermouth. You see, there was no upstairs room with a plumbed-in bath, a freestanding wash basin and, the thing that mattered most to him, an internal lavatory. His was in an outhouse in the backyard next to the cubby hole where the dustbin was kept. Everyone else in his form at school lived in posh semis with a bathroom and a modern loo in avocado, orange or pink. He was a working class boy and he felt like an outcast, haunted constantly throughout his teenage years until his parents applied for a local council grant to have a bathroom installed. But by then it was far too late. He was twenty one years old and he'd already left home for university. This is his story and it will explain all there is to know about him."

I was sitting in the lounge of my hotel in Watholme (pronounced '*Wottem*' before I forget), a bleak moorland village in West Yorkshire, laid up after a fall whilst out walking. It was the last Sunday in September 2015, the twenty seventh to be precise, and the dark nights were drawing in rapidly. As it was so late in the year, the hotel was almost empty, and a woman, Jane Dean by name, receptionist by trade, was keeping me company.

Foolishly I had ignored the weather forecast when, shortly after arriving, I set out to explore the nearby moors and I was caught in a sudden, heavy cloudburst in the middle of nowhere. I lost my bearings clambering down an almost vertical bank thick with treacherously brittle heather, and I went over on my right ankle. I was still on the ground in considerable pain when a gaunt, young man with shoulder-length hair came running through the rain and helped me back to civilisation, whereupon he vanished into the murk just as quickly as he had emerged from it. Despite being wet through, I telephoned for an ambulance immediately and spent the rest of the afternoon in hospital having ice packs applied to the sprained ligaments, after which my ankle was bandaged with what the nurse called a 'compression wrap'. She also informed me light-heartedly that if I ever recovered from pneumonia I would be unable to walk for at least six days and, extremely infuriatingly, drive my car, but she had helpfully made arrangements to have my ankle re-examined the following week at a hospital near my home in Chester.

When I returned to the hotel on crutches, I told an anxiously waiting Jane what had taken place and she turned ashen pale as I outlined the afternoon's events. She said that she had an idea who the mysterious man might be from my vague description of him. I had been unable to make out his features clearly because my spectacle lenses were spattered with rain, and I thought no more of it until she came and sat opposite me when she had finished her shift at nine o'clock that evening and launched herself into the story of 'Christopher'.

"As a youngster, he lived in a two-up-two-down, sandstone, terraced house at the edge of Oakgrove, a small conurbation that had sprung up at the end of the nineteenth century to become a suburb of Boughton, which itself was developing rapidly into an industrial town," she continued. "Boughton's pronounced 'Bothton' by the way, 'both' rhyming with 'cloth'. You can tell immediately that you're dealing with a stranger when you hear it called 'Bowton' or something equally alien. What once had merely been a collection of farm workers' cottages in open countryside near a wide river meandering through lush, green meadows, grew almost overnight by today's standards to meet the housing requirements of an unprecedented influx of tradesmen and manual workers in the mid-nineteenth century. Oakgrove or 'The Grove', as it came to be called by the locals, was situated north of the town centre two thirds of a mile away, and it had been built half way up a steep hill which flattened out into the basin of the glaciated valley through which the river ran. Close by, at the top of the street was a main road and at the bottom there was a railway line running, at this point, alongside the river. Rows of similar houses stretched away in parallel, cobbled streets, bisected by a central access road, for over a third of a mile until they ended asymmetrically at the far side where a Methodist chapel and a rambling, age-old cemetery were to be found. The graveyard's close proximity to a railway, a road and a river made it perfect vampire country according to a book Christopher read on the supernatural when he was ten years old, and he never went near it after sunset. As if to intensify this sinister atmosphere, at the far side of the railway line, accessed from one of the streets by an under-bridge passage, was a 'dark, satanic', woollen mill which, by dint of its totally incongruous location, added a spine-tingling, Gothic element to the semi-rural setting for anyone who had a fertile imagination."

At this stage of the story, I was most impressed by her eloquence and her remarkable facility for naturalistic detail delivered with only the faintest of traces of the Northern accent I assumed she would possess. It sounded as if she had told this tale several times before and had polished it almost to perfection. I could have been listening to a programme on the radio had she not been there in the flesh leaning back in her armchair. She was a small, plump woman, somewhere between sixty and seventy years old, her neat, grey hair done up in a bun, complementing perfectly her black receptionist's uniform, shoes and stockings. Her round face was rather flabby and her dark eyes were slightly hollowed, making her look stern. She might have been attractive as a young woman but time and gravity had inevitably taken their toll. Or perhaps it was something else, the harsh environment in which she existed, for instance.

"The house had two bedrooms," she went on, staring ahead of her as if she was studying the building itself from an estate agent's perspective, "the larger of which he shared with his two brothers, a reasonably-sized living room, and a small kitchen at the rear which also served as a washing place. Beneath these was a cold, damp cellar, which often flooded in wet winters due to rain-swollen, subterranean streams running down the incline. It was here that his weekly all-over scrub took place, weather permitting, in a metal bath filled with tepid water brought down from the kitchen in a steel lading can. A short passage led from the living room, past the kitchen to the right and the cellar door on the left, to a flagged yard at the rear which housed the dreaded privy. At the front was a well-kept, flower garden which, in the height of summer, resembled a miniature jungle of roses, lupins, marigolds, foxgloves, antirrhinums and small wallflowers and gave the impression of urban respectability. Incidentally, he'd not always lived there."

She paused again and shook her head. Her attention had been caught by something behind me and I turned round in my armchair to see a middle-aged woman who was waving at her from the foyer. Jane waved back, then she shook her head again and looked me full in the face.

"That's my sister, Agnes," she said, almost apologetically. "She works here as a Jill-of-all-trades and like me she lives in. When the restaurant shuts, she goes out for a breath of air, no matter what the weather. Now where was I?"

"You were going to tell me where Christopher lived before he lived in, er, Oakgrove, was it?"

"Thank you. Until he was eight he lived up here in this rugged, wind-swept village, in a similar stone-built terraced house with one major difference: it had a bathroom and an inside lavatory. Christopher's earliest memories were therefore mainly very happy ones. He had loving parents who doted on him and his two younger brothers, although at times they could be harsh disciplinarians on the rare occasions that trouble brewed. You won't be aware of course that Watholme resembles a much larger version of Oakgrove, in that it was built on the steep slopes of a valley bisected by a small river flowing next to a now disused railway line. As you discovered this afternoon, it's surrounded on three sides at its summit by vast tracts of craggy moorland, and it would be an isolated, harshly rural settlement if it wasn't connected on its northern edge to the sprawling conglomerations of rundown terraced houses, factories, shops and pubs that line the sloping descent to Boughton town centre four and a half miles away. Watholme itself nestles in a shallow glen at the summit of the southern incline of the glaciated valley in which Boughton itself is located. All the houses here were small and built from sandstone which had become blackened by soot as the years of coal-fuelled enterprise rolled by and many of the roads that weren't dirt tracks were still cobbled. A few more years would pass before Mr Macadam's boys were seen here in large numbers. The native folklore said that it often snowed in summer such was the severity of the prevailing climate. In the eighteenth century life expectancy had been very short and anyone who reached the age of forty was regarded as old – and very lucky. Some of the modern intellectuals even believe it was called 'the metropolis of the moors'. I hope that's a joke, because it was and always has been a largely inhospitable place. Yet it had a certain austere charm and many outsiders, braving the harshness of the elements and the prospect of being soaked to the skin, or, at worst, frozen to death, came to spend a few days here, more often than not to challenge themselves on the unforgiving, windswept moors. They also had to contend with the frostiness of the welcome they received from the dour inhabitants who regarded strangers as meddlesome intruders and hence not to be engaged in any kind of meaningful conversation. It was like this in the nineteen fifties and it hadn't changed much from pre-industrial times. It liked its privacy, which is no bad thing."

"But Watholme isn't like that anymore," I said, trying to avoid a tone that might offend her. "There are lots of charming, little shops and restaurants and at least four hotels, not including this one. Hundreds of thousands of tourists come here every year to see the village where the world-famous Ayre family lived. Many others like me come to walk on the moors. Don't you approve of how prosperous the place has become?"

"Ah yes," she laughed. "You've caught me out. I prefer to think of it as it was when I was younger, how it always had been and how it always should be. Many people think it's far too commercial nowadays. When I was a girl, there was one café, and the few shops that there were sold food and other things that we needed, not antiques, tatty souvenirs and magical pieces of rock. As for the authors, well, they're massively overrated, especially the oldest one, Catherine Ayre. She's mostly unreadable in my opinion. Her other two sisters didn't produce much, half a dozen novels between them and a few slim volumes of mediocre, self-indulgent poetry. They've been dead for donkeys' years, anyway. But the biggest farce of all is that the cottage where they lived doesn't exist. It burnt down over a hundred and fifty years ago and all that's left is that silly memorial stone across the road from here. To cap it all, it isn't the site of the original house either. This hotel is where it once stood, but they wouldn't put a plaque on an unexceptional structure like this, would they? If it hadn't been for those meddling, self-styled women's libbers back in the sixties who popularised the three writers again, very few visitors would come here, just as only a handful go to Knutsford in Cheshire each year to see where Mrs Gaskell lived as a child."

"I'm from near there," I said, grateful to have something to agree with. "I suppose you're right about Mrs Gaskell. That's probably because I happen to have heard of her but I didn't realise she was from Knutsford.

I thought she hailed from Manchester. That's where her house is. Even so you make most of your money from tourists, don't you?"

"The hotel seems to attract walkers like you generally, probably because it's closest to the moors, but they don't tend to spend much and they drag their filthy boots all over my carpets," she said, dismissing my crass comment with an impatient frown. "Some of them even injure themselves as well. However, let me continue with my story. It was in this grim, *middle of the twentieth century* environment that Christopher spent his early childhood, although by then, things were beginning to change as the young and newly-married baby-boomers moved in, seeking to take advantage of the low cost of housing compared to prices down in Boughton. The house he lived in was a three storey, back to back, stone-built, terraced dwelling which had been *modernised*. It consisted of a living room and a tiny kitchen, above which was a bedroom as well as the bathroom, and, further up, an attic. There was also a large cellar where, according to his father, a horrible monster called Murrr (spoken softly but in a guttural voice like I'm attempting to do now) dwelt unseen. Young Christopher was scared stiff of going down there on his own and it was the source of his first ever nightmare. He was woken one night by Murrr who was standing in the doorway of his bedroom, and when he tried to call out for help, he couldn't make a sound. Obviously he was fast asleep, shouting at the top of his voice, and he was very relieved when the bogeyman disappeared to be replaced by the comforting face of his worried mother."

Before I could react, she stood up and slowly smoothed her skirt. I was immediately struck by how frail she looked, as if recounting Christopher's life history was gradually sapping her strength.

"I'm thirsty," she said. "Would you like some liquid refreshment?"

"I'll have a pint of bitter please, to ease the pain," I replied. "Whatever you've got that isn't too gassy."

"I'll have something a bit stronger, just to wet my whistle, mind you," she said with a wry smile. "I'm not an alcoholic, you know."

She went off to the bar, a faded, ornate, semi-circular counter, behind which were two old-fashioned beer pumps (mild and bitter), three optics and an array of shelves containing several bottles of wines and spirits. It had probably been like that for the last fifty years. She returned a few minutes later with my drink and what looked like a large whisky and dry ginger for herself on a tray which she carefully placed between us on the low-level table.

"We keep the bar open until late," she said as she plonked herself down again. "It's my turn to be on duty and I may be called away from time to time. The next phase of Christopher's life is very crucial so I hope there aren't too many interruptions."

This was a peculiar statement to make, I thought, since I had not seen anyone other than myself in the hotel all evening.

"Is it a long story?" I asked, uncertain what I was in for.

"Oh yes," she replied rather irritably. "As long as you want it to be. Reality has no well-defined beginning or end, it just continues. It's a good job you're booked in for a week because there's no way that you'll be able to hike or drive anywhere. You can stop me whenever you've had enough."

"I didn't mean to be rude," I said, blushing. "It's very interesting. Please carry on."

"Christopher was a beautiful baby and he was perfectly formed," she resumed, her good humour restored. "All the neighbours admired him, and once, when on his first holiday in a seaside boarding house, he was actually mistaken for a little girl. That's not to imply that he was effeminate. Far from it. It demonstrates rather that he was very handsome, and you should always bear this in mind."

She bent forwards and picked up her glass and raised it in front of her face. I had my beer in my hand and I smilingly acknowledged her toast.

"Cheers!" she said cordially. "Here's to a good holiday despite the unfortunate drawback. Right, let's get back to young Christopher. He could only remember two things before he started primary school. The first was 'Coronation Day' when Queen Elizabeth II succeeded her late father, George VI. He went to a jam-packed, communal party in some large hall or other down in Boughton, where he was given jelly and ice cream, a union jack flag and a commemorative silver crown in a plastic box. I've still got mine in some drawer or other. The second significant incident involves a train, his father and another character, Pip, a black and white cocker spaniel. Pip was his mother's dog. It had moved in with the newly wedded couple and it was the household favourite until Christopher came along. By then, however, it was getting on in years and was going blind. Add to this the highly strung nature of the breed and an accident was waiting to happen – and it did one dark, winter night. The family, who'd been visiting their relatives in Oakgrove, had travelled home from Boughton on the last train. As they were getting off, the engine's boiler safety valves opened and a sudden, ear-splitting roar drowned out all the other, more commonplace sounds. Pip panicked and dragged so hard on his lead that he broke free from Christopher's father's grip and bolted along the platform – and off up the line into the infinite darkness. The guard was summoned and the train was held whilst he and Christopher's father went in search of the terrified dog. Luckily it hadn't gone far. It couldn't see where it was going and it had laid down on the track about two hundred yards ahead of the engine. It went to the vet one last time a few days later. Christopher cried. RIP Pip."

She paused yet again, this time to take another sip of her drink. The weather had taken a turn for the worse and the rain was lashing against the window panes to my right. It was pitch black outside and, apart from the splashes on the glass, all I could see was a distorted reflection of the lights illuminating the room in which we were sitting.

"I hope your sister took an umbrella," I said. "She won't have gone near the moors, will she?"

"She knows her way around," she rejoined waspishly. "Besides she loves the wind and the rain. I expect she's prowling through the village and looking in the shops. She's not afraid of the dark like some people I know, Mr Lockwood."

She yawned and picked up her glass and drank what was left in one gulp. It was getting on for ten o'clock and I began to wonder if she had had a long day. Nevertheless she pressed on with what was becoming a tediously convoluted account of the young man's early life. What was the point of it, I asked myself?

"Everyone can recall their first day at school," she said. "It's one the most significant rites of passage in the transition from irresponsible, carefree infancy to the first taste of the institutionalised, cast-iron discipline of childhood. Well, it seemed something like that then, before the advent of less formal, 'progressive' education, as they call it. All Christopher's playmates were as excited as he was as they skipped along, together with their mothers, on the short walk through the park and down the hill to meet the teacher of the infants' class, a diminutive, gnome-like spinster in her early fifties. That morning she was all sweetness and light as she showed the new intake around the playground and the spotless room that was to be their base. Christopher was thrilled. There was a wooden climbing frame, a sand pit and a reduced-size football cum netball pitch in the enclosure reserved for the five year olds, and all manner of toys, pictures and books in cupboards and specially laid out on the desks in the classroom. At the end of the tour, the gnome clapped her hands.

'Now children, choose a chair to sit down on and say goodbye to your mothers,' she drooled. 'They're far too big to stay here with us.'

Little, blond-haired, blue-eyed Christopher didn't hear this smiling instruction and, as he saw his mother leaving the room, he ran after her and grabbed her hand.

'Where are you going young man?' shouted the gnome, trying to sound like a good-natured pixie but not managing to sustain the pretence. 'Sit down on the nearest seat this minute.'

'I like playing here but I'm going home with my mummy,' came the innocent reply. 'I want to play with my soldiers now.'

Everyone laughed except the gnome, but she pretended it was funny, although, as Christopher was to soon find out, she already had it in for him. Sure enough, as time passed, another incident took place, one which was to have long-lasting consequences for his personality. It occurred during an unusually warm, fine afternoon in

October and the whole class had been outside collecting 'things from autumn' to draw. He was sitting at his table working on a painting of a desiccated sycamore leaf, next to his best friend Alan. The desks in the classroom were arranged in three sides of a square, in a sort of u-shape, and Christopher sat at the end of one line, facing the blackboard. He was aware that Janice Fisher, a frisky, spiteful girl if ever there was one, who had become his deadly enemy, wanted to sit next to Alan too. I believe, even at that age, she fancied him. When Christopher stood up and sloped off to a sink in the corner by the windows to refill his jam jar, she speedily moved her things onto his desk and threw his picture onto the floor. More pertinently she sat herself down on *his* chair and immediately started giggling.

'Miss, miss, Janice Fisher's sitting in my seat,' he wailed.

The teacher saw that Janice had indeed moved but, instead of rebuking her, she turned on him.

'Pick up your picture, sit down over there and get on with your work,' she growled. 'Go and sit in Janice's seat and don't be such a cry-baby.'

He fumed. He was the injured party and he was made to look like a whinging tell-tale. Worse was to come. Janice proceeded to wet herself all over his chair. Perhaps it was the excitement of getting one over on him that caused the mishap or perhaps she was marking her new territory. But girls don't do that. That's what the male of the species is for. The next thing he saw, as he stood transfixed at the injustice doled out arbitrarily by a biased, old witch, was Janice gathering up her things and trying desperately to return to her original desk. He was furious.

'Miss, miss,' he screamed. 'She's pissed all over my seat.'

'You foul-mouthed boy,' the evil goblin bellowed, her face strained and white with anger. 'What have you done, you stupid nincompoop? You've spilled water everywhere and you're trying to blame Janice? You're a liar as well. Go and find a cloth and wipe up your mess immediately. Then you can stand in the corner and recite one hundred times *girls are made of sugar and spice and all things nice, but boys are made of slugs and snails and puppy dogs' tails.*'

The girls in the class howled with laughter, but the boys didn't. That stupid woman had just created more than a dozen male chauvinists there and then. It took a long time for Christopher to get into her good books after that, but he did so eventually, purely by being the cleverest boy in the class. The gnome didn't turn out to be too bad after all. Her main responsibility, apart from settling them into the school's routines, was to teach the little ones how to write using a rectangular slate and a stick of chalk. Christopher loved it and he quickly excelled. He was particularly fascinated by the letter 's', chiefly because he could make a hissing sound and get away with it. He learned quickly that behaving himself and doing as he was told worked wonders with her, but if anyone stepped out line they were for it, especially the boys."

The wind was getting up, the bar lights flickered alarmingly and her flow was interrupted by something sounding like a large branch smashing against the window outside. She winced at this eerily disconcerting thud, and she stared at me to see if I had flinched too. However, my mind was elsewhere, dredging up similar examples of the negative influences of primary school teachers on working class children in that era of educational history.

"And so it was that, after his first year was over," she continued as if nothing had happened, "he bade her a cheery goodbye and after the summer holiday was over, he entered the reading class where he made the acquaintance of Miss Ada Barfield. She was another formidable, middle-aged spinster, but, if Christopher had ever felt intimidated by the gnome, it was nothing compared to the very physical presence of this unique, Dickensian individual. She wasn't what you'd call hefty but she was, to put it mildly, exceedingly difficult to look at. Her hair was a greasy, brown mess and she wore her national health spectacles provocatively on the end of her nose, which, upon first meeting her, immediately gave her an imperiously authoritarian demeanour. Her most striking feature was unquestionably her large mouth, which was framed by two fleshy lips and contained the biggest pair of ill-fitting dentures ever manufactured. Her voice was, to say the least, stridently stentorian, and as she spoke her false teeth moved about in her mouth so that her words were interspersed with a series of chillingly sinister clicks. Consequently there were no complications with discipline and she could get on with her job without any fear of disruption. To say that the children were scared of her is a massive understatement bordering on absurdity. After a few weeks she divided them into smaller groups according to the speed in which they learned to recognise words without much effort and this quickly led to their being allocated more or less to their future occupational categories and social standing. The quickest and most fluent were placed in the 'top group', those who stumbled over a few of the longer words or whole sentences were placed in the 'second group' or the 'third group', and those who struggled with most words – or wondered what all the squiggles on the page were –

were placed in the 'dunce group'. Each set of pupils sat at a separate table from the others and there was some movement between the tables as the weeks rolled by in a sort of promotion and relegation system. 'Come out the dunce group,' was invariably greeted with tittering and braying noises as the procession of misfits, some with snot hanging from their noses, trudged each morning to the front of the classroom to be ritually humiliated. No one ever forgot Miss Ada Barfield. This was, however, by no means the most bizarre example of her draconian, Victorian behaviour. There was yet another spectacular eccentricity: she possessed an extraordinary weakness for confectionary of all sizes and descriptions. Each morning after she'd taken the register she would ask in her most soothing voice: 'Now children, has anyone brought any lunch?' By 'lunch' she meant snacks for the morning break. During the first few days of their enforced stay in her classroom, those of her new charges who had brought sweets and biscuits and such like dutifully put up their hands. 'Be good boys and girls and bring it out to the front,' she trilled, smacking her thick lips. 'I'll keep it safe for you.' The rest of the morning until playtime two hours later consisted of a succession of children reading aloud to her at her desk. As they droned on through each pre-selected passage, she would carefully choose either a chocolate bar, a packet of crisps or a cream bun from her 'safe' store and munch and click her way through it. No one whinged to their parents. Luckily the children sussed this quickly and foiled her by refusing to admit they had any 'lunch', or by stopping bringing snacks altogether. Christopher was in the 'top' group and never took sweeties to school. Miss Barfield took a shine to him because he was an honest, angel-faced boy and the best reader in her class. He had curly, fair hair, blue eyes and the most gorgeous, little face you could imagine."

From somewhere outside I heard a long, drawn-out wailing sound as though some unfortunate person or some wild animal was in terrible pain. Jane recognised at once my temporary distraction and offered an obvious explanation.

"It's the wind, Mr Lockwood," she said gravely. "In these parts it blows constantly, usually accompanied by incessant rain. It's because we're high up in the hills. It can knock wheelie bins over and devastate trees and gardens. Sometimes it damages buildings. You'll get used to it. There's also another explanation but you'll have to wait and see what that is. It might include you, which is why I'm telling you this story."

"I'm not sure I *will* get used to that noise," I replied, shuddering. "I'm sorry I've stopped you again in full flow."

"The following year he had a new teacher, who taught Christopher his times tables," she went on, raising unsympathetic eyes to the ceiling. "He could have recited them at any time of day, probably in his sleep. If you asked him what nine sevens are, he would have instantly answered 'sixty three' without a pause for thought or a request to repeat the question. He learned them to the beat of a ruler drummed on the top of a desk. 'Tap-tap-ta-tap, tap-tap-ta-tap, tap-tap-ta-tap', that's how it went, from one to twelve right through each of the tables. 'One two is two', 'two twos are four'…'two twelves are twenty four'. His teacher was the youngest in the school, straight out of training college. She was also very pretty. Yes, Miss Helen Mountjoy was a stunner. Every child adored her because, not only was she easy on the eye, she didn't threaten them in any way. She read the works of the most famous children's authors to them in the afternoon to make up for the arduous mathematical problems (or 'sums') she set them in the morning. That was when they weren't painting whatever they wanted, real or imagined, or writing about whatever took their fancy. Christopher wrote the most exciting stories as well as excelling at mental arithmetic. Miss Mountjoy liked him because he was, you guessed, the best in the class and by far the best looking.

'It's your turn, Christopher,' she would say in her sing-song voice. 'What number is five times seven add eight minus thirteen, then times three?'

'Ninety!' came the instant response. Whatever fairly complex combination of numbers she asked him to calculate in his head, he was always correct."

"He must have been a *very* clever boy, then," I said, hoping that I had not spoken out of turn. "Did he become someone famous?"

"You'll have to wait a while for an answer to that question," she grinned. "If you're still keen tomorrow, I'll move on to the second part. Meet me here again after lunch at, say, two o'clock. I'm doing the early shift in the morning and I should be free by then. Meanwhile I'll give you a preview, although you'll have to judge whether I'm just whetting your appetite for more. When he was eight years old, he had to say goodbye to the school he loved during the spring term of his third year and move down to Boughton. On his last day there, the day before the removal men came, his parents received a letter from the headmaster, Mr Trueman, asking them to call to see him. His mother, who didn't work, had to go alone, fearing that Christopher had done something so awful that she had to be notified in person. Mr Trueman, a quiet-spoken, charming, old gentleman, offered her a cup tea and put her at her ease immediately.

'Thank you for coming, Mrs Heath,' he said reassuringly. 'I wish to tell you something about your son while I still have the chance. He's the most intelligent boy we've had at this school for some time. He has a first-rate brain and he'll go far in this world. He's also a very nice, quiet, helpful lad and all his teachers will miss him.'"

At this juncture, Jane stood up and stretched her body overdramatically, raising her arms high above her head.

"We'll leave it there, Mr Lockwood," she said as she stooped to pick up her empty glass. "I'll fetch you another beer before I go. When you've finished it, please leave your glass on the table and my sister will clear it away when she gets back."

CHAPTER TWO

Monday Afternoon

Let me say straightaway that I was totally perplexed by Jane Dean's outlandish behaviour on that first evening in The Green Man, the name of the hotel in which I was staying. My injured leg would give me plenty of time to evaluate why she had chosen to embark on what was no doubt intended to be the opening chapter of an exceedingly comprehensive history of the anonymous young man who had to all intents and purposes probably saved my life, which is doubtless why she said it might include me. Yet somehow it had turned out to be little more than a sketchy series of disconnected excerpts, and I was uncertain whether she was always referring to the same chap.

After I finished my beer I dragged myself off up to bed and spent an uncomfortable night trying fruitlessly to establish a suitable position in which to fall asleep with a tender, aching ankle. I'm a little overweight with quite a large stomach (hence my choice of a walking holiday) which intensified the pain every time I moved about on the mattress, despite the presence of a cardboard box lifting the duvet clear of my injured foot. At my age – I'm sixty six – I also needed to go to the lavatory, from memory two or three times, which necessitated struggling out of the bedclothes and hobbling off in my dressing gown down a chilly, poorly illuminated passageway to the communal bathroom on the landing at the top of the stairs. Once or perhaps twice I also heard shuffling noises and alarmingly hollow footsteps from somewhere above me, although I was not aware that the hotel had three storeys.

In retrospect I was regretting that I had selected this particular hotel. I chose it from the tranquil convenience of a tourist guide on the internet, since it was – as Jane had said – the closest one to the moors and above all the cheapest. It was predictably an old-fashioned, no-frills sort of lodging house, the kind that had offered me a spotless, single room consisting of little more than the basics required for a short holiday: a crisply clean bed, a small freestanding wardrobe, a dressing table and an armchair which had seen better days, but no mod cons such as a television or Wi-Fi.

Likewise, the layout of the hotel was uncomplicated: on entering there was a reception desk with the small, nineteen seventies style bar on its left, in between which there was a short passageway leading to the staircase to the upper floor. The lounge where I had spent most of the evening was on the right, made up of twenty or so fairly shabby, upholstered easy chairs arranged at right angles to each other around five or six low-slung coffee tables. There were numerous black and white photographs of rural Yorkshire on every wall. A narrow archway led to the breakfast-dining room at the rear of the building.

Upstairs there were twelve bedrooms, some of which were en-suite I expect, as the communal bathroom would hardly have served the needs of twenty or more guests. The wall tiles and porcelain fittings of this particular room were done out in white but they were so outdated that they were now back in fashion. Even the lavatory had a high, wall-mounted cistern complete with a dangling, metal chain. I should have opted for a more expensive establishment, one that would have afforded me a more luxurious convalescence. Despite its scrupulous cleanliness there was a lingering, musty odour pervading the place, and the grubby doors, scuffed walls and skirting boards throughout had remained untouched by an interior decorator, it appeared, for many years. I decided the best thing to do was to enquire about changing to a larger room, hopefully one with its own toilet.

To a great extent I was most annoyed with myself for venturing downstairs to the lounge on my first evening there. Sitting alone reading a book with my back to the foyer and my right leg propped up on a coffee table, I was a soft target for anyone who might infer that I needed cheering up. Perhaps Jane had come to this conclusion when I returned from hospital, or perhaps I was overestimating her and she merely wanted someone to talk to, since it was off-season and the hotel was predictably quiet. Indeed, I had only seen one other person and my waitress whilst I was eating dinner in the restaurant earlier. Whatever her reason, Jane had taken it upon herself to sit with me and had, without encouragement or preliminary discussion, launched into the biography of what I assumed was my erstwhile rescuer.

With these minor irritations circulating in my head and contributing to my sleeplessness, slowly but surely it occurred to me that there were many implausibilities and inconsistencies in her narrative so far, and the more I dwelt on these, the more I found there were a multitude of obvious questions I would have to ask her. Why, for instance, did she begin her biography with an anecdote about an outside lavatory and why had she not referred to this again? Why was there so much detailed description of the houses in which the young man had lived? What was the significance of his early schooldays? In essence she was recounting the tale of a boy who had grown up in the nineteen fifties, one who had to be roughly the same age as she was. Yet the man who had helped me from the moors could not have been more than twenty five.

As I mulled over these contradictions I realised that she might be having me on, that she might have been making it all up to entertain me and help me to forget for an hour or so my unconcealed discomfort. She might even be telling me a highly embellished shaggy-dog story to add a more sensational element to the 'native folklore' to which she had drawn my attention, to create a myth about a mysterious animal that wailed plaintively on the moors in bad weather. In reality, my Good Samaritan might simply have been a jogger or a fellow rambler hurrying home to escape the worst of the weather, someone who had come across me by chance. If this were the most common-sense line of reasoning, it would not have served her purpose to disclose his real identity immediately.

But what was her intention? Was it to drum up more custom to help swell the coffers of the hotel by giving me – and almost certainly there must have been others – an intriguing yarn to tell my friends when I returned home in the hope that they would come to investigate the mystery for themselves? Or did she have more wide-ranging reasons involving the identity of Watholme itself? What was it anyway other than a typical, small Pennine outpost, one that had been saved from semi-obscurity and commercialised up to the hilt on the backs of three illustrious, dead authors in the same way that Stratford-on-Avon has been popularised because William Shakespeare came from there? She might perversely want to put hordes of people off coming to the village so that it would be allowed to return a former, less venal age, a state of affairs that she definitely preferred. My final thought as I drifted off to sleep was that all she was actually trying to do was to keep my morale up for the rest the week out of the goodness of her heart.

The following morning I went back to bed after breakfast to read the newspaper I had ordered when I checked in. I did not see either Jane or Agnes as my meal was served by the same young waitress whose command of English was minimal, but enough to bring me a full English fry-up with toast and coffee which was excellent. There could be nothing better than good, traditional Yorkshire cooking to put me in a positive frame of mind for whatever the day had in store whilst I was temporarily housebound – a mild inconvenience however, when I saw the weather. It was bucketing down again and the moors were entirely obscured by the low-lying, impenetrable clouds and the silvery fusillade of raindrops falling diagonally from the heavens.

At one o'clock I limped my way downstairs for lunch (served again by the tongue-tied, young woman) and at five minutes to two I arrived in the lounge to be greeted not only by Jane but also by her sister Agnes. I was struck by how similar she looked to Jane, almost her spitting image, but she was slightly younger, taller and fleshier. She was dressed in a brown tweed skirt, a mushroom coloured jumper and a purple necklace; her hair, like Jane's, was entirely grey and done up in a tight bun. Since neither was wearing a wedding ring, they might have been two elderly spinsters, two Miss Marples maybe, sitting side by side on a sofa and taking afternoon tea, had Jane not been dressed in her receptionist's uniform. It was Agnes who opened the conversation.

"Good afternoon, Mr Lockwood," she said with a welcoming smile. "I hear that Jane has been telling you all about Christopher Heath. You should feel tremendously honoured. She's never breathed a word about him to anyone else and, as far as I'm aware, you're the only person outside this family who she's confided in. I must therefore insist that you swear not to tell another living soul about him. Do you promise?"

I signalled my agreement compliantly and turned my gaze onto Jane, who was pursing her lips. That was one question I did not need to ask and I deleted it from my mental list.

"I haven't heard much of the story so far," I said, looking back at Agnes. "We've done about eight years, isn't that so, Jane? I have a few questions…"

"So Christopher's about to leave here to go to live down in the town, I presume," replied Agnes, butting in. "Before he goes, did she tell you that an hour after he was born, there was a total eclipse of the sun? That could be highly significant, couldn't it?"

"Oh Agnes, do stop exaggerating," scowled Jane as she moved forwards in her seat. "You're going too fast. It doesn't mean that he was born unlucky."

"Did she tell you about the battle with the Ridgesiders and the vandalising of the old cars round the back of a garage when he was six?" continued Agnes remorselessly.

Before I could answer, Jane cut across me, after which they began to argue with each other as if I were not there although I was sitting directly opposite them, with my leg on the vacant fourth armchair and my back to the lobby.

"There isn't much point," Jane said crustily. "The battle with the Ridgesiders never took place. It was a typical immature boys' version of gang warfare, a kind of diluted tribal stand-off. After some of the bigger lads challenged each other, everyone went to their respective homes and armed themselves to the teeth with wooden swords and shields, catapults, peashooters and anything else they could lay their hands on. Then they stood on opposite sides of a field behind the primary school and yelled at each other. They ended up playing football! Christopher was disappointed because he wanted to be a knight in shining armour."

"What about the garage incident?" said Agnes, becoming more and more animated. "Christopher got the blame for that just because his father was a mechanic there. He was unlucky then, poor lad."

"He was a blameless bystander," replied Jane huffily. "He was led on by older boys. They got into an unlocked, old banger and started to smash it up. They'd done quite a lot of damage when a fierce-looking man in a suit, the boss unfortunately, appeared from nowhere. Then they all ran away. The man recognised Christopher and told his dad. Little Christopher was in serious trouble and the others got off scot-free. His father had to pay for the damage and Christopher wasn't allowed to play out for a month."

"I bet you forgot to mention the naked man who used to live under the bandstand in the park," grinned Agnes. "Tell Mr Lockwood all about him."

"That was tittle-tattle," retorted Jane. "I can't remember who started the rumour about this particular bogeyman. It must have been adults warning youngsters about paedophiles in nineteen fifties style or it might have been a children's prank. Either way it was a powerful reminder not to go into the park alone, especially at night. The bandstand was slap bang in the middle, surrounded on all sides by dense bushes and completely isolated from the outside world. A perfect place for murder, robbery or hanky-panky. They always referred to the mysterious weirdo as 'the bare man'. No one ever saw him though, did they? Adults lied about nearly everything in those days."

"Did you mention that day when his mum took him and his brothers for a picnic in a field by the river?" Agnes squealed, her enthusiasm getting the better of her. "There they were, sitting on a waterproof sheet eating their ham sandwiches and drinking their bottles of pop when two teenage women leapt over the hedge without seeing them. Quick as a flash they lifted up their skirts, dropped their drawers and let nature take its course. Even his mother giggled."

"What's that got to do with anything?" muttered Jane, rapidly becoming irritated by her insensitive sister.

"He didn't have a dirty mind, Mr Lockwood," cooed Agnes, now beaming like a doting grandmother. "A few years later when he lived in Oakgrove, he went to church every Sunday. He was eleven. He went to matins, afternoon service and evensong for twelve months and easily won the prize for best attendance among the juniors. He was a good, little boy, wasn't he, Jane?"

"Yes he was," returned Jane, winking at me. "That's where I finished the first instalment last night. It was exactly how Mr Trueman, the headmaster, described him, wasn't it? Christopher was a *very* good, little boy – too good really. That's the Christopher we think about with a lump in our throats. So much going for him academically."

"Mr T couldn't have got it more wrong though, bless him!" sighed Agnes. "You need far more than intelligence and a pleasant temperament to go far in this world. In fact, being bright can sometimes be more of a hindrance. I've got personal experience of that!"

"You must have an appropriate birthright..." echoed Jane. "It was finding out that he was working class when he passed his scholarship – the eleven plus – and went to grammar school that he lost most of his self-assurance and confidence. He met people a lot posher and more mature than he was, but I'll be coming to that later."

She hadn't observed that Agnes was now glaring at her. Her mood had changed without warning and her eyes were blazing.

"You've concentrated on highlights from the early days in Watholme, haven't you?" she said. "I bet you've missed a lot out. Have you mentioned his love of the moors?"

"I haven't got that far, my dear," said Jane, raising her index finger and shaking it slowly in her sister's direction. "He regarded himself as a wild spirit of the fells, that's for sure."

They both were alluding to events that I was manifestly not party to. I was beginning to feel giddy watching their verbal tennis match, and before I had time to ask what their heated exchange was about, Agnes stood up and grabbed her handbag.

"The countryside began a hundred yards or so up the street from his home in Watholme," she said as she prepared to leave. "There was a huge expanse of open grassland, divided randomly into fields, part of an age-old farm's extensive estate, with a dirt track leading down to the farmhouse and the barns. Now, there was also another dirt path going uphill in the opposite direction and the further you went along it, the closer you came to the moors about ten minutes' walk away. He was invited to the farm once to watch the cows being milked, but the smell in the cowshed made him retch and he rushed out to get some air. He went for a stroll to recover and sooner or later he came across the other path. All of a sudden he found himself trekking through heather into another world, a world of absolute silence, punctuated solely by the distant cries of birds carried on the wind. He liked it so much that he just kept on walking. At the very top of the highest ridge, he could see for miles, and if he spun himself around in a circle he could see the slate-grey roofs of the houses in the village in one direction, the green blob of the fields in another, and acre upon acre of dull-brown heather everywhere else. It was this sense of total freedom he missed the most when he moved down to Boughton."

A glazed look had come over her face as if in that instant she had fallen into a trance. She stood transfixed for a few awkward seconds then she snapped out of her reverie and smiled.

"I'll leave you to it then," she said directly to Jane, ignoring me yet again. "I'll get back to the kitchen. I hope Mr Lockwood enjoys the next, er, instalment if that's what you want to call it."

When Agnes was safely out of the room, Jane shuffled about on her chair and sat forwards, as if she had something of great importance to let me in on.

"She's a stickler for completeness," she whispered. "It comes with the territory, I suppose. She didn't know Christopher as well as I did, and she's only heard some of the things she said I'd left out from me. I expect she was showing off a bit."

I bobbed my head sympathetically, although I was now struggling more than ever to understand why she felt she had to exhibit such unconcealed familiarity to a man she had only known for just over twenty four hours. Had I not injured my ankle, I doubt she would have noticed me during my stay at her hotel or remembered me a few minutes after I checked out. I am not as a rule a gregarious person, and I have no striking physical features (other than spectacles) or peculiarities of personality which would make me attract her attention, although the size of my stomach might elicit a humorous comment or two. I have a conventional old man's hair style parted on the left, and I have it trimmed every month to keep it neat and tidy. I do not dress in a flamboyant way, jacket or pullover, shirt and slacks being my preferred mode of attire. Her directness had to be more to do with my unfortunate accident which had been the instrument that had drawn her to me. Nevertheless, I had to seek some answers to my lengthening list of questions.

"I don't mean to be discourteous," I said as assertively as I dared. "But before you get cracking on part two, I have a few queries from last night's segment. For example, why are you going into so much, er, detail about…"

"It might be best if you left them till later," she replied abruptly. "I've only got half an hour this afternoon and Agnes has already hogged ten minutes. We'll have to continue after dinner if that suits you."

I shrugged my shoulders and conceded defeat. If that was the way she wanted it, I had no choice but to concur. I could of course have withdrawn to my room but that would have smacked of petulance. Moreover, my delicate condition necessitated that I was on good terms with her. I had become too involved in her scheme to amuse me to do anything other than acquiesce and listen.

"Are you sitting comfortably?" she asked pointedly, still leaning forwards with her hands on her knees. "Then I'll get cracking on part two. When he was six, Christopher's grandmother had a stroke and the right-hand side of her body was paralysed, which meant she couldn't walk unaided, or do anything else for herself. At first she was looked after by Christopher's grandfather and every weekend Christopher's mother went to visit her in Oakgrove, the place I sketched out for you at some length last night, to give his grandad a bit of a break. On Sundays the whole family usually attended. Sadly, one Tuesday afternoon grandad fell asleep in an armchair and never woke up. A few weeks after his death, it came as an unwelcome surprise to Christopher's father when, in a spirit of supreme self-sacrifice, Christopher's mother announced that they would have to 'flit' down to Boughton so that she could become a sort of part-time surrogate nurse and housekeeper. As a married woman in those days, she didn't work and she was therefore expected by social convention to take care of her mother, but she couldn't do that from five miles away, with three kids and no transport. They ended up in Oakgrove in a run down, draughty house in need of modernisation – the one I alluded to yesterday with the outside loo – situated conveniently, for the local council in particular, only a few streets away from his grandmother's house. Its location signified that his grandmother didn't qualify for a home help. His parents hadn't realised that when they bought the house."

She paused and sat back, putting her right hand across her mouth in one swift movement.

"Oh dear me," she said. "I haven't offered you a drink. You must think me very rude. Would you like a cup of tea or coffee or something stronger?"

"I'm fine," I lied, conscious of the delicate state of my bladder. "I had a good lunch and I'm anxious for you to tell me more."

"Well, here are some more elaborate topographic features for you to digest," she resumed, the puckish grin lighting up her face yet again. "A few yards further up the hill from his grandmother's house a level piece of ground had been engineered, and, for some reason, the council had chosen to construct a children's play area there. It was really a large field, bordered by tall oak, lime, sycamore and horse chestnut trees, and it sloped gently up to the main road. It marked the boundary of Oakgrove and a dirt path led to a much larger, more exclusive semi-detached estate about a third of a mile away on the outskirts of the town centre. When Christopher was eight years old and on his weekly visit to his convalescent grandmother one Sunday afternoon in spring, something happened which he was never to know the real significance of. It was only a matter of months before he moved down to Boughton. The sun wasn't shining, as it always does in childhood memories. It was a dull, dreary day with rain in the air. He'd been sent out to play, God knows why, and he wandered into the playground, a strip of tarmac at the edge of the patch of grassy scrubland that had been predictably christened 'the field' by the local children. There were three swings, a roundabout and something which resembled a fairground swing boat. It consisted of a tall, tubular, metal frame in which a long, wooden bench, divided into seats, went backwards and forwards if one person pushed it or two stood on the platform at either end and 'worked it up' with their legs. However, only the roundabout is important. That's where he found himself alone with a girl for the first time. She was standing on it and looking very nonchalant, staring abstractedly into the distance. Yes, nonchalant. I can't think of another word to describe her. She was wearing a navy blue cardigan over a light blue, gingham dress. There was no one else around. Sadly, he could never bring to mind exactly what she looked like, except that she had short, mousey hair. Or perhaps it was darker? She was about his age, maybe a few months older. He sauntered up to her, buoyed by the confidence given by his brylcreemed hair and dapper,

Sunday best clothes: short, grey trousers, shiny brown shoes and a bottle green, home-knitted jumper. He stood next to her on the stationary roundabout and looked at her out of the corner of his eye.

'Want me to shove you?' he enquired casually.

'No,' she replied, continuing to gaze dreamily into the distance. 'I don't know you.'

'I don't live round here,' he said, pointing vaguely to his left. 'I'm visiting my grandma. She's very poorly. She lives down there.'

'Oh,' she said.

'She's had a stroke, whatever that is,' he said.

There wasn't much to add to their makeshift conversation and they stood in silence, as if frozen in time, for a good, few minutes. Then the girl moved her head.

'Do you want me to show you my knickers,' she said in a matter of fact sort of way in keeping with the tenor of the preceding dialogue.

Her facial expression didn't change. Without looking at him she calmly lifted her dress and there they were. White. Persil white.

'Give me sixpence and I'll pull them down,' she said

'No,' he said indifferently. 'Not today.'

'Why not?' she asked.

He froze. He didn't have any pocket money.

'You won't tell your mum, will you?' he implored, suddenly terrified that he might be in big trouble.

'No,' she replied. 'Come back tomorrow and you can look at my thingy for nothing.'

'I can't,' he mumbled nervously. 'I'll be miles away at home.'

He didn't recall anything else. He never knew her name. He often wondered who she was and if she remembered him. It was nineteen fifty seven."

Throughout this last part of her anecdote, she had affected the voices of a young boy and a young girl as if to bring them to life for me. She was clearly enjoying herself and I had never before come across such an enthusiastically singular raconteur. At this juncture, however, she became strangely solemn – and silent – for well over a minute. She sat back and stared, glassy-eyed, out of the window and onto the moors.

"But she does remember him," she mumbled. "But she's never really cared about him."

Then, as though this short interlude had not occurred, she brightened up again and launched herself as chirpily as before into her eloquent monologue.

"So now he's eight years old and he finds himself living down yonder in the town," she said, picking up from where she had broken off. "At this stage of his short life, he didn't worry much about anything. He wasn't worried yet about outside lavatories and he definitely didn't smoke, although most adults did, even doctors and nurses. Everything became a different, exciting adventure. He made new pals, he explored new places and he went to a new primary school in the next parish, an upmarket area called Highton, presumably, as its name suggests, because at its peak it was the highest residential area in the district. It consisted almost entirely of well-appointed, detached houses with gardens the size of a cricket pitch. If we hark back to my detailed description of Oakgrove, at the far end was a cemetery, flanked by the main road and the railway line which ran northwards to the Yorkshire Dales. Well, his new school was on the far side of the cemetery at its northern edge where it met the lowermost part of Highton. It was situated in its own grounds near the Anglican church, and it was a delightful contrast to the one he'd been at before. It was a compact but airy, single-storey, modern building with a large playground whereas its predecessor, if that's the right word, in Watholme was a forbiddingly grim, soot-stained, two-storey structure that would haven't been out of place in a nineteenth century horror novel. When you can walk a bit, you should go down and have a look at it. Take your phone or your camera if you've brought one. Highton School was where he came into contact for the first time with middle-class children, but they didn't stand out from the crowd except that they spoke differently. They were neither cleverer nor better dressed than anyone else and they had no airs and graces. It was when he went to grammar school that he found such people daunting. After a few weeks, because he was so intelligent, he was moved up a year to a class containing children who were at least twelve months older than he was. At the end of his first term then, he was popular with everyone and he was very happy. His best friend was Brendon, who lived in the posher housing estate near Oakgrove I referred to a few minutes ago, and they went everywhere and did everything together. Brendon wasn't what you might characterise as the rough and tumble type. He was quite chubby, he wore national health spectacles and he didn't like sport. He was, however, the more talented one of the two of them, truly a Renaissance man in the making, and, although being second best was a new experience for Christopher, it didn't affect their friendship one bit. On the contrary, he learned a host of new things from him, such as how to make and paint plastic construction kits and build a model railway. He became a keen train-spotter, like all of the other children in Oakgrove, including many girls incidentally, taking advantage of the proximity of the main railway line to Scotland and the Lancashire Coast that ran at the bottom of the streets where they lived."

I have to confess that I was becoming bored with, what seemed to me, an over-elaborate wealth of biographical and, in particular, geographical minutiae. I was also curious about how she knew so much about Christopher and where all this was leading. Yet what was puzzling me most was why she had reacted so peculiarly to the incident on the roundabout. It was one more thread of the saga that she had left dangling and I made a mental note to add this to my ever-expanding dossier of queries, should I ever get the opportunity to ask any questions. Perhaps she was deliberately refusing to give me any answers to ensure that I would remain enthralled, or perhaps she was merely a little scatter-brained. Nonetheless, she had brought up the subject of outside toilets and the grammar school boys again, although for what consequence I was still unable to comprehend.

"During his first week there, there were two or three bizarre events which will make you smile," she added. "The first involves another girl who made a fool of herself by doing something really silly. She was called Olive O'Brien and she was ten years old. She said she wanted to be a boy and boasted that she could wee into a urinal. She'd told just about everyone in her class, so by the time she entered the boys' toilets there was already a large group of tittering spectators waiting. Regrettably she only succeeded in wetting her legs and her knickers. She gave up the idea of changing gender from then on and when she grew up, she became a shorthand-typist and married a chartered accountant. It was Christopher's first day at his new school and, in light of the roundabout episode, he thought that all the girls in the district must be weird exhibitionists, although he wouldn't have used that phrase, would he? The next one involves a teacher. Christopher liked her very much and got on well with her for most of the time. She was young, like Miss Mountjoy was, but she was in no way as attractive, although most of the boys were probably having childish fantasies about her. In view of his first impressions of the fairer sex, he was astounded when, in order to help him do a sit-up in a PE lesson, she crouched down beside him with her legs spread wide apart. It was the first time he'd seen a grown woman in such a position."

She laughed quietly to herself as she was describing yet another, rather graceless tableau, although it seemed that I was the only one who was embarrassed. She watched my face for a few seconds, as if daring me to react in some way.

"I expect you're wondering how I know about this, aren't you?" she said eventually, when no response from me was forthcoming. "Well, he couldn't stop telling everyone about it. He was nine years old, for goodness sake, as yet incapable of rationalising his emergent sexual awakening. Until that precise moment he'd preferred watching trains or catching caterpillars. I wasn't there of course. Someone else in his class told me a few days later.

There's not much more to add about the early years, although I expect finicky Agnes would be able to think of one or two minor things to tell you about. It was going to grammar school that made him what he was."

She began to giggle again, and I could not be sure whether she was amused by these extraordinary reminiscences or whether she was sniggering at me. Suffice it say that it was self-evident that she had rendered me speechless.

"I'm not shocking you, am I, Mr Lockwood?" she enquired as she got up. "Your facial expression changed rapidly many times from polite interest to one of affronted incredulity as my latest chapter unfolded. I assure you that there will be many more disturbing things to alarm you if you want to hear the rest of the remarkable history of Christopher Heath."

"I beg your pardon," I returned, trying my best to smile. "It's just that everything about him so far seems to revolve around sex and toilets. I'm sure there are good reasons."

"Are you free this evening?" she replied, ignoring my muted protests. "I have some paperwork to tidy up and chores to do but I'll be available around eight if that suits you. In the meantime, if Agnes accosts you, please make some excuse...you know...tell her you have to make a telephone call. Her account of Christopher's journey is different from mine and I don't want her interfering."

CHAPTER THREE

Monday Evening

I spent the rest of the afternoon in my room attempting a cryptic crossword and reading a bit more of '*The Master and Margarita*' by Mikhail Bulgakov, which, for a mystical horror story, was very heavy going. Consequently I found it difficult to concentrate for more than a few minutes before my thoughts wandered back to the two eccentric sisters and naïve, little Christopher. As for Jane, I could at last make out some of the dominant themes of her long-drawn-out chronicle.

I supposed that she was emphasising the effects on him of his early encounters with girls to prepare the ground for some vivid, sexual revelation later on. Indeed all the major characters thus far had been female except for Christopher himself, and they had not been portrayed at all positively. Had the narrator been a man, he would unquestionably have been accused of being blatantly and typically misogynistic. Another recurrent theme had to be Christopher's working class background that had contributed to his transformation into the neurotic, middle-class snob she introduced to me at the very beginning of the story. When I connected these two themes with a third, the likely influence, impact even, of his early schooldays on his personality development, I assumed that this also would contribute to the vivid dénouement still to come. Furthermore, there was a plethora of other random factors to consider, and, as dinnertime approached, I had to concede that the more I speculated on them, the more I realised it was futile. Focusing on more practical issues such as seeking an upgrade to a more luxurious room, one with a bathroom, had to be a better course of action, and I cursed myself for forgetting to attend to this earlier. I did not wish to spend another minute in a cubby-hole, let alone another miserable night. I decided to rectify the matter immediately.

I made my way painfully down to the reception desk at about five o'clock, behind which, to my surprise, Agnes was sitting. She was wearing a green, cotton trouser suit with a string of white seashells around her neck and she looked totally out of place, as if she had recently jetted in from Hawaii or somewhere equally exotic.

"Good afternoon Mr Lockwood," she said cheerily as I approached the counter. "Or should that be 'good evening'. I never really know when one starts and the other finishes. I expect you're after Jane."

"Yes I am," I replied. "I was hoping to move to another room if there's one available."

"Is there something wrong with the one you're in now?" she asked defensively, getting to her feet. "I'm sure we can sort it out, whatever it is."

"No, the room's fine," I returned. "One with an en-suite would be much more convenient for me and my sore ankle."

"There's a splendid one at the front with a view of the moors or another at the rear overlooking the village." she beamed. "They're both more expensive though, twenty five pounds a night, but we can come to an arrangement. Shall we say seventy five pounds extra for the week?"

I quickly calculated that her offer amounted to a saving of fifty percent – I was here for another six nights

– and, in the circumstances, I thought it an exceptionally reasonable discount. It was not the fault of the hotel that I had become incapacitated and I was thankful that the matter could be resolved so speedily, hopefully within the next few minutes.

"I'll have the one with the view of the moors, if I may?" I said apprehensively. "Please put the difference on my bill. There's just one thing. Do you have the authority to do this?"

"Oh yes," she said, still smiling. "As a matter of fact, I own the hotel."

I tried to conceal my astonishment, but without success. I felt my jaw drop and my eyes open wide in one instantaneous movement, a reaction which caused her a great deal of amusement.

"Actually I co-own it with Jane," she chuckled. "I don't have to obtain anyone's permission to make financial decisions but I have to justify them whenever we do the books. However, as you can see, we're not busy this week and an extra room to clean will give Nadia something to do tomorrow morning after she's finished clearing the breakfasts away. Would you like her to help you move in now?"

"She could perhaps carry my suitcase and one or two other things," I replied gratefully. "I'll be ready in half an hour."

"Before you go, I have a message from Jane," she said as I turned to lumber off. "She's tied up this evening, not literally I hasten to add, and she sends her apologies. She's looking after a sick relative. She'll continue telling you about Christopher tomorrow if you're in the mood. She's forbidden me to carry on where she left off but I don't know which version she's been telling you anyway. Jane knew Christopher when he lived up here and when

43

he went to primary school in Highton, and she used to hang around with him when they were teenagers, so some of her information's first-hand but there are other sources. I was friends with his brother Paul and most of my knowledge has been gleaned from him. I could tell you about the famous Ayre sisters if you want, their real history, not the one that's in all the biographies and guidebooks. How about eight o'clock as arranged?"

Before I could think more about it, I heard myself agree and I shuffled off upstairs to get ready to move.

I had packed my things and I was sitting on the bed when Nadia arrived. She was a waif-like, young woman, in her early twenties I guessed, with pinched, angular features and blonde hair pulled back tightly into a pony tail. I pointed to my suitcase and a plastic bag and she picked them up obediently and walked off, motioning with her head that I was to follow her. I limped down the corridor behind her for a few yards until we came to my new room, the door to which she had already opened and left ajar in anticipation that she would have her hands full. She placed my things on the floor as we entered and stared at me for a split second before pushing past me rather brusquely to make a speedy exit. I held out my hand and offered her a two pound coin but she shrank back in horror and shook her head.

"No, no," she mumbled in a thick Slavonic accent. "I don't want money. I go now."

"This is for you," I insisted. "I'd have struggled to carry my belongings without your assistance."

"I go now, I go now," she repeated as she hastily ran off back downstairs.

I stood there for at least a minute, bemused by her odd behaviour and wholly at a loss to understand why she had bolted so dramatically. I had discovered inadvertently why she never spoke but I would have to ask Agnes later if there were another major reason, the effect of some deep-seated psychological disorder, for instance. My bewilderment was further intensified when, shortly afterwards, Nadia served my evening meal with her customary courtesy as though nothing had taken place between us earlier. Perhaps it was the presence of other diners that made her feel more secure. I had thoughtfully been given a table (which I occupied for the whole week) nearest the entrance so that I did not have far to walk for my meals. There was a family of four and an elderly couple sitting separately at the far end of the restaurant, none of whom I had seen before and I did not see them again during my stay. They must have been non-residents, or perhaps they had booked in for one night only and left before I took breakfast the following morning. They did not acknowledge my presence despite my attempts to catch their eye, leading me to conclude that they were locals openly demonstrating what Jane had referred to as 'frostiness' to 'outsiders'.

Nevertheless, my new bedroom cheered me up somewhat; it was four doors down from my previous room and it was spacious and luxurious where its predecessor had been cramped and spartan. Apart from the standard items of furniture, there were old, black and white photographs of Watholme on the walls, and there was a television, a king-sized double bed with room enough for me to spread out at night, and a coffee table complete with packets of biscuits, a kettle and sachets of tea, coffee, sugar and fresh milk. My window overlooked the front of the hotel and if I bent forwards I could see the street below, my car on the hardstanding, and any passers-by strolling past. However it was the sight of the moors that took my breath away. Since the empty plot of land opposite had been left vacant as the site of the Ayre memorial stone, there was nothing to obstruct a striking, panoramic view of the rolling, dark-brown terrain that rose forbiddingly to meet a correspondingly sombre skyline whether it was dark or broad daylight. My original room had been at the side of the building and I had been able see nothing other than the gable end of the next block of houses. I had made the right decision for once and my money had been well spent.

* * *

"How much do you know about the Ayres?" said Agnes, when I was comfortably ensconced in the lounge at five past eight. It was pouring down outside again and a gusty wind was, as always, lashing the rain against the windows. I was sitting with my bad leg propped up on a chair, and she was facing the lobby so that she could keep an eye on reception in Jane's absence. She had already seen to it that we had a bottle of red wine to share.

"Not very much," I replied. "I watched a documentary about them on TV. Their names were Catherine, Elizabeth and Amy, weren't they? I've an idea what they looked like from their portraits. Long hair done up in a bun a bit like yours, plain, unsmiling faces and very slim waists – typical Victorian women. I read 'The Stone Seat' when I was a boy and I think I may have seen a film of it, the original nineteen forties, Hollywood version not one of the more modern interpretations made for television. I watched a bit of the serialised TV production of 'The Governess' in the seventies, but I don't know about any of their other novels or their poetry."

"That's par for the course," she laughed. "It's probably two more than most of our American visitors. I expect you're also familiar with their biographical details."

"If you asked me to give you a potted history, all I'd be able to tell you would be that they all died tragically young, and were outlived by their father," I said. "He outlived his wife as well. She died giving birth to the youngest daughter, Amy I believe. Didn't they die of typhoid or was it cholera?"

"So the guidebooks tell us," she sneered. "Don't you think it's coincidental that Amy and Elizabeth died within two weeks of each other and that Catherine lived on for a couple of years afterwards? Then she snuffs it when all their best work's been published. Have you been to the cemetery? If so, you'll have noticed that they're buried in one grave. That's spooky isn't it? Shortly after Catherine's six feet under, their cottage burns down but a memorial stone's erected on the opposite side of the street. Getting creepier by the second, isn't it? Finally, their grieving father, tremendously healthy, old Patrick, builds this hotel, leaves Watholme and more or less disappears without a trace."

"Hang on a minute," I cut in. "You're losing me. I thought that the two younger sisters died in the typhoid epidemic. It was typhoid, wasn't it, caused by poor sanitation? The water supply was somehow polluted by bacteria in contaminated human waste."

"Yes, there was an outbreak of typhoid fever, which was fatal in those days in remote areas like this, but it didn't last long. So why didn't Catherine die of it?"

"She died of influenza, didn't she?"

"The doctor recorded 'pneumonia' on her death certificate, although, like most of their other possessions, it was lost in the fire. We only have the doctor's word for it. Fortuitously their original manuscripts and other drafts of novels and poems survived. Another interesting happenchance, don't you agree?"

"I'm not sure I do," I said a tad too antagonistically. "What's more, you support Jane's view that their cottage was sited here and not where the memorial is. What evidence do you have?"

"I have an old map," she grinned. "It's over a hundred and fifty years old."

She sat back and continued to smirk. As she spoke she had been leaning forwards with her hands on her thighs, a posture which suggested that she was about to divulge some electrifying scandal.

"I thought our conversation was going to be more about their writing," I said after a moment's reflection. "I'm aware that Catherine wrote 'The Stone Seat' but which one of the other two wrote 'The Governess'?"

"Catherine wrote 'The Governess', she replied authoritatively. "It was Elizabeth, the middle one, who wrote 'The Stone Seat', although Amy probably gave her the idea and contributed three or four chapters. However, the original manuscript's in Elizabeth's handwriting. It doesn't really matter, because what I'm going to tell you will make it irrelevant who wrote what. What matters is why they became so famous so quickly after their unfortunate deaths."

"Do you mean to say that the text books are all wrong?"

"Oh yes, yes, Mr Lockwood, yes, oh yes," she intoned sardonically. "Now listen carefully and try not to interrupt. Patrick Ayre was a very ambitious man. He moved here from Leeds when the children were young. Catherine was eleven, Elizabeth was nine and Amy nearly eight. His textile business had gone bust and he needed somewhere cheap to escape to, to rebuild his life. He had enough money left to open a draper's shop in High Street and it's still there, although it sells antiques these days. If you turn left outside the front door of our hotel and make for the post office, it's at the bottom of the hill opposite the park. While we're about it, if you turn right there, about two hundred yards further on you'll come to Sharp Street where Christopher Heath used to live. Patrick also bought the cottage where our hotel now stands, and later on he acquired the land opposite where the memorial is. That's very important. As for the three sisters, he didn't send them to the local school because, in his very biased view, it was a rough place, a cross between Dickens's Coketown School in Hard Times and Dotheboys Hall in Nicholas Nickleby, but nowhere near as brutal. He hired a governess from Ripon who was extremely well-educated and very refined, and she produced the young adults that became three of the most celebrated literary icons of the nineteenth century."

"I have a statement to make and a question to ask, if I may?" I said politely when she paused to take a swig of her drink. "Most of what you've just told me is in the biographies but I'd be interested to know where Patrick got all his money from if he was broke?"

"He was a shrewd man, old Patrick was," she laughed, as she refilled her glass. "It was well-known that he had multiple bank accounts when he began to prosper in Watholme and his creditors in Leeds mustn't have done their searches very thoroughly. He always kept back sufficient funds to make a bolt for it if he got into financial difficulties, and this is what he made use of when the typhoid epidemic broke out. You see, the Ayre siblings didn't die, they moved out. They went to Bronte, near Taormina in Sicily, and only one of them came back."

I shook my head, not in amazement at this startling revelation, but in sheer disbelief at her assumption that

I would find it amazing in the first place. I have never been the bookish type. I left school when I was fifteen to become an engineering apprentice, and I graduated through the ranks within the same company as I grew older, and I ended up as the north regional sales manager in my mid-fifties. Consequently I have a reasonable pension to go with what I was able to squirrel away as the years went by and I have enough savings in the bank to guarantee a free and easy retirement. Even so, if I do find myself in a situation where reading is the most suitable means of killing time, I would choose something with a supernatural element to it, anything by Stephen King for example, which is the only reason why I brought Bulgakov's disappointing, so-called masterpiece with me. In short, this is not how I envisaged my walking holiday would turn out and I shuddered at the prospect of having to listen to yet another of the sisters for a few days longer, especially when I had a television in my room.

"Did they emigrate to escape the epidemic or for some other reason?" I asked, trying not to betray my indifference and praying that this was an appropriate response.

"To make more money in a similar way that paintings appreciate in value after an artist dies," she replied obligingly. "The sisters were gaining in recognition among the bourgeois metropolitans down south, consisting largely of impressionable, young women who liked racy love stories such as 'The Stone Seat'. The steamier the better, but done in the best possible taste."

"Then why didn't they stay in this country and write more of them?" I exclaimed.

"The simple answer is that none of them liked writing very much," she countered. "That's well documented. They'd already written several novels, Mr Lockwood, but they weren't selling in large numbers outside the Home Counties, were they? Elsewhere they were virtually unknown – even up North. Sales were flagging and an untimely death always boosts an artist's reputation and hence sales figures. That's what Patrick, sharp businessman that he was, calculated would happen – and it did! After the sisters' fictitious deaths, there was an instant reappraisal of their novels by a group calling themselves the Pre-Raphaelites. They demonstrated that 'The Governess', for instance, was actually a denunciation of the subjugation of women. This and similar themes were shown to pervade the other novels so they weren't schmaltzy romances but serious *romans à clef* which every woman should read. Sales rocketed and demand also soared for their other, less accomplished stuff. Their publishers in London even travelled up here to buy up their unfinished material. However far-fetched it sounds, it worked, didn't it? There was also another very good reason why they had to disappear. Incredible as it may seem, Amy was really Amos. She was a bloke and today she would be called a 'transsexual', if that's what it means by being a girl in a boy's body. A man dressing up as a woman was a serious crime then, and the punishment was harsh if you were found out. I have a newspaper cutting from 1860, which describes how the police were looking for a 'queer', as they called such men in these parts, after a distasteful incident on a train in Boughton station involving a man I believe to be Amos and another gentleman. Luckily he wasn't identified and he made a clean getaway."

I raised my hand as a signal that I wanted to cut in again but she anticipated my question and continued on regardless.

"The newspaper story names the suspect as an effeminate young man with long, blond hair, which came to light when his hat was knocked off in a struggle. The police also found a paper bag in the railway carriage from 'Ayre's, Drapers of Distinction of Watholme'. When they followed the trail here, they came to a dead end. No one knew of any *man* who fitted their description. Amos as Amy – getting confusing, isn't it – would have been able to change to her alter ego very quickly by tucking her longish hair into a cap, and from contemporary portraits Amos was fresh-faced enough to pass himself off as a woman without anyone having the slightest suspicion that she was a he. That was when Patrick hatched his plan. Amy-slash-Amos had to disappear for a while. It was documented in the parish records that Amy passed away a few weeks later, followed shortly afterwards by Elizabeth, allowing the two of them to slip off incognito to Europe, eventually ending up in Sicily. Catherine stayed on to put their affairs in order. She helped her father sort things out in Watholme and purchase a small villa in Taormina. Patrick had already been in the process of borrowing quite heavily to acquire and develop the land across the road where the monument now stands, deceiving the bank into believing that he was going to expand his drapery business on it. He guessed that people might come to Watholme to see where the two dead sisters had lived, but most of the accommodation on offer was in pubs with rough and ready rooms that were hardly suitable for refined young ladies. A new, purpose-built hotel would be required to accommodate the visiting gentry, but developing the plot across the road as anything other than a large shop would have broken the terms of his loan, so he had to acquire more land to build one – and all he had was his cottage. Two years later, in 1862, Catherine '*died*' of pneumonia and her empty coffin was buried in the cemetery in the same grave as the other two, probably to save money on separate headstones. When the cash started rolling into his bank account from the sales of the posthumous three authors' books, and people began to come here as he predicted, he burnt down the cottage in 1864. He'd already contracted a firm of builders to replace the cottage with the hotel we're now sitting in, and it was finished a year later in 1865. Three years afterwards he sold it at a huge profit as a thriving concern through an agent. In the meantime, he'd already erected the stone monument on his empty plot and gone off to rejoin his family. Job done!"

"I can see why they chose somewhere off the beaten track like Sicily," I said, when she picked up her glass to take another mouthful of wine, "but how did they get away with it? They would have had to show their passports and surely someone over there would have recognised their names."

"Amy travelled as Amos and Elizabeth posed as his wife," she explained patiently. "There was no requirement to have a passport to travel around Europe in those days. You've also forgotten that Catherine was married by then and if she had obtained a passport it would have been in her new name. Her husband, George Carlyle, was away on business when she faked her death and she was buried before he returned…"

"Where were the three bodies that went in the coffins then?" I said, throwing my arms out wide in exasperation. "They had to have some bodies to bury."

"Not necessarily," she laughed, leaning forward again. "They could have filled them with sand or soil, or stones and even lead. The corpses of people who died of typhoid weren't pretty sights. The undertakers may have dropped off some coffins for Patrick to deal with and been mightily indebted to him for doing so."

"What were the doctor and the local vicar doing while Patrick was topping up the coffins with bricks? Someone had to complete the paperwork."

"I suppose they mustn't have seen the bodies either. Maybe they were paid off, I don't know. This was a small village in the middle of an epidemic. Times were difficult then and people were dying every day. As for Catherine, well, Patrick must have been allowed to deal with her coffin as well."

I was about to ask her how she had discovered that the Ayres had chosen to live in Taormina as well the details of the journey made by Amy as Amos and Elizabeth, but it seemed pointless to press her further on this implausible flight of fantasy. It would have been of no consequence anyhow, since Jane had appeared out of nowhere behind me. As I twisted my body round to say hello, she beckoned to Agnes, who stood up and scuttled towards her.

"She'll see you now," she whispered mysteriously. "You'd better be quick before she goes back to sleep."

With that Agnes was gone as speedily and silently as her sister had arrived. I saw neither of them again that evening. For the next half an hour I remained on my own in the lounge and finished the wine, leaving the empty bottle and a note at the reception desk informing them that I would pay for the drinks. Slowly I made my weary way back upstairs to spend what was left of the day watching television, God willing, without any irksome distractions.

When I entered my room, I went over to the window to close the curtains without switching on the light so that I could take one last look at the ominous wilderness that stretched out ahead of me. It had just stopped raining and, as my eyes wandered over the moonless blackness behind the streetlamps in a vain attempt to separate the horizon from the vast swathes of heather, my gaze was inexplicably drawn downwards to the indistinct outline of a figure of a man standing by the Ayre monument across the road. He was dripping wet and panting heavily. All at once he stepped forwards into the light and I saw a dishevelled young man who resembled the one who had come to my aid when I turned my ankle in the thunderstorm. He looked up at me for a few seconds, then he ran off into the darkness and away from the village towards the moors, without leaving me time to do anything other than watch him dissolve into thin air as the night consumed him.

CHAPTER FOUR

Tuesday Morning

As I have already indicated, this was not how I imagined my short autumn break would go. I had planned my week's itinerary thus. Starting on the Monday morning, I had intended to spend the first two days walking on the moorland. There is a narrow road splitting it conveniently into two contrasting halves. On the side nearest to Watholme are marshy lowlands, punctuated by undulating, heather-covered hillocks and hollows rising steeply upwards to their highest point about half a mile away. On the opposite side the heath is flatter and slopes gently down to the horizon to meet the vivid lushness of uncultivated, treeless fields in the far distance. There are no sheep, no cows or horses, and no sign of human habitation on either side, or anything to suggest that there ever will be.

I would then have spent the next day more restfully, exploring the village and its bygone and contemporary attractions without, I state adamantly, dwelling too long on the Ayre sisters. There is a disused railway line down in the valley with most of its gravel trackbed still intact. It leads to Boughton about five miles away and it is used these days as a nature trail and cycleway. Hiking briskly into the town and back would therefore have been my fourth day's activity. On the last two days I was looking forward to driving first to Sleighton, a small market town on the edge of the Yorkshire Dales, followed, to round off my holiday, by another car journey through the surrounding villages and hamlets in search of a good, old-fashioned, country lunch in a picture-postcard inn.

Instead, I was cooped up in a second-rate hotel with a gammy leg, no Wi-Fi and two women of questionable decorum who had me at their mercy, tormenting me at every opportunity with a gritty biography of some nondescript young man, and a fanciful concoction about the duplicity of three sisters who happened to have written a few blockbuster novels that, frankly, bore me to tears. How many other unlucky guests had suffered a similar fate to me, I wondered? Would the braver ones have avoided them both at all costs after the first session or, like me, would every poor martyr to good manners have listened patiently to their ridiculous assertions and been too polite to pour scorn on them as utterly absurd – or senselessly long-drawn-out as with Jane's muddled epic? To add insult to injury they had sworn me to secrecy over the subject matter, a clever ruse, I supposed, to convince me that I was the only person they had confided in.

What would the vast army of Ayre experts, the feminist writers in particular, have made of Agnes's allegations? Surely it was the sisters' artistic merit, not their premature deaths that had led to their being placed among the literary giants of the nineteenth century. Popular wisdom decrees that they highlighted, among many other things, the inferior status of women in those patriarchal days, preparing the way for many other authors to champion their cause and lead ultimately to the emancipation movements of the next hundred years. This may be too much of a generalisation, for I am no intellectual, but I cannot stomach the notion that their pioneering spirit was sacrificed merely to increase sales and hence their royalties. I can easily believe that Patrick Ayre may have been the prime mover in such an underhand scheme but not that he wielded such a powerful influence over the strongminded sisters as to make them deceive everyone into believing they were dead, and then furtively slip out of the country.

What sealed it for me, however, was the sensational tsunami that would surge through academic circles, were Agnes's controversial disclosures true and she turned whistle-blower. The repercussions of their fraud would make the front pages of every newspaper in the country, if not the world. What would the effects of the aftershock of such an exposé be on Watholme? Would their notoriety make it less or more popular? Could Agnes handle the responsibility, let alone the publicity, for possibly ruining the livelihoods of so many small businesses, no matter what Jane may have thought of them? Having said that, would anyone take her seriously, without any scholarly pedigree or hard evidence? If the Ayres had covered their tracks well enough not to cause one scintilla of suspicion in academic circles after a century and a half, it was easy to understand why no one had unearthed their well-kept secret by now – because there was nothing to suspect, ergo no one suspected anything.

On the balance of probabilities, I concluded that Agnes had made everything up, but why? As a result, in contrast with my expectations of a relaxing change from my habitual mooching around at home, my head was now aching, awash with hypotheses about dead authors whose existence I had not regarded as significant for a nanosecond before. Furthermore, I had lied to her about reading 'The Stone Seat' and 'The Governess'. If I had been able to finish them as a schoolboy, I should most certainly have placed them in the category of Mills and Boon bodice rippers which, in my humble and untutored opinion, would appeal in the main to highly introverted, middle-class schoolgirls. Jane herself had admitted something similar already. I cannot remember what happens in either novel except, as my cynical, old English teacher would have said, they are little more than contrived, mushy tragedies with a serious, social message – the significance of which as a teenager had completely escaped me.

Was this the thing that I had been missing, a clue – a simple explanation even – to what had befallen me? Were the Dean Sisters merely two romantically inclined old maids, living their twilight years vicariously by regaling gullible visitors with tall tales about imaginary people who either were long dead or did not exist all? As if to reinforce my line of thinking, I had this frighteningly surrealistic dream during the night. My car had run out of petrol in the middle of God knows where, and I was straining myself pushing it along a country lane until suddenly it became stuck because the offside front wheel would not move (my injured right ankle?). In a flash I found myself in a gloomy school assembly hall (this hotel?) with several display cabinets built into the wall facing the windows. There were trophies and other artefacts, belonging to former pupils, I fancied, in all of them, and the labels describing the contents of each cabinet were not of the printed cardboard kind but had been carved quite exquisitely onto wooden blocks. I was standing looking into one that had caught my attention, as it contained nothing more than a photograph of two elderly women (Jane and Agnes?), a slim volume of a book and a label on which my name, Douglas Lockwood, was printed. As I stood pondering how it happened to be there, three giggling girls came to stand by me and, without acknowledging my presence, said quite clearly in ghastly sinister voices 'We want you to kill those two interfering, old bitches'. I woke up in a cold sweat at this juncture, not having to think very hard as to who the three girls might be, and I took this to signify that my subconscious mind was warning me to disassociate myself from Jane and Agnes from then on.

And what of the elusively shy young man? The more I thought about his baffling reappearance in the street below, the more I became convinced that he was no more than a keen jogger out for a late-night run. He was dressed in a grey sweat shirt and what looked like grey tracksuit bottoms, and he must have been taking a breather in the street outside the hotel. I had assumed that, because he was looking upwards, he must have been looking at me, when in reality, he was probably gazing at the sky. Why would he have been there otherwise? It was much too late in the day for him to be seeking a casual meeting with me to ask after my health. It had to be what Agnes would have termed an 'interesting happenchance' and nothing else.

On the Tuesday morning I was determined to sneak furtively down for breakfast and return similarly stealthily to my room where I hoped to spend the rest of the day, leaving again only for meals. I would still have to pass through the foyer on my way to and from the dining room but I could avoid eye contact with Jane if she were there and trundle on as fast as possible. I would have to play it by ear if I was accosted, depending mainly on whether I received an invitation to sit and listen to the next episode in the life story of Christopher Heath. I had not seen much of Agnes during the daytime, and, for this reason, I was not at all worried about bumping into her. I do not think that she had a great deal more to add to her preposterous cock and bull story about the Ayres in any case. The best laid schemes o' mice an' men…! I managed to avoid Jane quite easily since the reception desk was unstaffed as I shuffled by.

My breakfast was served as usual by the tight-lipped Nadia and I was reminded that I had yet to enquire about her background. All was going well until I asked her if she would bring me my newspaper, which I had neglected to pick up from reception on my way in, such was my haste to avoid Jane. When she returned she was smiling sphinx-like as she placed it on my table. I gave her a quizzical look but naturally she said nothing and went about her business. I did not have long to wait to find out what her uncharacteristic exuberance signified. Inside the newspaper was paperback copy of Elizabeth Ayre's 'The Stone Seat' and a beautifully handwritten note from Agnes recommending that if I were to read it again, what was undoubtedly puzzling me from my 'tête-à-tête' with Jane would to some degree be clarified. Needless to say, I had absolutely no intention of doing so. The note also invited me to meet her again at eleven o'clock in the lounge. What was I to do? As it was, my decision would be an easy one. I had two hours to kill and just as many options: I could return to return my room or I could attempt to make my way into the village. Mercifully it was not raining and this swayed me towards the walk option.

Ten minutes later I left the hotel, having twice again successfully avoided the absent Jane. It was not easy to make much headway on crutches. They were of the more modern, metal design, where support for the legs is via the forearms and elbows rather than under the armpits, and it took me some time to get used to them when wearing a thickly padded, waterproof jacket. I shambled along slowly and self-consciously past two or three detached cottages and a prosaically designed and dilapidated Baptist church to my left, before the road became narrower, now flanked on both sides by numerous short, cobbled streets of tiny, terraced houses built at right angles to the thoroughfare. As I approached the end of the road, which began to slope gradually upwards, I could see the first shops, the post office that Agnes had broached before, and another hotel in the distance. The incline became too much for me and I had to stop, frustrated at not being able to explore what seemed, from the number of people milling about, to be the focal point of the village. Later I learned that I had indeed been correct in my assumption. It marked the beginning of the commercial area where numerous shops, cafés and restaurants proliferated, most of the names of which made some reference to the Ayres directly, or, more discreetly, by reference to their novels. Hence a fish and chip restaurant had been crassly christened 'The Ayres' Plaice', an expensive women's boutique styled itself pretentiously as 'Emily' after the heroine of 'The Governess', and there was even a pub called 'The Stone Seat'.

Defeated but not too deflated, I returned to The Green Man and sat in the lounge reading my newspaper to await the arrival of Agnes. It occurred me as I lay back in my armchair and closed my eyes, that there may be another solution to my current problem: I could telephone my next door neighbours and ask them to come here and take me home. I had fleetingly considered leaving by taxi before, but I had dismissed this as a possibility because I would have to abandon my car and return at some later date to pick it up. But would either Ron or Jean be able to drive my car back for me? They were both in their seventies and this would entail a difficult journey for both of them, which they would not relish. I was not convinced that I could place them in the delicate position of having to refuse and make an embarrassing excuse, and I dropped the idea, at the same time racking my brains for another couple of individuals who might be able to travel here and back during daylight hours. My brother and his family live in the south of England and most of my long-standing friends live in equally far-flung locations throughout the country. As I have already mentioned, I am not a gregarious person and, as I have grown older, I have been more than satisfied with my own company. In addition I never married for similar reasons. Consequently no one from the suburb of Chester where I live sprang to mind and I resolved to stick it out in Watholme, resigning myself to a few more days of misery.

At ten past eleven, Agnes, dressed in the same green trouser suit she had worn the previous evening, duly emerged from the dining room, her face flushed as though she had just stepped out of a hot bath. I saw her coming because I was sitting facing the foyer. She sat down heavily, ran her fingers through her hair and blew out her cheeks.

"I'm sorry I'm a trifle late," she said breathing deeply. "We've used up all the bread and I had to do an emergency dash to the bakers to buy some more. Otherwise you won't have a basket of rolls with your lunch or your evening meal. We moved onto off-season staffing last week. That leaves us with the chef plus Jane, Nadia and me, so it's all hands to the pumps when necessary."

I tried to smile sympathetically but I felt my lips tighten, disobeying my brain's command to appear relieved that she had been able to keep our appointment. To make matters worse my choice of words to exonerate her tardiness betrayed feelings better suppressed, but she did not seem to notice.

"Take your time," I said clumsily. "I'm a captive audience. I'm not going anywhere else, am I?"

"How are you this morning?" she said jauntily, indicating that she had taken no offence. "Is your ankle any better?"

"About the same, thanks," I replied, and, to add effect, I grimaced theatrically.

"If I remember correctly," she went on. "I'd just finished describing how the Ayres sisters had pretended that they were dead and moved clandestinely to Sicily. You were sceptical, I recall, and were asking all sorts of questions about how they got away with it. Well, Mr Lockwood, it doesn't matter what you think because it happened."

"That's the kind of thing that people who believed the Earth was the centre of the universe used to say," I retorted. "Where's your evidence if it's true and why hasn't any literature specialist discovered their fraud?"

"Oh, that's easy to answer," she came back excitedly. "They got married. Catherine married a rich merchant..."

"That's bigamy?" I snapped. "She was already married to a chap called, er...the name of a city, wasn't it?"

"Yes, she was married to George Carlyle, a wool merchant from Boughton," she laughed. "She must have been attracted to merchants. All the same it's a moot point whether a woman certified as dead can commit bigamy. Within a year she became Carlotta Mancini. Elizabeth got married too, to a notary called Borelli and changed her Christian name to Lisa, Lisa Borelli. They went to live in a small town called Bronte, situated a few miles due west of Taormina. They're both buried with their husbands somewhere in a little churchyard south of the town, in separate, marked graves. That, in a nutshell, is why no one has ever doubted the veracity of their deaths in Watholme. They became other people, abandoned writing altogether and lived quiet, undistinguished lives as conventional, bourgeois wives and probably mothers."

"What happened to Amy then?" I glared. "She can't have married to change her name...can she?"

"Amy didn't like Taormina or Bronte one bit," she continued. "She went there as Amos, had to remain a man and found life hard – Taormina hadn't yet developed into the town that attracted writers, artists and broad-minded people of a similar persuasion. So *she* became a he who couldn't find a job because, unlike her sisters, she didn't speak Italian. This didn't help her with her identity either. She was trapped in her birth body, which unsettled her tremendously. She was probably too scared in an alien environment, a staunchly Catholic society, to solicit men and, as she wasn't interested in women, she had to live a lie. Her father, still in England, didn't mind supporting her, especially when Catherine and Elizabeth moved out of the family villa, but Amy as Amos became very lonely and depressed, and above all terribly homesick. She lasted four more years until Patrick, now also in Bronte, agreed to pay her return fare to England on condition that she didn't go anywhere near Watholme. She travelled about a lot at first and finally settled down in Leeds as Amos Heath, a clerk on the railways, and, wait for it, *he* had a wife called Fanny and a lovely, blue-eyed baby boy, George Benjamin Heath. Yes, he'd changed his name, and, for some unknown reason, his sexuality. No one checked up on things such as birth certificates in those days and, well, like Charlotte and Elizabeth, he got away with everything because history records that he did."

"Hold on a second," I interrupted, almost shouting. "There's a huge credibility gap here, Agnes. Apart from inexplicably transforming himself conveniently into a heterosexual, conformist pillar of society, how old was he? Mid-thirties? Forty?"

"He was forty two when George was born."

"That would be in the early eighteen seventies, wouldn't it? And he changed his name to Heath, did he? Isn't that the same surname as Christopher's?"

"Yes, yes and yes," she returned, a wide grin lighting up her face. "Now you're finally catching on."

"I expect you mean that facetiously," I said. "So Amos was Christopher's great, great grandfather."

"Something like that, yes," she said. "Jane knows the exact number of 'greats' because she's more precise than I am. That makes George Christopher's great grandfather and his son, William Henry, was Christopher's grandad. Robert Henry, William's only son, was Christopher's dad and he married May Davies, Christopher's mum. Jane will show you the family tree she created for him, although it doesn't go as far back as Patrick Ayre for obvious reasons."

"That's all well and good, but how do you know this Amos Heath was *actually* related to the Ayres when no one else in the whole wide world does?" I asked crossly.

"I'll reveal that when I'm ready to," she muttered sheepishly. "Until then you'll have to be patient. On another matter, did you get my note about 'The Stone Seat'?"

"Yes, thanks," I said calming down. "It was a book I had to study in English lessons at school but to be honest I haven't read it from cover to cover. It isn't exactly my cup of tea and I can't remember a great deal about it other than it's set in a moorland village much like Watholme."

"Exactly!" she exclaimed. "That's why you must have a go at rereading it."

"There'll be a synopsis on Wikipedia," I said. "I can't access the Internet from your hotel, so can you recommend a café with Wi-Fi near here?"

"I can't, I'm afraid," she replied, sounding as though she thought she had let me down. "There are some brochures and things over there next to reception that might help. Failing that Jane will be able to fill you in on the novel, or, if she won't, I'll try. She loathes the Ayres but, being a contrary so-and-so she adores this novel, and if she ever gets round to finishing telling you about Christopher, you might understand why."

That marked the end of her lecture about Christopher and the Ayres. From then on she seemed more interested in finding about what my plans were for the remainder of the week, and we discussed what I might do were I ever able to walk more than a hundred yards from the hotel doorway.

"That's given me an idea," I said as she stood up to leave ten minutes later. "You've made me realise that I have to stop moping about and get my backside into gear. Those brochures you suggested should come in very handy."

When Agnes had gone, I made my way slowly over to the leaflet rack and thumbed through the many delights that were on offer in and around Watholme. There were, as expected, numerous fliers for anything that could pass itself off as relating to the three authors, including a wide variety of small Victorian villas, ancient smallholdings, churches of several different denominations, and bijou cottages that might have figured in any of their novels. I was looking for three fliers in particular: the one advertising the Ayre Information Centre, another from any local taxi firm, and lastly, one from any place that offered hopefully free Wi-Fi. To my delight I found all three fairly quickly and limped back upstairs to my room to make an important telephone call.

CHAPTER FIVE

Tuesday Afternoon

If I can't walk very far, I reasoned, then something should take me where I want to go, and I wanted desperately to pay a visit to the Ayre Information Centre. Since there was no bus service past the hotel, I telephoned the first of two local taxi companies whose leaflets I had obtained and asked if they hired out cabs by the hour. The man on the other end of the line said there was a car available that very afternoon and I booked it without bothering to ring his competitor. It cost forty two pounds, which was rather more than I wished to pay, but it amounted roughly to a slow, return journey on a heavily congested road to the nearest city ten miles away, the taxi man told me. I had no real alternative but to accept since it was my only chance to speak to someone who was a genuinely knowledgeable expert on the Ayres and their truncated history.

The taxi, a smart, silver Toyota, arrived at two o'clock. The sky was still overcast but there was a fresh wind blowing hard enough to keep away the rain. We drove to the top of High Street and slowly threaded our way through the pedestrians walking up and down the steep, cobbled road until we came to the Centre situated at the very bottom of the thoroughfare opposite the park gates. It was set back in its own grounds and, from the look of it, it had once been a rich man's mansion. Like most of the other buildings in Watholme it was made of sandstone but it stood out from the majority of other dwellings due to its sheer size. The ground floor had been converted into one very large room serving mainly as a souvenir shop, but there were notices on the walls pointing to a museum and a coffee shop on the first floor. At this time of year on a weekday there was only a handful of tourists about. At the far end to the right was a counter predictably marked 'Information', behind which sat two long-haired, young women visibly exuding boredom. They were chatting to each other as I approached their desk.

"Good afternoon, sir," the first one said politely. "How may I be of assistance?"

She was about twenty four years old, bespectacled and wearing a dark blue cardigan over a black, woollen dress. This was probably her first job since leaving her university English course, I thought mischievously.

"Good afternoon to you too," I replied cheerfully. "I haven't been to Watholme before. I know quite a lot about the Ayre family but I'm still a bit vague about the circumstances surrounding their deaths. I wonder if you can help me?"

"Certainly, sir, I'll do my best," she replied. "It was widely reported in the national newspapers that Elizabeth and Amy Ayre died in the typhoid epidemic of 1860. Catherine died of pneumonia two years later in the winter of 1862. It was very cold that November actually. They're all buried in the family grave in the churchyard down by the school. If you cross the road from here and walk through the park, you'll see it in on your left as you approach the far side."

"Thank you," I said raising one of my crutches. "I'll bear that in mind."

"I'm terribly sorry," she replied, looking flustered. "I hope I haven't offended you. I didn't notice your, er, disability. I do most sincerely apologise."

"Think no more of it," I smiled. "I understand that what happened to their father is still a bit of a mystery."

"Yes, it is," she nodded. "We haven't been able to find anything on paper to substantiate what he did or where he went after Catherine's funeral. He might as well have vanished into thin air. The only thing we can be certain about is that there's no record of his remaining in Watholme after the Ayre cottage was destroyed in a fire in 1864. Shortly afterwards the memorial stone was erected although, to this day, it's not known whether Mr Ayre commissioned or paid for the work."

"How soon after the fire was the hotel 'The Green Man' built?" I asked earnestly. "It's on the site of the cottage, isn't it?"

"Oh no, it isn't," she returned, sounding like a character from a pantomime. "The cottage stood where the memorial is. The inscription is quite clear about it and I quote: 'In loving memory of Elizabeth and Amy Ayre and Catherine Carlyle nee Ayre, novelists. Taken away from us too early'. Then in smaller letters below it reads: 'This stone is also in remembrance of their cottage, which was lost in the disastrous conflagration of 1864'. If you look closely at the enlargement of the early nineteenth century parish map on the wall behind you, you'll see the exact position of the cottage on the empty plot of land on the opposite side of the cart track past the hotel. The hotel was built there around 1865, but I regret to say that we don't know by whom. There are no documents at the Land Registry referring to its building or who acquired the land from what source. The first names on the deeds are those of Samuel Bracewell and Sons but they were a firm of solicitors in Boughton, and that was in 1871. The Land Registry wasn't established until 1862 but registration wasn't compulsory until the turn of the twentieth century. So, all things considered, the credentials of the hotel are pretty vague."

"Could you tell me where the memorial is? I've not been there yet," I said. "Is it far?"

"Turn left outside the Centre and go to the top of High Street," she said. "Follow the road to the end of the village and the hotel's the last house on the right hand side. You can't miss it because the moors start there. The memorial's on the opposite side of the road. All the other major attractions, such as their graves and the school they attended are marked on a more modern map on the wall below the other one."

"One final question," I said confidently. "Do the sisters' death certificates still exist or were they burnt in the fire?"

"Phew," she replied glumly. "No one's asked that before. The short answer is no they don't exist and we can't be sure what happened to them. They will have been signed by a Doctor Ackroyd, the family physician and a friend of Mr Ayre, and he mustn't have retained them for some reason. We do know that they existed because, according to the parish archives, the vicar verified them before the respective interments. Doctor Ackroyd wasn't very well organised and he left his medical records in rather a mess. He blamed it on the mountain of paperwork he had to do single-handedly during the epidemic. Shortly after the fire in 1864 he retired and moved to Liverpool and most of his documents went astray, or else he must have taken them with him by mistake when he left. The new doctor was up in arms about it and, to protect his own back I suppose, he told the local newspaper. The article's still on microfiche in the library down in Boughton, unless it's been uploaded onto their new database. However, as you said in your question, they were most likely burnt in the fire. I must write that down and look into it."

"Thank you very much," I said warmly, hoping to cheer her up. "You're a veritable mine of facts and figures."

"You have to be in this job, sir," she beamed. "We get asked all sorts of questions, but I've never dealt with such a specific one as your last one before. Most people want to know about what the sisters did before they were famous or where they went to school, for example. That sort of thing."

I was laughing to myself as I struggled to get back into the passenger seat of the taxi. I was delighted that I had ascertained in five short minutes that Agnes had indeed been spinning me a yarn as I suspected. This left me in a quandary. What was I to do if she persisted with her claims that her version was true? I would have to go along with it until she ran out of steam, and, in any event, it might make it more enjoyable to see where it went. I was not going to upset her by challenging her. Nevertheless the authorised explanation given by the young woman at the Centre was only slightly more feasible. If I confronted Agnes with my findings, I did not doubt that she would maintain that there was a conspiracy afoot to cover up what actually happened, because she would remind me that *what actually happened* would have dire consequences for the modern Ayre money-making industry.

"You look pleased with yersel," Derek, the taxi driver, said jauntily in his strong Yorkshire accent as I slammed the car door. "Learn owt useful, did you?"

He was a thickset chap of African heritage, somewhere in his mid-forties, I guessed, judging by his middle-aged spread and receding hairline. He was wearing a short-sleeved sports shirt and casual trousers, the archetypal taxi driver's uniform. His beige, cotton zipper jacket was on the back seat.

"Yes, I did," I replied. "I'd like a tour of the village for the rest of my hour. Please take me to Sharp Street first."

It was a short journey. Derek reversed the car and turned left onto a tarmacked road, taking the next right to our destination. He drove slowly past identical rows of terraces, each with two back to back houses at the end facing us on our right as we progressed up the moderate gradient. There were no buildings on the other side, only mud-churned fields with a few sorry-looking sheep munching away in them.

"Looking for somewhere in particular, are you?" he enquired.

"I was until we got here," I said. "But all the houses look alike so I'm none the wiser. Let's go to the church and the primary school and have a look round there."

"Are you checking out the places where the Ayres went?" he said. "There's nowt 'ere if you are. I'll show you around if you want. I've worked out a guided tour because I get a lot of requests for one. Keeps me in business in winter."

"Go ahead," I said, waving him onwards like an arrogant aristocrat in a hackney carriage.

"I'll take the bypass, if that's okay with you," he said as we went along. "It leads straight to the church but it takes a bit longer. I don't like driving up High Street with all those pedestrians milling about. It's a toe and heel job and it burns out the clutch."

"That's fine," I said, suppressing my laughter. "We don't want to break down, do we?"

"Have you read their books?" he went on as taxi drivers are wont to do. "I tried once. I reckon nowt to 'em. Too soppy for me but the wife likes 'em. They're written for women who like strong female characters, she says. That's her opinion anyway. I prefer a gory murder thriller, the more bodies the better."

When we arrived at the church, he dropped me off at the gates as there were no parking spaces in the street. I followed a sign pointing to the burial site of the Ayre Sisters which was at the rear in a surprisingly extensive graveyard. It was not difficult to locate. The headstone was relatively new and it stood out, like the beacon it was, from the weather-beaten rows of the other crumbling sandstone slabs. It was made of grey, polished marble and the names of the authors had been carved into it in gold-inlaid letters.

"The original's in the Information Centre," whispered Derek, startling me; he was standing directly behind me and I had not heard him approaching. "It's in pretty bad nick so they replaced it. It's the amount of bad weather we get here. It even snows in summer, you know."

The school stood in the same grounds and it was exactly as Jane had depicted it. It was a bleak, forbidding structure and it was separated from the church and the cemetery by a high, stone wall.

"Did you go to the school?" I asked him. "Do you remember any of the teachers?"

"Yes, I went there," he replied blankly. "I don't have many happy memories. The teachers were all dry-as-dust tyrants and none of them was wed. It's part of Boughton College now. The kiddies go to a new school down there in the valley."

"Have you ever heard of a Miss Barfield?" I said tentatively

"The late, great Ada Barfield!" he exclaimed, his mood brightening appreciably. "Everybody in Watholme has heard of her. 'Come out the dunce group' and 'Has anybody brought any lunch?' were her catchphrases. She was the last of the genuine characters who taught there. She'd have been in big trouble these days but the wife's father liked her. He was in the top group for reading."

"Shall we go somewhere else?" I said and limped off to the taxi which Derek had left in the school playground, subsequently converted into the College's staff car park.

"I'll take you the long way back and show you a couple of the more interesting sights," he said as he started the engine. "Then you can see what you've been missing."

We drove back down the bypass and into the lane which we had taken previously when we went to Sharp Street. After about half a mile, we left the village behind and came to the western edge of the moors. The road narrowed considerably, hardly wide enough for two vehicles to pass in places, and I was overwhelmed by the speed in which my surroundings had been transformed. I had been transported to a silent, featureless, ageless region which had remained unaltered since time immemorial. At the first road junction, about a mile further on, we turned right and followed a similar tarmacked track, climbing steadily as we cut a path into the upland.

"We'll be there in a tick," Derek said unexpectedly, waking me from my reverie. "I'll drive slowly so that you can take a look at summat spectacular."

As we approached the crest of the summit I recognised the contours of the hills where I had my accident. We were approaching them from the opposite direction to my ill-fated exploration on Sunday afternoon and it took me a few seconds to gain my bearings.

"If you look to the left you'll see some huge blocks of concrete on the next bend," he continued grim-faced.

"They're known as 'The Stone Seat' by us locals, if that means anything to you. They serve as a barrier to prevent vehicles crashing into a bog which is treacherous if you're unlucky enough to go off the road there. No one's ever marked its boundaries because no bugger dare do it. That's what all the warning signs are for. Keep well away if you know what's good for you, that's what they should say. When I was a little lad, a young man lost control of his car on the bend and careered straight into the swamp. It was late at night in one of the worst storms we've ever had. He must have been driving too fast. It was the lad's unexplained disappearance, the tyre tracks on the soggy ground and the skid marks on the road that made the police reach that conclusion, and the coroner recorded accidental death. Summat like that, anyhow. That's why they put the blocks there. A tragedy, a bloody tragedy. He'd had a row with his girlfriend and the daft sod must have wanted to get away as fast as he could. Why he chose to take this road is still an unsolved puzzle. He lived down in Boughton, you see, which is the back the other way. Maybe he wanted to top himself."

"Who was he?"

"I don't know his name but Jane or Agnes at The Green Man might be able to tell you. Folk in these parts say that you can hear him screaming at night when the wind blows. They lock their doors, they close their curtains and they turn the lights out. I think that's stupid because the clue's in the word 'wind', isn't it? Whipping off the hillsides and blowing through the crags. But they believe it's him wailing because they never found his body or the car. They didn't even try looking because the bog's supposed to be bottomless. That's what the old fogeys say. Silly buggers, the lot of 'em."

CHAPTER SIX

Tuesday Evening

When I returned to The Green Man at ten past three, Jane was back in her usual position behind the reception desk reading a magazine. She did not look thrilled to see me.

"Good afternoon, Mr Lockwood," she said gruffly. "I hope you enjoyed your trip out. Have you've been anywhere special, as if I need ask?"

"The taxi driver, Derek Earnshaw, showed me around," I replied, sounding like a police suspect accounting for his movements. "I can't drive and I can't walk very far – I tried this morning and only managed about a hundred yards. It seemed logical, therefore, to hire a vehicle for the afternoon and take advantage of someone who's familiar with the area. I had a circular tour of the village, starting in High Street, and we came back here via the new bypass. I went to the cemetery to see the Ayre grave and I saw the school that Christopher went to. Then Derek took me to the moors and we stopped at the concrete barrier by the bog that swallowed up a car in an accident forty or fifty years ago. Oh yes, I nearly forgot, I also went to Sharp Street but I wasn't able to identify Christopher's house."

"Haven't you left somewhere out?" she muttered sarcastically. "Nadia spotted you going into the Ayre Centre."

"Well, yes I did," I said, feeling my hackles begin to rise. "Isn't that one of the main reasons why people come here? Why are you giving me the third degree?"

"What did Derek tell you?" she persisted, ignoring my protest.

"Nothing extraordinary," I heard myself saying. "Typical taxi driver stuff. He told me about where the original gravestone is and he knows about Ada Barfield. Apparently she's quite famous, or should I say *infamous*. You might be delighted to hear that he doesn't like the Ayre novels. Have I passed my examination?"

"You've passed with flying colours," she laughed as if the foregoing exchange had been some kind of childish game despite its spiteful quality. "He's not struck on this hotel and I was checking if he'd said anything derogatory about us."

"He didn't mention anything about you other than you might know the name of the young chap who died in the accident at the Stone Seat several years ago," I said. "Do you know what he was called?"

"I might do," she replied uneasily, as though my question had touched a raw nerve. "I'll tell you later if you'll meet me here at eight thirty. Agnes won't be coming. I've torn a strip off her for lying to you about the Ayres and she's sulking because I've banned her from speaking to you again. She tries to upstage me whenever I get chatting to visitors. This time she's gone a bit over the top, I fear. Are we on for eight thirty?"

It is no exaggeration to say that I was extremely annoyed by her impudence. I was a guest in her nondescript hotel and I was not duty-bound to have to account for my whereabouts whenever I went out. I did not, however, let my irritation show and I quickly accepted her offer simply to get away from her. I had to take stock of what

I had discovered during my afternoon's excursion and, most of all, I had to devise a subtle strategy with which to confront her about why Agnes had manufactured such an outrageously contrived scenario concerning the Ayres – which made no sense to anyone but her.

When I reached my room I became aware of how much my afternoon trip around Watholme had taken out of me. I lay on my bed, switched on the television with the sound off and quickly fell into a deep, dreamless sleep, which was as much a testament to the quality of daytime TV as my energy-sapping excursion had been. I awoke at ten past six with a dry mouth and intense pain in my bruised ankle. I was also very hungry. Twenty minutes and two pain-killing tablets later I took my seat in the restaurant, waiting expectantly for Nadia to bring me my dinner and half a pint of best bitter with which to slake my thirst.

I have so far not been very kind to the quality of the accommodation at The Green Man but I could not grumble about the cuisine on offer. It was what the blurb on the area website had referred to as 'traditional English cooking' and it was excellent. On Sunday evening I had feasted on roast beef and Yorkshire pudding followed by apple pie and custard, on Monday I had polished off rack of lamb with seasonal vegetables, and today chicken casserole was on the menu. The chef must have been catering exclusively for me, since, once again, I was dining alone and it made me feel pampered for the first time. Perhaps I was being too harsh, too demanding for my own good. On balance, although Jane and, to a lesser extent, Agnes had been entertaining me with two fatuous, if thought-provoking tales, whatever their unfathomable motives, they had so far prevented me from enduring two days of abject boredom, isolated in my room with nothing to do other than to watch TV or feel sorry for myself, which amounts to the same thing in my book. My spirits were also lifted by the hangdog expression on Nadia's face every time she came to my table. I was not paranoid enough to believe that she had been sent to spy on me in Watholme that afternoon, but it goes without saying that she had reported my presence at the Ayre Information Centre probably without prompting, revealing her steadfast loyalty to the two sisters without necessarily being in league with them.

At eight thirty on the dot I took up my usual position in the lounge to wait for Jane as arranged. A bottle of red wine had, as now seemed customary, already been placed on the table. A few short minutes later, she materialised from the dining room, as ever in her black outfit and looking like the cat that had already eaten the cream. She was almost running towards me.

"Hello again," she purred, "I have something to feel cheerful about. I've just taken umpteen reservations from a party of schoolteachers for half term. Every room's been taken and they've booked full board for the whole week. The drinks are on me."

"Congratulations," I said, forcing a smile. "When's half term?"

"In two or three weeks' time," she replied, forcing a corkscrew into the neck of the wine bottle. "They're going to walk the length of the moors as well as enjoying themselves taking in the delights of Watholme. That usually means getting drunk a lot. I'll have to hire a couple of extra staff, probably two or three of my trusty locals. We'll get more enquiries about the week after now that half terms are staggered. We're very popular with teachers. That's why we stay open the whole year round."

I continued to smile until my face ached, not because I was pleased for her but because I was pondering what my holiday would have been like if the hotel had been full. I would not be sitting on my own in the lounge humouring the owner, that much was certain. I was brought back to reality by the explosive sound of the cork being removed.

"I must apologise for Agnes's behaviour last night," she went on, filling our glasses. "She'd no right to tease you with such complete poppycock! She's got a fertile imagination and unless you know her well, there's no way you can possibly sort out the truth from her fantasies. It's not your fault that you were taken in enough to consult the experts. That's why you went to the Ayre Centre, isn't it?"

"What she said had a kind of plausibility that was easy to swallow," I said defensively. "The official facts of the matter are likewise vague and open to closer scrutiny. I'm surprised that no one's done any research or come up with a conspiracy theory similar to the one proposed by Agnes. It doesn't matter anyway. After I'd been to the Centre, I was convinced that no one suspects that there's anything fishy about the deaths of the sisters, Patrick Ayre's abrupt disappearance and the circumstances surrounding the building of this hotel, although no authoritative evidence for any of them seems to exist."

"I thought you'd reach that conclusion," she returned. "Why don't you delve deeper?"

"Now you're being silly," I grinned. "I wouldn't know where to start and who'd pay any attention to an amateur sleuth like me? Besides the woman at the Centre disagrees with what you told me about the original site of the cottage. There's a large map on the wall in the Centre showing quite clearly the existence of a cottage where the memorial now stands. Their version's obviously much more likely to be authentic, so I'm prepared to go along with it and let sleeping dogs lie."

"Well, that seems to be the end of that but your young lady's mistaken about the location of the cottage!" she laughed. "Let's get down to a bit of business before we do anything else. Agnes says you've upgraded to a front view, double room and she's charged you seventy five pounds extra."

"Yes, that's correct," I said, nodding my agreement. "Is there something wrong with the arrangement?"

"No, she's behaved perfectly appropriately," she replied. "It's in keeping with our normal practice. However I'm letting you off the surcharge – for three reasons before you protest!"

"You sound like Scrooge on Christmas Day when he fooled Bob Cratchit into thinking he was going to be sacked," I joked. "And what pray, my good lady, are those three reasons?"

"The first one's for Watholme's sake," she declared. "The second one's because I'm in such a good mood this evening, and, lastly for what Agnes put you through."

"She got me out for some fresh air and a bit of sightseeing so don't be too harsh on her," I said, stretching forwards to pick up my wine. "And she told me where you've been for the past twenty four hours. How's your sick relative bearing up?"

"She's not too well," she frowned, her broad smile evaporating. "She's a long-term invalid and she's going through a bad patch. It's all my fault because of something I told her about you."

"About me?" I laughed. "What's so special about me?"

"She's very poorly," she repeated quietly.

"I'm sorry to hear that," I said, hoping that I didn't sound insincere. "Does she live in with you?"

She shrugged her shoulders ambiguously leaving me none the wiser. She clearly did not wish to discuss the matter and a burgeoning frown turned into a full-blown scowl. We sat silently at this temporary hiatus, staring anywhere but at each other until I hit upon an idea to brighten up the proceedings.

"Am I the only guest for the whole week?" I ventured.

"Apparently," she said unhelpfully. "We had a cancellation yesterday because of the weather. There isn't much to do when it's squally."

"Is that why you're telling me all about Christopher Heath?" I asked, hoping that she would not think that I was patronising her.

"No, of course not," she said coolly. "It's relevant to your, er, recent misfortune, isn't it? It also does me good to share a good yarn of an evening. I miss having someone interesting to chat to when I've finished my duties. Agnes prefers to go out for a stroll. Neither of us watches much telly and if you weren't here, I'd have had an early night."

"Have you told anyone else about him?"

"No, as I said on Sunday. Why should I?"

"I was just curious."

"Shall I get on with it, then?"

"I have two more questions first," I said more firmly than I had allowed her to be accustomed to. "Why didn't you tell me you owned the hotel?"

"I thought you knew," she replied coldly. "My name's on the licence plate above the front door. Does it matter?"

I could feel that she was losing her patience with me. Undoubtedly she preferred to be in charge of our conversation, judging by the number of times she

83

prevaricated whenever I tried to seek clarification of anything remotely enigmatic. All the same I pressed on.

"Why doesn't Nadia say anything?" I said. "I'm well aware that she's a foreigner but she seems reluctant speak to me."

"She's Kosovo-Albanian," she said, tilting her head to one side and raising her eyes. "She came to this country when she was a child, a refugee from the Kosovo War in 1999. She's the only survivor from her family who were systematically 'ethnically cleansed' – I believe that's the appropriate phrase – along with thousands of others by the Serbs. She must have witnessed atrocity upon atrocity and she's still pretty traumatised. She doesn't like being alone with a man unless it's somewhere open like the dining room. We've had her for the last four years and she regards Agnes and me as surrogate aunts. She's a hard worker and generally she's okay. Sometimes she has flashbacks at night, but she's steadily getting better. She'll go out on her own nowadays but only as far as the village."

She put her empty glass on the table, uncrossed her legs and inched forwards to be closer to me, as if to suggest that she was about to reveal something even more earth-shattering about Nadia. Our faces were only a few inches apart and, involuntarily, I pulled myself back into my chair.

"She told me about the little incident when you moved rooms," she said. "She thinks you're a nice man and she likes you. I'd count that as a small victory, if I were you."

I smiled another insipidly thin smile, not because I had obtained a straight answer at last, but because Jane had saved me from additional embarrassment. I had fully intended to ask Nadia at breakfast the next morning why she had run away from me, but thank goodness I had had the common sense to ask Jane first. Jane, however, was becoming visibly more edgy.

"Shall we get on?" she added, sitting back and folding her arms. "Christopher's about to go to grammar school."

"I'm all ears," I said wryly, cupping the said organs. "Fire away!"

"This is the part of his biography that I don't have first-hand knowledge of, so it'll be more disjointed than before," she announced solemnly. "The grammar school was an all boys' school. I say 'was' because it was replaced by a state of the art, new school forty years ago, in the green belt area on the Sleighton road. The 'old' school, like most built over a hundred years ago, was a grimy, four-storey edifice bang in the middle of the town centre with a small, tarmacked area which was used at break times as an exercise yard – there isn't a patch of grass or a tree anywhere within its grounds. If you ever get down to Boughton you can't miss it. It sticks out like a sore thumb from all the other buildings that surround it. It's been empty for a number of years. It can't be long before it's demolished and replaced by a suite of offices or something. There's a consortium of businessmen interested in buying it, I hear. In its heyday in the middle of last century the school had a reputation for academic excellence and sporting prowess, mainly in cricket and rugby. Many of the teachers had degrees from Oxford or Cambridge but when it went comprehensive in the nineteen seventies you'd be hard-pressed to find some of them with any kind of degree. The brain drain had started at the end of the sixties when the staff got wind of the sweeping changes in educational policy. Let me say from the outset that I believed in the three-tier system – grammar, technical and secondary modern – which I'm sure you experienced, didn't you?"

"I failed my eleven plus and went to a technical school," I replied. "I wasn't intellectually inclined so it didn't bother me. I liked working with my hands and I went on to do an engineering apprenticeship with day release at the local college. I ended up as a fairly senior manager by time serving rather than through qualifications."

"There you are then," she continued. *Quod erat demonstrandum*. There's no need for me to browbeat you. I went to public school when I was twelve. I was a day pupil at a small place called Broadacres, near Sleighton. It closed down years ago when it couldn't attract enough boarders."

"If you don't have first-hand knowledge of this part of your story, where did you obtain your information about the boys' grammar school?" I said, trusting that I was not trying her patience again.

"Yes, I ought to clarify that," she replied. "I went to school in Watholme until I was seven. After that my father removed me from the primary school down the road because he considered it too rough and ready. He had social pretensions because he owned this hotel so he used his influence with the council and he had me transferred to Highton. The children from its catchment area were more suitable for 'sophisticated young ladies' like me. Those were his very words. Their parents were solicitors, accountants, bank managers and the like. He drove me there every morning and picked me up in the afternoon. He did the same when I passed my scholarship and started at the girls' grammar school, but that wasn't good enough either. He decided I had to have a proper education and found a place for me at Broadacres. I had to catch two buses to get there though, starting at seven o'clock from here."

"What about Agnes?" I said when she paused for another mouthful of wine. "I didn't get the impression that she went to Highton."

"No, she didn't and she was quite miffed about it," she laughed. "Daddy regarded her as less bright than me, which was horrible of him. She stayed in Watholme till she was eleven when she also passed her scholarship. She had to go to the girls' grammar though, where she got three good 'A' levels and subsequently ended up at Hull University. It worked out for her in the end too."

"You still haven't told me where you obtained your information about the boys' grammar school?" I asked.

"I was coming to that, wasn't I?" she answered in a manner that suggested she regarded my question as yet another impertinent intrusion. "I was at the same school as Christopher only during my last year at Highton. I was three years older than him, so we were never in the same class together even when he was moved up a year. When I was eighteen I started going out with his pal Brendon. He'd lost all his puppy fat by then and he was quite a charmer, even though he was a year or so younger than me. We met at a folk club and became friends until we went our separate ways a couple of months later. He told me a few things about Christopher's junior school days that I wasn't aware of and some of his experiences at secondary school. I picked up other bits and pieces from what I observed and what Christopher told me himself. The rest came from one or two other boys who went there."

She rubbed her eyes for a few seconds and let out a long, deep breath. Without looking at me, she shook her head from side to side rapidly. A few more seconds later she regained her composure, finished her wine and smiled apologetically.

"This is going slower than I expected," she continued. "So many people. So many people. Let me press on. Christopher was immensely overawed by grammar school. It was ten times larger than both the junior schools he'd attended put together, and it was much more old-fashioned than he expected, reminding him of Rugby School in *Tom Brown's Schooldays*, a black and white film he'd seen on television during the summer holidays. It became a frightening ordeal for him at first. Every boy was taller than him, they wore identical uniforms and the teachers wore smart suits, half hidden by their academic gowns. The cacophonous noise at morning assembly made by hundreds of shouting boys unsettled him until he got used to it. Previously he'd been an enthusiastic and jolly pupil, but now he encountered three new, negative emotions. Shyness, inhibition and fear, which combined to make him neurotic. He worried about anything, especially when he thought he might get into in trouble. In his first year he was the youngest boy there. Since he'd gone up a year at primary school and he'd passed his eleven plus underage, many of the new intake were two years older than he was. Quite a few were from Watholme, but they were the older boys he vaguely recollected from in and around the village, and he'd only come across them occasionally in the junior school yard. Brendon was placed in a different form from him, as were all his friends from Highton, some of whom came from Oakgrove. In the early days he endured an unfamiliar loneliness, but gradually he made new acquaintances and settled down to a different world of sights, sounds and smells, and, of course, learning. Yes, I did say smells, starting with the pungent, leathery pong of his new satchel. He once told me that his earliest memories of the grammar school consisted of draughty, high-ceilinged classrooms, narrow, windowless corridors and the sterile aroma of freshly polished, wooden floors everywhere he went – except the toilets of course. They smelled of smoke because they were situated near the boiler house. When he walked past the staff room for the very first time, the door was opened suddenly, and the reek of cigarette and pipe smoke nearly bowled him over, it was that strong. It's funny what your initial impressions are, isn't it?"

"You're an excellent storyteller," I said in all sincerity, making every effort not to sound too fawning. "With a memory like yours and such a way with words, you should have been an actor or an author, or, failing that, a TV presenter."

"I've been two of those," she replied light-heartedly. "You'll have to guess which two, but here's a clue. I've never been on television. That's surprised you, hasn't it?"

"It would be a really boring day if you or Agnes didn't stagger me at least twice an hour," I laughed. "I bet if I ask you to explain yourself, you'll say 'I'll tell you later'."

"Thirty odd years ago I wrote a pamphlet entitled 'Nineteenth Century Watholme'," she replied, grinning wickedly. "It's in its fourth reprint and it's still on the bookshelves at the Information Centre priced competitively at three pounds ninety nine. As for being an actor, I used to be into amateur dramatics when I was a teenager. Sorry to disappoint you."

"Okay, I'm not shocked," I said. "I'll buy a copy of your booklet if I get the chance."

"That's the ticket, now where was I?" she continued, resuming her more formal tone. "When he started at grammar school Christopher was placed in the B stream. Brendon went into the A stream and from then on their strong bonds of friendship weakened as the differences in their ability, which weren't too noticeable at junior school, began to manifest themselves in their annual reports. A year later Christopher was promoted to the A stream where he continued to keep his head down and work hard, but he could never match top of the class Brendon, despite achieving a top ten position each year. To complicate matters the A stream had been selected to be an elite cohort which was known as the Fast Lane. This was one of those educational experiments whereby for the next three years the brightest boys in that particular year studied eight academic subjects for their O levels, dropping what were regarded as peripherals such as art, carpentry or metalwork, biology and geography. It was scrapped the following year without explanation but I imagine it was because it was too narrow a curriculum, or someone genius had worked out that most of the boys would be fifteen when they started their advanced levels. That meant they'd have to spend an extra year at school at the wrong end of their studies, most likely with nothing much to do other than kick their heels doing meaningless extra subjects until they could go to university, or leave and take a gap year. Whatever, the Headmaster's decision to continue to run with it for this particular group, had a monumental effect on Christopher's future. On paper he was successful. He achieved eight good passes and, at the ripe old age of fourteen, he went straight into the sixth form, two years ahead of the normal schedule. That was when he changed completely. The sixth form was a term used to define a block of students aged sixteen to nineteen doing advanced studies, and at the grammar schools that meant, ninety nine times out of a hundred, taking two, three or four 'A' levels. These days it's referred to as years twelve and thirteen, so I'm told. Now take Christopher, fourteen and a half years old, physically weedy with newly sprouted pubic hair, in with lads who were not only bigger than he was, they were far more mature in both body and mind. Picture him on the rugby field! Many had long-standing girlfriends and went out drinking, whereas Christopher wasn't too familiar with female anatomy and still liked trainspotting. He could just about compete with them academically but in every other aspect he was like a fish out of water, until he fell in with some 'wrong-uns', that is. He'd chosen to do Arts subjects, one of which was French, and he started knocking about school with three or four of his classmates from this course, who were all two years older. They taught him more about the opposite sex and teenage life than he would have learned naturally and in many ways he did benefit, as you'll soon see. Brendon had plumped for sciences, although he could equally well have followed the arts route had he so wished, and from here on in his and Christopher's paths diverged considerably."

As Jane spoke these words there was a tremendous clap of thunder, followed almost immediately by streaks of sheet lightning which illuminated the outside world like a speeding police car's flashing blue lamps. The lights in the bar flickered for a few seconds until normality was restored. We were both momentarily stunned by this inauspicious sign from the heavens until we burst out laughing simultaneously at the ridiculousness of our reaction.

"Someone's angered the gods," she shrieked. "I hope it isn't me!"

"You've managed to add sound effects to your narrative," I said, shaking my head in mock admiration. "What's next, background music?"

"There's another storm brewing and my voice will probably be drowned out by the rain splashing the windows," she replied. "That means another confounded delay."

Her prediction proved to be correct. For the next few minutes the rain lashed down and she got up to shut the front door.

"I'll go and check everything's all right at the back," she shouted from the foyer. "I won't be long."

I stood up and stretched, raising my arms high above my head and arching my spine. I felt more relaxed than I had done for the past few days and I must have yawned half a dozen times. The pain in my ankle was also easing and I hobbled over to the windows to see what was happening out in the street. The rain had slackened and all that remained to testify that there had ever been a squall were rippling torrents of water being swallowed up by the drains. There were no people about. Even the clouds had vanished, leaving a black, starlit backdrop high above the roofs of the houses across the road.

Jane was gone for over half an hour. When she returned her face was strained and she was wiggling her fingers in agitation for no apparent reason. I was still standing by the window and the sound of her footsteps had made me turn round.

"Are you okay?" I enquired politely, ensuring that there was no trace of any emotion in my voice other than one of mild concern.

"I'll be fine after another drink," she replied as she hesitated beside the bar. "The crisis is over, for the time being anyway."

"It's not serious, I hope," I said, slightly startled by her ominous words. "Has there been any damage?"

"Nothing physical and nothing for you to bother about," she muttered edgily. "Pour me a drink, please and fill my glass. Let's get on with story, shall we?"

She did not sit down immediately. Instead she went to the reception desk and leaned over it to search for something. She rummaged around and a box of tissues materialised in her hand as she withdrew it from behind the counter.

"I'm sorry," she said enigmatically after she blew her nose. "I don't like storms. They unsettle the horses."

"I beg your pardon," I grinned as I poured her wine. "Which horses would they be?"

"Nothing to concern yourself about," she repeated. "Christopher's waiting patiently."

Why was she deliberately talking in riddles, I wondered? Something serious must have happened backstage to unnerve her to such an extent but I had no time to dwell on this. She sat down with a bump, picked up her glass and drained it in one.

"That's better," she declared, whereupon she launched straight into continuing saga of Christopher Heath.

"Let's go back to Christopher's time in the A stream," she continued. "There isn't much to report about his four years in the lower school. In the second form he stood as the Liberal Party candidate in a simulated election and received no votes other than those from himself and Brendon, his loyal 'agent'. This was due to a disastrous speech he gave because he was shaking like a leaf and he couldn't string two words together. He was also beaten for misspelling the word 'pamphlet' and every time he saw that word thereafter, he winced. He enjoyed the railway society trips to places he'd never heard of in the North of England and when he went on holiday with his family, he spent most of the week alone either trainspotting or watching cricket matches. He made two new friends in his second year, Richard and Steven, the little and large of the class. Titchy Richard, a dapper, little chappie, was a bit of a wide boy. He was also a smoker and it was he who encouraged Christopher to take up the filthy habit a couple of years later. Steven was a great guy, however, despite what happened when they first met. His surname was Lumb, and, totally out of character, Christopher made a crude joke over and over again about what it rhymes with. This irritated Steven no end and he warned Christopher that he would thump him if he repeated it once more. Christopher did and Steven blacked his eye. They always laughed about it afterwards, believe it or not. Christopher also met Philip, the brainbox of the class, and for a while Christopher was drawn to him because he was shy and a worrier to boot. This was the gang that grew up together until they split apart in their late teens. Brendon, the cerebral, suave charmer, Philip the intellectual philosopher, Richard the dapper spiv, and lanky Steven the easy-going optimist. Brendon and Philip went to university, Richard got a job in London and Steven, who remained in Boughton with Christopher, went to work as a trainee accountant."

As she spoke, she had a fond, faraway look in her eyes as though she was visualising the four young men one by one as she slowly described them to me. It must have been a very happy period in her life and perhaps she wanted somehow to turn back the clock and be with them again. I, conversely, was beginning to lose patience, finding it difficult to make sense of why she was going into so much detail. She was packing too many anecdotes and new characters into this second or third part of Christopher's life – I was losing count – and it had become an incoherent mess of woolly-mindedness. I could no longer follow who was who, and I have had to rack my brains to recall all their names, some of which I may have got wrong.

"Christopher's now found himself in an established circle of friends," she continued. "When you add these to the new lot he met in the sixth form, he was prepared for the next stage of his life, and that was, as if you can't guess, girls. Not academic brilliance, oh no. It was girls, and, to put it crudely, they came by the bucketful. They threw themselves at him. He'd always been attractive as a child and his good looks blossomed when he was fifteen. Without a word of a lie he looked a lot like Michelangelo's statue of David with clothes on, but much more handsome. He never realised what an overpowering effect he might have because he was still shy and nervous, and up till then his favourite pastimes were watching rugby, cricket and football and collecting train numbers – girls weren't at all important to him. It started at a church disco and, extremely reluctantly, he asked a young lady to dance. Richard, ciggie in hand, had pointed out that step by step she was moving closer to Christopher as she bopped away with a female partner, and he bet him that he didn't dare cut in. Christopher plucked up courage and she accepted with a lovely smile but he was instantly confused, because he hadn't thought things through. He assumed he'd be rejected and he didn't know how to dance or what do after the music stopped. Well, she showed him what to do and started to chat him up after the record had finished. She made it that easy for him. They spent the rest of the evening together and he walked her home afterwards. His first ever snog came on her doorstep where she made two big mistakes. She told him how good-looking he was and she asked if she could see him again. Her name was Dorothy, while we're on the subject. He ran all the way home, bursting to tell his mates what had happened. The next day, in a coffee bar in Boughton town centre, for the first time in his life he looked at girls, and he noticed that they stared back for longer than they should have done. The following weekend he finished with Dorothy at a party, and took up with Margaret, who lasted two weeks.

She was followed by Beverley, Christine, two Jeans and a Susan, a string of new girlfriends who were lucky if they saw a full cycle of the moon."

Jane smiled constantly as she reeled off many more names to add to this preliminary list, as though she were proud of her ability to dredge them all up in the correct order. Nonetheless, how could I have judged if any this was accurate? Soon, however, it became apparent why she had gone to such lengths.

"He'd started smoking by then because he said it made him feel older," she added, looking at me in vain for confirmation. "But he couldn't fool the others, particularly Brendon. No, he started smoking because he suffered from anxiety which comes in many forms. In this case it was because he found the thrill of the chase incredibly stressful and a cigarette or two calmed his nerves and made him look cool, a classic case if ever there was one. But there is no pleasure without pain of some kind, is there? He slowly but surely became aware of one thing that was to haunt him. He came from a *working class* family, whereas every single one of his friends and conquests hailed from the posher side of the tracks. Their fathers worked in offices and wore suits and ties; his dad worked in a garage and wore overalls. Whenever he visited one of their houses, it was always a smart semi or even more grand – and they all had bathrooms. This presented him with a problem, the problem I alluded to right at the start of my story: his house had an outside toilet, and it had be kept a closely-guarded secret for fear of ridicule by his well-to-do friends. He could easily pretend that he too was middle class because he went to grammar school. He was *an articulate, clever boy*, and he became adept at fooling them all by avoiding answering direct questions about who his parents were and where he lived. He'd become a terrible snob and he took great care *never* to invite anyone home. He was especially ashamed of having to invent deceitful excuses to prevent any of his school buddies or sweethearts from gaining access to the horror lurking in the backyard. 'Why can't I ever come to your house?' was a question that always terrified him. 'Because – insert 'mother', 'father' or the name of one of his two brothers – is poorly,' was his instant, well-rehearsed reply, depending on which one of the four possible responses he'd used before. Illness was therefore suspiciously rife in his family, more so when his invalid grandmother came to stay and she brought with her a commode, a piece of furniture resembling a large, backless dining chair, lurking inside which was a large chamber pot. It was an inside toilet of sorts, but it was on public view and it left foul-smelling odours for hours after she had 'done her business' in it. That was his mother's explanation, a typical euphemism for which she was legendary – and she had a rich store of such niminy-piminy phrases. His grandmother had had a stroke, if you recall. A bed was set up for her downstairs and a whole array of new complications and a further set of unwelcome embarrassments reared their ugly heads, although it did provide perfect grounds for keeping outsiders at bay for as long as she remained alive. 'We can't go in,' he would say. 'My grandma's bed is in the living room and it might upset her if she sees a stranger.' Bingo. A new challenge threatened, however, when he started to go out with girls. A year or so after his grandmother died, one of them insisted that he invited her for Sunday tea so that she could meet his family, mistakenly presuming that, as they'd been seeing each other for a few weeks and fully aware of his reputation as a fly-by-night, they were well on the road to engagement and marriage. She was so insistent that he couldn't get out of it. His mother put on quite a show: a ham salad, tinned fruit with Carnation milk, and a large pot of tea served in their best china cups. She even used a tea strainer. He prayed that the girl's bladder was a strong one.

'It's time to go,' he whispered surreptitiously after half an hour. 'The film starts soon and we've just got time for a coffee beforehand.'

'I'll just go to the toilet then,' the girl replied, startled by this impulsive announcement of imminent departure.

'You can go at the coffee bar,' he growled tyrannically. 'Come on, get your coat.'

He finished with her that very evening. The young woman had seen an unsettling side to his character and she thought he was weird. He didn't care. His secret was safe and he'd repelled another boarder. He'd become a snob, Mr Lockwood, a social climber, although the pretentious, young so and so referred to himself as *déraciné*. He was an arrogant prat, a traitor to his heritage and his upbringing, though, deep down, he loathed himself for it. Pride comes before a fall, as you shall discover. We're back to where I began on Sunday, aren't we? I told you that there's a rational method in my madness but I'm not finished yet, not by a long chalk."

She was about to drink up the remainder of her wine when the telephone in the reception area rang. She did not go and sit behind her desk to answer it; she leaned over the counter again with her back to me and picked up the handset. She seemed mildly annoyed at first as she listened to whatever was being said, but her posture changed as the call progressed. She grabbed a notebook and scribbled a few words and when she replaced the receiver, she turned round and raised her left fist in triumph.

"You're going to have company tomorrow," she shouted. "Two Belgian couples. I'll have to stop there for tonight, I'm afraid. I have to make sure everything's shipshape. Good night Mr Lockwood."

"You should have the Internet installed," I yelled back. "That way you can take your bookings without having to…"

"Oh no, no, no," she interjected impatiently. "I don't want that. I'd be forever checking my website. Besides I haven't got a computer. Good night!"

She was gone before I could bid her goodbye, leaving me once more with two fifths of a bottle of undrunk Rioja. My head was still spinning after being bombarded for the best part of three days with so much unwanted information about Christopher Heath, a man whose life story I cared not a jot about, and I needed to reward myself for enduring its inexplicable futility for so long, despite her insistence that there was some coherent purpose to it. I decided therefore that Jane owed me the pleasure of having one last drink on her and I would take the bottle to bed with me. It would not be easy to manage my crutches and carry a glass and an uncorked bottle but I was determined to try.

Ten minutes later I was sitting in the armchair in my room watching television with my bad leg propped up on the lukewarm central heating radiator under the window. I must have dozed off soon after downing my first few mouthfuls of the wine because I was jerked abruptly back to my senses around midnight by the raucous sound of someone banging a dinner gong repeatedly downstairs. As I struggled woozily to get to my feet to investigate the source of this nerve-jarring hullabaloo, it stopped, and a blood-curdling, high-pitched howl reverberated through the very fabric of the building. It was, without exaggeration, the most spine-chilling sound I have ever heard, and the mere thought of it still makes my hair stand on end.

CHAPTER SEVEN

Wednesday Morning and Afternoon

I did not sleep much that night. After my initial panic subsided, I poked my head cautiously out into the corridor but there was nothing in sight. It was as silent as the proverbial grave, and the only sounds I could hear were my shallow breathing and the rapid beating of my heart pounding in my ears. I did not venture further since I could not see what I would be able to do if I were confronted or attacked by whatever it was that had wailed so harrowingly. No wild animal had made that scream, not even a wolf, of that I was sure. It had come from deep inside some wretched human being who was suffering intense pain, an agony that could just as well have been psychological as physical. Was it one of Nadia's flashbacks, I pondered, that had caused her to wander around in the dark, reliving, albeit temporarily, the excruciating nightmares she had witnessed in Kosovo? But why should she bang the dinner gong so manically? No, it had to be the action of a madman – or more likely a mad *woman*, for as far as I knew I was the only man in residence. Jane had said I would hear frighteningly strange sounds in or around Watholme during the storm on Sunday night.

As this thought flitted through my mind, I suddenly realised that there were no other guests in the hotel and that I was alone in the building. Had anyone else been present, surely they would have come out of their rooms to investigate what was going on in the same way that I did. Slowly it dawned on me that I may be in great danger, that I could be robbed or even murdered, and no one would be the wiser until my dead or injured body was found when my room was cleaned after breakfast. I would have to speak to Jane as soon as possible about this and what, for instance, I might do in the event of a fire.

I closed the door quickly and locked it, testing the handle several times before I was certain that it was shut tight. I spent the next few hours lying on my bed with one of my crutches beside me to use as a weapon. I was determined not to nod off but I was very drowsy and I felt myself drift away on frequent occasions. Or so it seemed. I was jolted back to torpid consciousness at seven o'clock by the rasping buzz of my alarm clock, to find myself on my left side, with my back facing the door and saliva dribbling out of the corner of my mouth. I had been out cold for more than four hours!

After a quick wash and a complete change of clothes, I made my snail-like way down for breakfast. I was most anxious to speak to Jane to seek an explanation about who or what had caused that awful racket, and to report an important aspect of health and safety that she had failed to acquaint me with. While I was about it, I also intended to point out that since it had no elevator, the hotel was required by law to install a stair-lift for disabled guests and staff. Naturally she was nowhere to be found! Another surprise was waiting for me when I entered the dining room. A radiantly smiling Nadia was standing by my usual table holding my daily newspaper.

"Good morning, Mr Lockwood," she said, sounding like she was reading from a script. "How are you today?"

"I'm fine, thanks," I stuttered. "Do you know where either Jane or Agnes is?"

"They are not here," she added robotically. "They are indisposed for the time being. Here is your morning paper which I hope you will read with some pleasure."

With that she spun on her heels and scurried off to the kitchen. It was obvious that she had been coached, right down to the pirouette, although she had fluffed her lines slightly at the end. But why? Perhaps she was acting out of character to convince me that it was not she who was responsible for the macabre disturbance during the night. If so, it was beyond doubt that she had been put up to it by the Deans. On the other hand, it could have been a clever trick, overegging the pudding to make me believe that it had indeed been Nadia. That would neatly put me off the scent that someone else could have been the guilty party, say Jane or Agnes or even the 'sick relative' that they had referred to on numerous occasions.

Until now I had surmised that the invalid lived elsewhere in the village and that Jane's unforeseen absences were caused by her having to leave the hotel. Then again, I had failed to absorb fully something that Jane had mouthed to Agnes when she called her away on Monday evening, something presumably I was not supposed to catch. 'She'll see you now,' she had said, before adding, 'you'd better be quick before she goes back to sleep.' Was there another woman living here, someone they kept out of view in the staff quarters, which I had not yet seen? What did this accommodation consist of, I wondered, as I munched away at my cornflakes? Did someone live in a room above mine, an attic, say? That would explain the eerie shuffling noises I had heard so clearly the other night. Or was there an annexe in the form of a block of chalets or another suite of rooms attached to the hotel building? I would have to go through the kitchen area to access whatever it was, but that would be out of bounds to an inquisitive lodger. Since my bedroom looked out onto the front street, the rooms at the opposite side of the corridor would afford me a view to the rear, but they were always kept locked. The only way to find out was to ask Jane.

After breakfast I returned to my room and sat down on the unmade bed to read my newspaper which I had not yet opened. I was about to peruse the front page for an article of interest, when my eyes fell on a brown envelope which had been pushed under the door. I picked it up carefully, assuming it to be a bill or some other kind of formal communication, since the hotel address was printed on it. I was wrong on both counts; it was a map of Watholme or, rather, an extract from the early nineteenth century parish map which adorns one of the walls in the Ayre Information Centre, showing the eastern edge of the village only. There was a yellow post-it' attached to it which read:

> *'This is part of the genuine map of Watholme, not a forgery like the one you saw yesterday down at the Centre. If you don't believe me, go to Boughton Library and verify it for yourself.'*

The message had been signed by Jane. A closer inspection of the map revealed that the road on which the hotel is situated had been circled in faint, red ink, with an arrow pointing to an extra cottage at the end leading to the moors. There was only open land on the other side of the road, indicating that a portion of it must have been the plot that Agnes said Patrick Ayre had purchased and where the monument now stood.

I tossed the map away in despair and slumped back down onto the bed. I leaned forwards and put my head in my hands, wishing for all the world that I could escape this prison I now found myself in. Why could Jane not allow me to spend the rest of my holiday in peace waiting for my sprained ankle to heal sufficiently to enable me to drive? Why was it so important to her that I trusted her judgement about the precise location of the cottage in any case? If she and Agnes were so confident that they could prove that the Ayres were scoundrels, why had they already not done so? Moreover, why were they involving me? Surely they would have chosen some highly qualified bookworm to help them, not a retired engineer who had not read one single novel to the end by any of the famous sisters. I did not get much further with these muddled objections. They were driven away by the jangling of a key in the lock followed by Agnes's sing-song voice asking me if I were 'decent'. I pulled myself together and told her calmly to come in and I had to smile when I saw that she was wearing an orange, floral patterned housecoat over her green trouser suit.

"I'm sorry I'm a little late this morning," she said as she entered. "Jane's in a tis-was about some new guests who are arriving this afternoon. They're Belgians which makes them special in her eyes. She worked in Belgium after she left university, teaching English at a school for sophisticated young ladies. She speaks French fluently so she'll want to get in some practice tonight, you wait and see. Personally I hope they're Flemish. Poor old Nadia's making up their rooms at the other end of the passageway as I speak."

For once I did not regard Agnes as an unwelcome intruder; it was a fortuitous opportunity to ask her about the goings-on that had scared me half to death in the middle of the night. I laughed politely to humour her because I wanted her to retain her high spirits.

"What was that awful howling at about half past midnight?" I said resolutely.

She did not answer straightaway. She placed a finger on her bottom lip, as if trying to recall such a memorable event.

"An awful howling? No, you've got me there," she replied in due course, looking slightly amused. "At about half past twelve you say. Nope, I didn't hear anything and no one's said anything down below this morning. Are you sure you weren't dreaming?"

"Someone banged the dinner gong over and over again at the bottom of the stairs, then everything went quiet again," I snapped back. "A few seconds later…you don't believe me, do you?"

"I sleep in the lodge behind the kitchen," she said. "The sound might not have carried…"

"You'd have heard that howl at the top of High Street," I broke in. "I couldn't have dreamed it."

"We've had no complaints from next door," she returned, shrugging her shoulders and shaking her head. "Nadia's a very light sleeper. If she'd have heard something like that, she'd have freaked out."

"Not if it was Nadia, not if she was freaking out already!"

"I'd know about that…"

"Having one of her flashbacks…"

"It wasn't Nadia, Mr Lockwood. It wasn't me and it wasn't Jane."

"What about your so-called sick relative, the one you've not told me anything about. She lives here, doesn't she?"

"Yes, she does," she said without batting an eyelid. "It's not a secret. She's bedridden, as bad luck would have it, and drugged up to the eyeballs for most of the day. She doesn't interfere with the smooth running of the hotel so we don't deem it necessary to inform our guests about her. She can hardly speak, let alone howl the roof off."

I did not persist. The only person I had not mentioned was the anonymous chef, whom I had never seen, and, as far as I knew, he or she did not live in. It was Agnes who changed the subject.

"Is that a map on your bed?" she said as she bent down to plug in her vacuum cleaner. "Is it by any chance an old map of Watholme?"

"What makes you say that?" I replied, curious to ascertain the full extent of her sham clairvoyance.

"Jane's going to send you one," she said evasively. "It will confirm everything she told you on Monday but I'm not supposed to bring the subject up again."

"Why is it so important that it *confirms* something?" I said, failing to disguise the irritation in my voice. "I'm here on holiday not for a literary investigation. Why should I give a damn about the blasted Ayres? I've not even read any of their books and, until this week, I'd never given them more than a passing thought, if that."

"A trip down to the library will do you good," she insisted. "Give Derek a ring. He'll be happy to take you there and bring you back in one piece. The library's a beautiful, listed building and it's opposite the old boys' grammar school."

"You've read the note attached to the map as well, I presume," I retorted. "You're working together, aren't you? What I don't understand is why."

"Well, for one thing, you haven't had much time so far this week to sit about and feel sorry for yourself, have you?" she offered equably. "We're giving you a reasonably complex puzzle to solve to take your mind off your discomfort. I bet you'll remember your stay chez nous and look back on it with fond memories. Go on, give Derek a ring."

* * *

As the taxi drew up outside the hotel, it started to rain. "Does it always pour it down in Watholme?" I asked Derek as I eased myself into the front passenger seat.

"Aye, lad, it does," he replied as we set off. "It even snows in summer round these parts."

"And, in the bad old days you could expect to live till you were forty, if you were lucky!"

"You've been doing your homework."

"You used that joke yesterday. Jane at The Green Man said something similar when I arrived here."

"She must have overhead me chatting to a customer. I'll have to change my patter from now on if she's nicking one of my routines. Now, where are we off to today?"

"The library in Boughton."

"Looking for something to read?"

"No, I want to use the reference section."

"That's on the first floor. There's a lift so you'll have no trouble with any steps. I think it's called the humanities and science library, but I'd ask a librarian if you're after something more exotic."

"I want to see the old grammar school as well."

"Another school? Did you used to be a teacher?"

"Agnes and Jane recommended it. Apparently an old friend of theirs called Christopher Heath used to go there."

"That name rings a bell, but I can't place him. Is he famous?"

"I don't think so. She's been giving me his life history. He's somehow connected to the chap who helped me when I hurt my ankle."

The journey down to the town centre was exactly as Jane had described it: sprawling conglomerations of rundown terraced houses, factories, shops and pubs on both sides of the road. There were, additionally, a church or two and at least three petrol stations which she had not included. As we drove, I gave Derek an abridged account of how I had sprained my ankle and he listened patiently until I had finished.

"It's a good job the young man was coming your way," he said. "There's a lot of moorland and you could have caught your death limping back in that weather. That is, if you could have found your way in a storm."

"I had my mobile with me," I said. "I'd have called the police. They'd have sorted things out."

"Not straight away," he countered. "You'd have been hanging around a long while before they located you, probably from your signal."

"Jane and Agnes have also been entertaining me with anecdotes about local people past and present," I went on, not wishing to discuss how long a hypothetical rescue operation might have taken. "They've given me a brainteaser, which can only be solved by a visit to the library."

"I can't park outside," he said, returning to more mundane matters. "It's right next to a set of traffic lights but I should be able to drop you off quite near. I'll hang around in a supermarket car park. Ring me when you're done and I'll pick you up unless I get another fare. Ring me anyway and I'll tell you where I am."

"I'll be an hour at most," I promised as the taxi came to a halt about fifty yards away from the library.

We had arrived in Boughton less than fifteen minutes after we left Watholme. The library, a two-storey structure, was exceedingly impressive, just as Agnes had said it would be. Like most of the older buildings it was made of sandstone, which had recently been shot-blasted clean. I glanced over the road and saw the old grammar school, which, regrettably, was in a sorry state, its neglected condition intensified by its soot-stained exterior. It *did* stand out from all the other buildings, but for entirely the wrong reasons. It was an eyesore, a 'monstrous carbuncle on the face of a much loved and elegant friend', to paraphrase Prince Charles. The contrast between the two testaments to a more prosperous, bygone age was, to say the least, highly alarming.

The humanities and science section of the reference library was, as anticipated, on the first floor. It was high-ceilinged and covered a large area, about sixty feet by sixty, divided into two parts by a counter which ran across the whole width of the room. There was a bank of computers to my left as I entered and the remaining public space was taken up by a series of broad benches, three chairs to each side, which would be ideal for spreading out charts and broadsheet newspapers, if they were still available. A photocopier and a series of wooden cupboards and drawers stood behind the counter, which augured well. There was no one else there. After about a minute I was greeted by a middle-aged man in a crumpled, brown herringbone suit, complete with black leather patches on the elbows of his jacket and spectacles attached to a string round his neck. When I asked if he had an early nineteenth century map of Watholme, he chuckled to himself.

"You're the second person in the past few days who's requested this," he said. "I can't remember the last time that happened."

"Was it an elderly woman?"

"Yes, it was Agnes Dean. She took a couple of copies of extracts from the originals. She wouldn't use the computers because she claims she doesn't know how they work. I recommended one of our courses for beginners, to no avail."

"So you know her," I said incredulously.

"Oh yes," he beamed. "She comes in here now and again looking for the odd bit of information about The Green Man hotel. I used the word 'odd' deliberately. A few weeks ago she was trying to determine if the stables at the back were part of the original construction."

"I understand there are two parish maps in existence from the middle part of the century," I said attempting to sound authoritative. "These are the ones I'd like some information about."

"Indeed there are," he replied, the broad grin now permanently inscribed on his face. "In fact there are four. Let me tell you about them and then you can choose the ones you want to study. The most accurate is the eighteen eighty impression, the only map that's dated."

The librarian was clearly in his element, enjoying the role of erudite expert in cartography, but I had neither the inclination nor the time to listen to him waffling on about unnecessary details.

"Sorry to interrupt," I said assertively. "I'm only interested in one specific part of Watholme and that appears to be the one Agnes enquired about, the area around The Green Man."

"That's easy then," he exclaimed. "Hold on a tick, and I'll get them up on my laptop."

It took him less than five minutes to locate the relevant file from the archive's extensive database. He leaned across the counter and turned the laptop round so that we could look at it together.

"Here's the eighteen eighty map which shows the location of the hotel next to a row of four ancient cottages that were demolished at the turn of the century to make way for the terraced houses that are still standing today. Across the road is the Ayre Memorial. The remaining three examples can be dated approximately by tracing the minor changes to the landscape that we know took place, the railway line for instance. The Boughton Railway Company was established in 1843 to construct a route to the West Coast but it ran out of cash very early on. It was one of the first railways to be built in Britain and one of the first to go bust. They only got as far as Cowburn, a small hamlet a couple of miles north of Watholme and optimistically it was double tracked. It was singled to an eight mile branch line in the eighteen fifties, and the dotted lines showing the proposed extension to Sleighton were removed in the eighteen sixties. Now, if you look at what I believe to be the earliest map, probably from the eighteen thirties or forties, you'll see that there's an extra cottage where the hotel is on the eighteen eighties map, making five in total, but it could easily be a mistake. Otherwise everything's more or less the same, except the Ayre Memorial grounds are marked on the later map, where previously there was nothing but open fields. Example three...shows cottages on both sides of the road, three to each side...and example four...shows one cottage only directly opposite, where the Memorial site is on the eighteen eighty version. In the last instance this would tally with the accepted account of the fire that destroyed the Ayre cottage, that is, it's on the opposite side to where the hotel was built. However I believe this to be a representation only of this part of Watholme, because the other cottages on the hotel side, which have been omitted for some reason, definitely existed. There's a rumour that this map was, shall we say, *tampered with*, by person or persons unknown to support the growing tourist industry in the late eighteen sixties, if you get my drift. The cartographer may even have been influenced, shall we say, by Patrick Ayre, the father of the famous sisters. That could tally with another explanation which is likely to be the more reliable. Some of the cartographers were notoriously lazy devils, especially the more corpulent ones. The chaps who drew up the three undated maps might not have actually charted the whole region. The hotel's at the top of a very steep hill and at the edge of the village. It was common practice for them to interview locals like old Mr Ayre about outlying areas rather than do the footwork if they could arrange it. What was much worse, they altered bits at random to make it look like there had been changes from earlier charts, thus justifying the need to keep on surveying and keep them in work. There are also blatant mistakes on each of the undated maps, guess where. Yes, on the peripheral areas. If I flick from one to the other…note how that farms mysteriously appear in the middle of the moors and then…disappear on the next map, only to reappear again on the third… and are gone altogether on eighteen eighties map. There were never any farms there. So, to conclude, the most accurate two-dimensional representation of Watholme is the eighteen eighty version. Unlike the others it corresponds to all existing building records. Shall I go over that again?"

"No, I get the picture – literally," I replied. "It's as clear as crystal. Is that why the Ayre Centre has chosen to display that map on their wall?"

"I recommended it," he said self-importantly. "And I know what you're going to say next. The memorial might be in the wrong place. That's what Agnes is attempting to demonstrate, but she's on stony ground, to coin a phrase. Everyone will suspect she wants to use the presence of the extra cottage on the earliest map as a marketing ploy for her hotel."

"You're psychic as well as remarkably well-informed," I laughed. "You've saved me a lot of unnecessary effort and I'm extremely grateful. I've a taxi waiting so I'll be on my way. There is one other thing. If I come back again may I use one of the computers?"

"Of course. I'll give you a log-in and a password and it's yours for an hour."

I gave him a cheery smile as I turned to leave, because my brief, peripheral research at his library (and the day before at the Ayre Centre) had put me in a position where I could no longer believe that there was such a thing as the Ayre conspiracy, and that I could challenge Agnes's version of facts and events, should she ever attempt to force them on me again. I called Derek immediately after I had limped down the steps at the library entrance. He told me to walk about a hundred yards away from the traffic lights to make it easier for him to stop long enough for me to struggle into the passenger seat. He would then be able to turn left at the lights and give me a grand tour of Boughton.

The town itself was a curious mixture of fading Victorian grandeur and present-day shabbiness. The library stood half way along the main road eastwards towards Leeds, called confusingly and pretentiously Sleighton Boulevard, next to the town hall and the police station, both magnificent buildings which owed their unquestionable splendour to their status in the community financed by the long-gone prosperity of the wool industry. As I hobbled off to my prearranged pick-up point in the pouring rain, I observed a row of equally imposing, expensive-looking boutiques, in the middle of which was a recently revamped shopping arcade. On the other side there were more modern shops, perhaps an interwar rebuild, and these were relatively mundane in comparison. The road to the left of the traffic lights led to the railway station and was similar in design to the Boulevard, probably Edwardian in origin.

"There used to be a huge railway goods yard behind the shops on the right," said Derek as we crawled behind a lorry past the station. "It's a supermarket now, complete with the usual hundred acres of parking. Somewhere on the left there used to be one of the town's ten cinemas, so my dad tells me. It was nicknamed 'The Ranch' because it showed nothing but westerns. It could be that household appliances' showroom about three doors up from the pub on the corner."

We turned left again at the next set of traffic lights into what might be termed 'an area in need of investment'. The shops that were still trading were much smaller and grubbier and dealt mainly in second hand goods or cheap clothing. There were two or three hairdressers, all with catchy puns on their signage, and several sleazy takeaways and cafés with foreign names.

"This is the old-fashioned quarter," he declared half-jokingly. "The council's planning to go through it with a dose of salts to smarten it up. When we reach the end, we'll be back almost where we started."

We spent the journey back to Watholme in thoughtful silence. Derek looked more drained than he did when we set out, and understandably I did not want to talk, since I had a lot to chew over.

"Sorry for being miserable," he yawned when we approached The Green Man. "My boy's got flu and I was up most of the night with him. The wife's not well either, so I'm calling it a day after I've dropped you off."

"I didn't get much sleep myself," I replied, rubbing my eyes in sympathy. "I must have had a bad dream or something. I hope I'm not coming down with a cold. I forgot my umbrella and I got soaked while I was waiting for you."

As we drew up to the hotel, I noticed that there was another car parked next to mine outside the front door. It had foreign number plates, presumably Belgian.

"I might get some peace tonight," I said as I got out into the drizzle. "Mine hosts will doubtless be distracted by the newcomers and leave me alone at last."

"They've been fussing after you, haven't they?" he laughed. "Watch out for yourself. They're a pair of randy, sex mad, old maids, and they'll be competing to see which one of them is going to ravish you before the weather improves at the weekend. Enjoy the rest of your holiday, old son."

CHAPTER EIGHT

Wednesday Evening

I did not go to the lounge after dinner. As I plodded through on my way upstairs at quarter past eight, I heard Jane chatting to the Belgians in what sounded like French, and I could not resist smiling because Agnes's prediction had come true. I would have myself to myself that evening, giving me the opportunity to have a couple of drinks in front of the television, a hot bath and early to bed. Nadia had already agreed to bring a bottle of red wine to my room and I settled down in the comfort of my armchair, with my feet perched on the radiator as usual, to watch a documentary about global warming. About a few minutes into the programme, at ten past nine, there was a knock at the door and a shout of 'room service'. It was Agnes, now dressed in a pink jumper and matching trousers.

"If you've got a minute, there's something – or, rather, someone I want to show you," she said as she placed the serving tray on the dressing table. "Jane's going to be occupied for the next hour or so with our new guests, and we'll easily be able to sneak past her. She's got her back to the foyer and the Belgians won't know what we're up to, will they?"

Reluctantly I swung my legs onto the floor and steadied myself with one of my crutches. She must have spotted my involuntary grimace and interpreted it – quite correctly I hasten to add – not as the pain in my ankle, but as a sign that I was reluctant to accompany her to wherever she was about to take me.

"You won't regret it, Mr Lockwood," she cajoled. "It will put your mind at rest about one aspect of your nasty experience last night."

We must have appeared quite comical as we crept past the bar area, Agnes on tiptoe with me shuffling along behind her on my crutches. We relaxed when we reached the dining room and made our way through to the kitchen. She did not switch on any lights but I could still see clearly enough that the place was well equipped, and that the glinting, stainless steel work surfaces, a dishwasher and an industrial-sized gas oven were tidy and, as usual, spotlessly clean. There was a faint aroma of roast meat, pork in this instance, which I had enjoyed an hour earlier, accompanied by 'seasonable vegetables', apple sauce and gravy. At the far end we came out into the open air and to a long, narrow single-storey building across a cobbled courtyard. It had to be the staff accommodation which, according to the librarian in Boughton, may once have been the hotel stables.

"This is where Jane, Nadia and I bunk up," she whispered. "Please keep your voice down. Nadia may be asleep and I don't want to waken her up. Actually it'll be better if you don't speak at all."

There were four doors located in the middle of the windowed, barn-like structure, about twenty feet apart from each other. She took out a bunch of keys and opened the door to the second apartment from the right. She beckoned me to follow her inside, into a faintly lit room and pointed to a bed next to the wall at the rear. I could just make out the back of an elderly woman wearing a white nightdress, half hidden by a dark-coloured duvet which covered her below her waist. Her black hair was streaked with grey and plaited into a single pigtail that came down two or three inches beneath her shoulder blades. She was breathing deeply and rhythmically. There was a strong, foetid aroma of cigarette smoke.

"This is Violet, my younger sister," said Agnes, speaking more normally. "She's the 'sick relative' you referred to this morning. She had a nervous breakdown many years ago and she's been in and out of, erm... hospitals ever since. I don't like the other words they use, like 'institution' and 'care home' because they imply that she won't get better. We brought her here to live with us in April, permanently from now on. As you can see, she's heavily sedated, so there's no way that she could have caused the commotion that you said woke you up after midnight. She has the occasional period when she's lucid and appears normal for a short while, but if she ever goes out for some exercise, she's always accompanied by one of us. It's strange what life does to us, isn't it? You'd never believe she used to be very beautiful when she was younger, and she fantasised about marrying a handsome prince when she was a child. I can see by the disapproving expression on your face that you've guessed she's a smoker. She's smoked since she was a teenager. It's her one and only pleasure in life, she says, so I don't mind. Jane's tried to stop her but it's far too late. Let's nip into my chalet, shall we, and leave the poor unfortunate in peace. I've something else to show you which I'm sure will make you come round to my way of thinking about what became of the Ayre sisters."

A few seconds later, she opened the door to the second of the middle apartments and led me into what had to be her studio flat, if that is the correct term for a bedsitting room with a bathroom and a tiny kitchenette. There was a large glass-fronted bookcase and a battered old escritoire to the left, and a small dining table with one chair in the middle of the room. Her bed was on the right hand side and, like the table and chair, it was almost entirely covered with handwritten sheets of paper of all sizes and several textbooks with strips of paper protruding from each of them, no doubt marking the pages of some key excerpts she was using to support her dissertation about the Ayres. On the wall above the bed was a large map of nineteenth century Watholme. For a second time the faint stench of cigarettes made me screw up my nose when we entered, which surprised me since I had not seen her smoke.

"Jane's chalet is the one on the other side of Violet's," she said as she switched on the light. "That's so that one of us will be able to hear if Violet needs us during the night without disturbing Nadia. We gave her the room furthest way from my sister's because she's a light sleeper. The three of us take it in turns to keep an eye on her but Nadia never minds her after ten o'clock because she has to get her beauty sleep."

"That explains why Jane has had to stop half way through telling me about Christopher Heath," I said as I looked round for somewhere to rest my aching ankle. "Her cryptic message to you now makes perfect sense as well."

She cleared the clutter from the dining chair and indicated that I should sit down. As I pressed past her, she bent down and picked up a grubby, brown A4 envelope from the floor.

"This is what I wanted to show you," she enthused as she pulled out three small pieces of yellowing paper. "I found these in the hotel cellars in a tin box full of documents of incredible historical importance. It's what made me start my research into the Ayres again. I've been at it seriously for nearly ten years. I reckon I've gathered enough evidence to blow Watholme sky high, although I'm going to make a lot of enemies."

"What are they?" I asked, summoning up as much enthusiasm as I could with Derek's light-hearted words about being 'ravished' by one of the oddball sisters ringing in my ears.

"They're death certificates," she whispered, tapping her mouth to remind me not to raise my voice. "I can't confirm their age exactly but some of the other stuff in the tin is definitely early Victorian. Perhaps they're the ones that Doctor Ackroyd misplaced, so to speak. There are also some shares in the Boughton Railway Company, the deeds to a cottage of unspecified address, two or three newspaper cuttings relating to the typhoid epidemic in the eighteen sixties, a traveller's guide to Italy, and a piece of a map of Watholme, regrettably not of this part of the village. The cottage's title is given as 'Moorview' on the deeds, and in all probability it's the one that belonged to the Ayres. Is all that impressive enough for you?"

"It looks intriguing," I replied softly. "What else was in the tin?"

"Some other odds and ends. They're early twentieth century. A couple of unused diaries, one or two old bills, an invitation to a wedding, and a battered, old hymn book."

"Sounds like somebody was tidying up, Agnes, and they bunged the whole lot in the box, probably to sort out later. Do you know any of the previous owners of the hotel?"

"My family's had it since the end of the last war. I can't remember who had it before that, but their names will be easy to find. Jane and I have been the owners for the last eleven years. When Daddy died he left it to us on condition that we took care of Violet. Mummy had walked out on him when we were kids and he didn't want Violet to rot away on her own in some sanatorium."

"What were the cellars used for? Storing beer and wine?"

"There are six separate cellars of varying sizes. The largest used to be the kitchen. There's an ancient, rusty cooking range and a cracked, porcelain sink still down there. One of the smaller cellars was a meat safe and the remainder were probably used for doing the washing and general storage."

She put down the envelope and went over to her writing desk.

"Here's a plan of the hotel," she said as she returned and passed it to me. "It dates from the nineteen forties, when my parents bought it and it was very run-down. The lounge used to be the dining room and the previous owners still cooked in the cellars. We lived in the four attics at first, which you probably aren't aware of because we closed them to guests a few years ago. They were luxury suites until they needed redecorating. You get to them via a staircase at the end of the first floor passageway through the emergency exit by the shared bathroom. We still use them from time to time in winter because they're the warmest rooms in the house. Daddy had the present dining room and kitchen built as soon as we moved in, and when the extension was finished we went to live in these chalets. They used to be overspill guest rooms. Jane, Violet and I had a bedroom each, and my parents slept where Jane now lives, at the far end."

"When did you find the tin box then?"

"Two of the cellars were full of old junk which had been down there for ages, long before we came on the scene. I was sifting through it after Daddy died to see if there was anything interesting and I came across the box. The rest went to the tip. That was about ten years ago."

"Who do you think put the box down there?"

"I haven't a clue. Some of the stuff could have belonged to Patrick Ayre, if you accept that the hotel building used to be where his cottage was. The rest might have been added by someone saving family bric-a-brac. Does it matter?"

"Not really. One last question. The man down at Boughton library said what you call 'chalets' had been stables. Why did he say that when it's obvious they weren't?"

"That was my fault," she laughed. "I haven't told him about my real research because he'd make fun of me. He thinks I'm investigating the history of the hotel. We've lived here all our lives, so it's the classic thing to do, isn't it?"

She paused and raised her eyebrows as if waiting for me to make a judgement.

"Well?" she said impatiently. "What do think of my find? I'm going to write a book about the Ayre's deception based on the death certificates and the copy of the old map on my wall over there as well as the other material I've already told you about."

"You mean you got your whole idea from these documents and a few other bits of circumstantial evidence such as the communal grave?" I asked sceptically. "How did you work the rest of it out?"

"There is more," she said calmly. "I admit it must appear speculative so I need to run it past someone. I'm not in the habit of talking to residents but you appear to be a very nice man. I saw it in your face on Monday afternoon when you were listening to Jane and me rabbiting on about Christopher Heath. You looked bored to tears and if you hadn't been incapacitated, you wouldn't have thought twice about making an excuse and doing a runner, would you?"

"You're wrong there, Agnes, I'm afraid," I grinned indulgently, bearing in mind I was alone with her. "I'm much too easy-going to do anything like that. Yes, I was bored to tears because I couldn't understand why you were giving me so much information about him. All I wanted was the name and address of the bloke who helped me when I had my accident. Can we continue this discussion in the lounge over a glass of wine?"

She looked at her watch and shook her head.

"I'm on Violet-watch so I'd better stay here," she sighed. "Give me two more minutes and then I'll let you escape. Have you heard of Emily Grace Harding?"

"I can't say that I have," I laughed. "Is this yet another character to add to your ever-growing list of infamous scoundrels from the past?"

Without answering she went over to the bookcase and took out a brown, badly scuffed, hardback book.

"She wrote this, 'A Mountain Daisy', published in 1888," she said eagerly. "It belonged to Christopher. I haven't read it but the novel's not relevant. It's what's written on the inside that's central to my argument."

She opened the book and brought it over to where I was seated. There was a dedication on the title page: *'To Billy on his eighth birthday. Lots of love Aunt Lisa, Bronte 1898'*.

"That would have clinched it for me," she added. "But I asked Christopher's dad, who's still alive. He'd never heard of an 'Aunt Lisa' and we couldn't ask his grandad – remember he was called William in the family tree – because he died in the nineteen fifties. His wife, Christopher's grandmother, had shoved the novel in a cardboard box and stowed it in the loft. When she died, Christopher's dad gave it to Christopher and he passed it on to Jane without opening it when they were at primary school. A few years later I was doing an English project on Victorian writers and Jane thought it might be useful."

"I presume you're saying that this 'Aunt Lisa' was Elizabeth Ayre," I gasped in utter amazement. "How on earth did you connect them?"

"From this letter," she grinned, producing it from behind her back like a magician at a children's party. "It had been used as a bookmark in 'A Mountain Daisy'. It appears that no one had got further than page twenty because the letter had remained wedged there, probably since 1898! I came across it again when I was moving my things out of the hotel into the bedsits. I thumbed through it to see if it was worth keeping and couldn't believe my eyes."

"What does it say that's so conclusive?"

She handed the letter to me and stood back to watch my reaction.

"Read it for yourself," she said. "If you're still unconvinced afterwards, I'll never broach the subject again."

The flimsy piece of paper smelled musty and its edges were badly stained. It had been folded neatly in half and there was writing on both sides. The ink had faded and some of the words had almost disappeared but it was not difficult to fill in any gaps. However, the letter itself was not dated and the sender's address was absent. More frustratingly, the top left hand corner had been torn off and there was no salutatory opening. At first sight then it appeared that a page was missing or that either the author or the recipient was deliberately concealing someone's identity. The content of the letter, which I have reproduced as faithfully as possible, was much less ambiguous.

> *'It is with deepest regret that I have to inform you of Catherine's death in Bronte. She passed over peacefully today in her sleep. She will be interred as Carlotta Mancini. We assume that you will not be attending the funeral because of your pecuniary hardship. I cannot assist you as I have been forbidden by my husband to send you any more money.*
>
> *She had hoped to see you one more time, as do I. She spoke of you constantly as she faded, and your name was on her lips as she breathed her last breath. It would be best for all concerned if you destroyed this letter immediately to protect my anonymity.*
>
> *My love to you and kind regards to your family.*
>
> *Your devoted sister*
>
> *Lisa Borelli.'*

"Well, what do you think of that, Mr Lockwood?" said Agnes excitedly, as I finished reading the letter. "It's obviously been sent to Amy Ayre in her new persona as Amos Heath. Now do you believe that I'm onto something?"

"Taken as a whole, it's very compelling evidence," I replied as I gave the sheet of paper back to her. "But taken item by item I doubt it will stand up in court."

"My case's watertight!" she protested. "The letter's the *piece de resistance*!"

"If it's genuine," I countered. "It will have to be subjected to tests to have it dated accurately like they do with suspicious paintings. All it proves really is that someone called Lisa was informing an as yet unidentified person about a woman's death."

"A woman called Catherine!"

"And what else have you got? The death certificates are blank, I notice. The deeds to 'Moorview Cottage' could refer to numerous dwellings in Watholme even if the name of the road is specified – which doesn't appear to be unless you've forgotten to mention it. Do you have any documentary evidence, other than your nineteenth century map, to corroborate where you think the original cottage was? Patrick Ayre could have tampered with the source of that map. I could go on, particularly about how you're so certain about the details of Amy's and Elizabeth's escape to the continent. That has to be sheer guesswork, it's so far-fetched. Nevertheless, before you become cross with me and lose your temper, taken as a whole, the letter does suggest that Catherine Ayre changed her name, and there's no doubt that someone somewhere had an Aunt Lisa in Italy, or rather, Bronte in Sicily, who wished to conceal her whereabouts. So, working backwards from that and factoring in the dedication in the book and the name of the cottage, the link with Christopher Heath's family tree plus the deeds and the death certificates, et cetera, et cetera, you do appear to have a *fascinating* case that the Ayre sisters did fake their deaths, but no more than that. There's far too much extrapolation and conjecture, a bit like finding the foundations of a house, a few silver coins and pieces of ancient pottery with some Latin words on them and claiming they prove the existence of an undiscovered Roman city. It may be there but you'll need to do a lot more digging and you'll have obtain more substantial proof, such as witness statements from any surviving relatives in Bronte who are aware of

Catherine and Elizabeth Ayre's real identity. Then you'll have establish that Amos slash Amy Ayre became Amos Heath. Christopher's family tree is the weakest link by miles. His great-something grandfather could simply be plain, old Amos Heath from Leeds whose ancestral records have been lost. And how do you know that Amy was Amos in the first place and later became heterosexual, bisexual or whatever the modern terms are? You've masses to do yet, Agnes."

"You're a hard man," she scowled. "But it's what I needed to hear. I'm not cross with you actually. I'm very grateful for your comments even if they've disappointed me."

She walked over to the door and opened it, holding it ajar as my invitation to leave.

"I need a fag," she said hoarsely. "I won't detain you any longer. Thank you once again for a frank opinion."

CHAPTER NINE

Wednesday Night

When I left Agnes's apartment I felt elated that I had out-argued her magnificently and proved that her contentious notions about the Ayres being crooks were nonsense. Even her own sister had used the word 'poppycock' and had tried to prevent her from discussing the topic with me. On my way back to my room I decided to investigate the exact whereabouts of the hitherto unseen emergency exit and the flight of stairs up to the attics, and this too had increased my high spirits since I had resolved the issue of what to do in the event of a fire. Jane was still chatting to the Belgians in the lounge area and no one paid me the slightest attention as I hobbled by, which was another refreshing change.

However as I climbed up step by painful step to the first floor it occurred to me that I had no right to have behaved so impolitely when dismissing Agnes's evidence. Instead I should have humoured her, agreed that she was probably onto something and left it at that. Any publishing house worth its salt would have done my job for me anonymously and much less acerbically. I had fallen into the same trap of overconfident familiarity that I had accused Jane of when I returned from my ride around Watholme on Tuesday afternoon. I promised myself that from then on I would keep my distance from them and restrict any future meetings to the hotel lounge if possible.

The only crumb of comfort was that I had spared myself further awkward sessions with Agnes but I would almost certainly receive a frosty reception should I ever need to ask her for help.

On reaching the landing, there, directly in front of me, stood the door in question which I insist I had not spotted before, displaying at eye level the appropriate sign in two inch high letters adjacent to the standard green health and safety symbol. I pushed it open with one of my crutches, and in the semi-darkness I could make out another short landing, on the left of which was a large, square, portable board barring the way up to the top storey rooms with '*No Entry to Guests. Staff Only*' printed on it. Two thoughts immediately wafted into my tired brain. Had the upper floor been closed down to avoid further expense on disabled access arrangements, and, more disconcertingly, were any of the rooms occupied by someone? Someone who was given to creeping about and howling during the night, someone deranged, a mad woman in the attic they kept locked up who had somehow managed to get out and create havoc. Agnes had said that she and Jane – and ostensibly Nadia too – slept there during a cold snap, which meant the rooms were still habitable. I had to find out, but I could not go back downstairs and barge in on Jane or, because of my insensitive behaviour, return to the chalets and interrogate Agnes. Then the most chilling thing hit me. I had heard movements in the attic on my first night in the hotel. Was I in any danger? If so, what would I able to do in my present vulnerable predicament?

I let the emergency exit door shut itself and fled. I was getting the hang of the crutches and I astounded myself by how speedily I was able to hop along when I needed to. I felt like a terrified teenager running away from imaginary muggers when out alone at night in deserted, half-lit streets. In vindication, I endeavoured to rationalise that it was the dark and the dread of the unknown that was scaring me but I have to confess that I failed miserably to do so. I was shaking as I locked myself in my bedroom and switched on the light, half expecting that the 'something' outside would any minute hurl itself against the door and begin howling like a badly wounded animal. Nothing of the sort happened of course. It was far too early, not yet ten o'clock, and there were other people around. Soon the Belgians would come upstairs and go to bed and I would feel more secure. Until then I would sit in my armchair and read, while listening out for the noise of their arrival down the corridor. Thankfully they must have been early risers because in a matter of half an hour or so I heard them whispering and laughing as they said their goodnights at the top of the stairs. Soon afterwards silence was restored and I felt confident enough to put on the television, turning the volume down so that I did not disturb my neighbours. I was about to pour myself a glass of wine when there was a light tap at my door. Before I could even begin to speculate who the unknown person might be, a muffled but familiar voice instantly solved the mystery.

"It's me, Jane," it declared. "I've brought you a nightcap."

She was grinning from ear to ear when I let her in. She was carrying a bottle of wine and two glasses.

"I've come to congratulate you," she said as she sat herself down on the edge of the bed. "You've given Agnes a flea in her ear about her damn obsession with the Ayres."

"Oh hell," I replied gravely, still standing by the door. "It was very cruel of me. Is she very upset?"

"Quite the opposite," she laughed. "She's more determined than ever to press on. You've given her some useful pointers. There are more holes in her arguments than in a Swiss cheese but she never listens to me. You've done us both a huge favour, Mr Lockwood."

I limped quickly over to the armchair at the opposite side of the room and reached down for the remote control to switch off the television set. She swivelled her head round to see what I was doing and frowned.

"If you're going to stay there, I'll have to sit with my back to you and bend round," she said irritably. "Come here and park yourself next to me."

Once again I found myself in an intimate, possibly problematic situation with one of the Deans, a situation I had promised myself I would seek to avoid at any price less than an hour previously. Even if Derek had not joked about their supposed promiscuous tendencies, I would have felt very uncomfortable, although nothing untoward was likely to occur between two people well past their prime.

"I should have recommended that she posed questions rather than supplying her with answers," I said, remaining where I was. "In my humble experience, that's what gets people thinking. They will then have to provide counter arguments to demolish her suggestions rather than dismissing her work merely as another vindictive conspiracy theory. I do actually believe that she may be onto something, except for her spurious notion that Amy Ayre was a man and reverted to her birth gender and became a husband, a father and a distant relative of your Christopher Heath."

"Quite so," she agreed. "The family tree I constructed is genuine. I can trace Christopher's lineage to a chap called Amos Heath but I can't get any further. That's what set her off again after she found the inscription and the handwritten letter in that mushy novel I gave her. As it happens, Agnes has never really grown up. As a girl, she was always fascinated by romantic fiction after she graduated from Enid Blyton and Edith Nesbit. It started with the Ayres, because they were our resident folk heroes, followed by Jane Austen, Thomas Hardy and Charles Dickens – Estelle in Great Expectations was one of her ideal role models, whereas I'd compare myself to Emily Ryder in Catherine Ayre's 'The Governess'. She was a champion of the working classes. I suppose both Agnes and I identify with strong, female characters rather than feminist characters, although I've never been sure where you draw the line between the two. At school she did project after project on each one of the Ayre sisters, and she read English Literature at university. Guess what the topic of her thesis was. She was a successful English teacher at an all-girls' schools in Nottingham until Daddy persuaded her to quit and help him run this place. She's never shown much interest in men and she's never been married, but she's never shown any lesbian tendencies, not to my knowledge in any event. In short, Mr Lockwood, she's not a woman of the world. She constructed her own cocoon many years ago and she's not made any attempt to force herself out of it."

"I should have kept my mouth shut and humoured her, shouldn't I?" I replied. "I'm a temporary guest here and I'd no right to be so critical."

"On the contrary," she said soothingly. "It's easier to hit and run than have to put up with the constant moaning and self-pity accompanied by her unrelenting justifications that each piece of evidence is equally valid. *'Find the forged death certificates'*, *'Go to Sicily and interview some people'*, that's what I keep telling her. *'Only if you come with me to interpret for me'* she retaliates, and she knows full well I'm not going to do that."

She closed her eyes and sank sideways onto the bed, resting her head on her elbow. She was still clutching her bottle of wine but both the glasses slipped out of her hand and landed on the duvet. I had not suspected that she might be a little worse for wear, so to speak, and the last thing I wanted was for her to fall asleep. I leaned forward as far as I could and tapped her shoulder.

"Don't get too relaxed, Jane," I said firmly. "Would you like a cup of tea before you go?"

"I'm not drunk, I'm tired," she yawned. "Romantic fiction's too airy-fairy for you, isn't it? I bet you haven't read anything by Jane Austen, have you? I can't see her being one your favourite novelists. I'm not impressed myself, and, as I already told you, I can't stand the Ayres."

"Yes, you're right there," I said. "If I were stuck on a desert island with only one book, I'd pray it was science fiction, preferably an omnibus by Isaac Asimov or Stephen King containing no less than a thousand pages."

"What did you do for a living before you retired?" she asked, clearly not interested in my choice of genre.

"I was an engineer of sorts but I moved off the shop floor to a suit job as soon as I could," I said, humouring her. "I ended up in sales management, which wasn't where I wanted to be, but there you are. It's all done and dusted and I don't miss it for one second."

"I was right. You were behaving according to your instincts as a technical man. You demand tangible facts."

"The company I worked for made conveyor belts and escalators, and motors and gear boxes for heavy industrial applications, including lifts. It was hardly the most riveting of jobs, and I don't mean that as a joke. If I demanded anything, it was increased sales figures. Have you done anything interesting?"

She sat up again and picked up the glasses which, along with the bottle, she lowered carefully onto the carpet.

"I went to Newcastle University after I left school, learning to be fluent in French and Italian. It was a very intensive course and I studied Dante, Rousseau and Sartre as well as a lot of other giants of European literature. Newcastle was the place to be at the end of the nineteen sixties. There was a vibrant night life in the city centre, especially at weekends. I went a lot to the famous Club a'Gogo, and I hung around the University Union most Saturday nights during term time. All the big groups played there and some lesser known ones too. Heady days! After I graduated, I got a job teaching English as a Foreign Language in a private school in Belgium but it only lasted a year. I left under a bit of a dark cloud and came back here."

She fell silent and that by now all too familiar faraway expression flitted slowly across her face. Then she shook her head and frowned, as though some painful memories had momentarily troubled her before being consigned again to some deep, dark recess in her subconscious.

"I've opened a bottle already," was all I could think of to say. "It's Rioja. Would you like to join me?"

"Just a splash," she laughed as she sat up. "Then I'll stop depressing you and leave you to your *telly*, Mr Lockwood. I enjoy reminiscing about those years. They were the best years of my life."

She stayed another ten minutes and we did not resume our conversation about ourselves. As I passed her half a glass of wine she began to tell me about her convivial evening with the Belgians who were leaving the following morning after breakfast. They had come to Watholme specifically to take photographs of the village where the Ayres had lived and died. They were, of course, their biggest fans, Jane had thrown in sarcastically. I let her rattle on. It had spared me the dilemma of whether to tell her that Agnes had allowed me to go into Violet's apartment to confirm that her invalid sister was entirely incapable of marauding around the hotel late at night. Nor did I want to mention the incident itself, for Jane would undoubtedly have given a similar explanation for the howling as Agnes had done, namely that I had dreamt it.

However I was most relieved that I had gained some much desired breathing space to fathom out how to put an end to the increasing intimacy between the two sisters and me. It would not be easy to maintain my distance from their two-pronged assault on my companionship while I was, as Agnes had remarked so aptly, a disabled captive in their hotel. My spine tingled at those last few words. I was reminded of Stephen King's novel 'Misery', in which author Paul Sheldon is terrorised by the severely unhinged Annie Wilkes in her isolated backwoods cabin. He has broken both his legs in a car crash and cannot escape. He had it easy. Although not yet in danger, I was at the mercy of *two* irrational women. Jane saw me shudder but made no comment. She probably assumed I was tired.

She left shortly afterwards, just before eleven, taking her bottle and the two wine glasses with her. I went straight to bed. I switched the television back on and turned down the volume to watch an American psychological thriller starring Clint Eastwood. I must have drifted off but I cannot have been asleep for very long – the film on the television was still running – when I heard someone whisper my name accompanied by scratching on my door. This was not a nightmare. The most shocking thing was that the phantom was whispering my Christian name, and I do not recall one occasion when it had been used before in the hotel. With some difficulty I staggered over to the door and flung it open, but there was nothing to be seen.

CHAPTER TEN

Thursday Morning

The following morning, before I had had my breakfast, I telephoned Derek the taxi driver. I had to speak to someone about the two chilling incidents in the night and to find out if the hotel was haunted. However there may have been a simple explanation for the scratching on the door. If I fall asleep while watching TV, the extraneous sounds somehow become incorporated into my dreams. Was this what had happened? In *Play Misty for Me,* Eastwood plays a deejay who is stalked by a deranged woman. It was a very bad choice in the current circumstances. Derek did not answer his phone and I left a message for him to ring me back. He did better than that; he came to the hotel while I was in the dining room. I spotted him in the lobby browsing through the leaflet rack next to the unattended reception desk. He was dressed in his usual outfit, complete with trainers, I noted.

"Morning, Mr Lockwood," he said, as I plodded over to him. "I got your call. I was just passing so I thought I'd drop in and see if you wanted a ride somewhere. My next scheduled passenger isn't due for another hour at ten fifteen."

"No, I don't want a lift," I said, lowering my voice. "I'd like to pick your brains about something that's bugging me about this hotel. Let's sit down so we can talk without being overheard."

I was about to point to a table that was furthest away from where we were standing when Jane appeared on the staircase behind us.

"Good morning, gentlemen," she shouted as she came down. "Off anywhere exciting today?"

"We're going up to Porterfield Nature Park," Derek growled back, taking my crutches from me. "We're just leaving."

We both nodded and smiled up at her. Derek took my arm and helped me limp out to his car which he had parked by the front door.

"Why the sudden, dramatic exit?" I said when I deemed it safe to speak again.

"That woman doesn't like me, and the feeling's mutual," he said, as he threw my crutches onto the rear seat. "We had a row a few years ago about public relations. I wanted her to recommend my company exclusively to guests, and in return I'd fetch any punters who wanted a bed for the night straight here. She knocked it back on two accounts. She said it sounded very dodgy because she didn't think many people who wanted a hotel in Watholme simply turned up without making a reservation. That meant the arrangement would be of greater benefit to me than The Green Man. The other thing was that she took care of her own advertising and she suggested I did the same. She reckons I'm a chancer but at least she still takes my leaflets."

"Are we really going to Porterfield Nature Park?" I said as we sped off.

"You've been there already," he said. "It's on the other side of the road to the bottomless bog. I want you see it, not as it is now, but how it used to be. That's why we're going there. By the way, have you noticed yet that there aren't any trees around here, not even in the fields opposite the moors? There's nothing holding the clouds up, that's why the weather's always so bad."

We drove for about five minutes on the same road bisecting the moorland that we had taken two days earlier but we were travelling in the opposite direction. When we reached the concrete blocks which the locals referred to as 'The Stone Seat', we turned left onto a dirt road that ended a few hundred yards further on in a large, pot-holed expanse of waste ground which served as a car park. It was raining hard as usual, so we resigned ourselves to sitting and chatting, since getting out of the car was out of the question.

"This is the only bit that the council didn't touch when they landscaped the whole area," said Derek with a great deal of bitterness. "They've transformed what was once a magnificent wilderness into a wishy-washy, health and safety officer's dream world."

He reached over me and opened the glove compartment. He rooted about for a few seconds and eventually pulled out a small wallet folder.

"Here, have a butchers at these," he said. "They're photographs of what it looked like before the bulldozers and the wagons came. My dad took them in nineteen seventy five. Most of them are in black and white to accentuate the bleakness. He fancied himself as an amateur photographer and one of them won a competition in a national magazine."

As I thumbed through the pictures, he continued to describe the features of the original terrain that fixated so many people and which had been immortalised by Elizabeth Ayre.

"It was a desolate, inhospitable expanse of hidden traps, Mr Lockwood," he said gloomily. "You could follow the paths made by carts and human feet, or you could wade knee-deep through the heather, up a steady gradient to the top from almost any direction. Okay, from the side nearest your hotel it's a very steep climb, but as young lads it was an achievement to scramble up to the top, like conquering Everest. It was when you reached the summit that everything changed. From here it looks innocuous enough, doesn't it? A series of picturesque, undulating mounds, like the sand dunes outside Blackpool. What you couldn't see were the canyons, and I use that word deliberately because it's no exaggeration. They were deep, crater-like ravines with sixty degree sides filled with bus-sized slabs of slippery, black rock and treacherous scree. My dad took several shots of them, as you can see. Breath-taking, aren't they? Extinct volcanoes, that's how he referred to them when I was a kid. He warned me never to try to go inside them, because I'd never be able to get out again. He was right. I got stuck one afternoon on my way home from school. I was eight years old. Some bigger boys had dared me to do it and they left me there, the rotten bastards. I tried to struggle out but each time I slid backwards on the greasy rocks and rolled back down to the bottom. I was shit-scared and cried my eyes out. One of the twats must have felt sorry for me because he came back and helped me. Young kids were always getting stuck. That's what made it so exciting and frightening at the same time. It's a good job you didn't have your accident in those days. There were no mobile phones then and joggers hadn't yet been invented."

He looked at me meaningfully no doubt reminding me of a conversation we had the day before.

"It was always an adventure to go up there," he continued. "I remember one time when I was at junior school, me and a mate found a rusty piece of metal in the fields across the road from The Green Man that probably came from an old, iron bedstead. It was shaped like the grab-handles on the front part of a chariot – I had a fertile imagination before you take the mick. We'd be doing the ancient Romans with Miss Simpson and we honestly believed we'd found an artefact of great historical significance. We took it to the top of the hill and surveyed the countryside down below and do you know what? We could see vehicle tracks in some deep grass down near the village and we were positive they'd be left by Roman chariots. They'd obviously been made by a tractor but we didn't care. We were laughed out of class the next day when nasty Miss Simpson burst our bubble and gave us the more common-sense explanation. She was wrong. What she didn't understand was that it was the magic of the moors that made us believe it, even though there's no record of the Romans ever being in Watholme."

"Why is it called Porterfield Nature Park?" I asked. "It's Wildheath Crags on my map."

"Your map must be out of date. That was the old name. The council rechristened it because Wildheath Crags sounded too wild and uninviting. They wanted to create *family spaces*, their words not mine, to attract young parents and children for picnics, and a healthy walk in the fresh air, not woolly-hatted hikers and old stick-in-the-muds like you. So they removed the boulders and filled in the craters and took away all the fun and the danger. You could hear the dynamite explosions from miles away. They grassed it over so efficiently that there's not even a pebble left to remind traditionalists like me that the Crags ever existed. The Nature Park's named after Daniel Porterfield, in honour of the chap who built the Victorian half of Watholme in the middle of the nineteenth century. Originally the village was split into two parts. There was the mediaeval bit at the very top of High Street where your hotel's situated, made up of farm workers' cottages, a few shops and a pub. Most of the land was farmland during the nineteenth century, mainly used for pasture because not much else but grass would grow in the cool, damp climate. The other part was down in the valley by the river where the mills and the railway line were. Porterfield owned all the land in between, and he built his house at what was then the highest point in the lower village and redesigned the side of the hill as his estate and gardens. The house is now the Ayre Centre. He bequeathed his gardens to Boughton Borough Council for '*the enjoyment of decent God-fearing citizens*', and they converted them into the local park. When the demand for millworkers' housing increased and shops to provide goods for them were needed, he joined the two settlements together. He built a long row of terraced houses up both sides of High Street and included, at various points, a grocers, an ironmongers and a drapers, as well as two pubs-cum-hotels and a restaurant. The Green Man wasn't built by Porterfield, while we're on the subject. It was commissioned by Patrick Ayre opposite where his old farm cottage stood before it burned down, and it was erected by a firm from Leeds."

"You should work at the Ayre Centre," I said appreciatively. "How do you know so much?"

"I did an assignment in history at secondary school," he laughed. "It got a distinction. Porterfield also built the junior school I took you to on Tuesday. He placed it next to the church and the cemetery on purpose to ensure that the pupils were good Christians and aware of their mortality. When the expansion was under way, he moved to his ancestral home near Bradford and died there years later, a very rich man, at the ripe, old age of eighty eight in 1903."

"How certain are you the Ayre's cottage used to be on the memorial site?"

"From the map in the Centre."

"Did you know that there are four nineteenth century maps in existence? The librarian in Boughton showed them to me."

"No, I didn't. So what?"

"The Ayre's cottage isn't in the same position on any of them. It seems to move about a lot. That may mean that it wasn't on the site of the memorial but on the opposite side where The Green Man is."

"Does it matter which side it was on?" he said suddenly raising his voice. "It's the memorial that counts, commemorating three talented sisters who brought prosperity to Watholme as well as a diverse, transient population. Otherwise, it would be a shrinking, dormer village or, even worse, empty and dying with most of the houses second homes for the well-off, out-of-town invaders. I'm Yorkshire born and bred, Mr Lockwood. I was born in Boughton but I grew up in Watholme, I went to school in Watholme and I married a woman from Watholme. I like a pint, I like cricket and football, and I support the Boughton rugby league team. If it wasn't for the Ayres I'd be a bus driver like my dad was."

As he spoke I could see that he was becoming agitated. I must have touched a raw nerve, and I was not about to probe more deeply, not sitting so close to him at any rate. Furthermore I had other, more personally relevant questions for him which concerned the midnight prowler. He shuffled around in his seat and wound down his door window. Then he pushed his hand out, palm upwards, to determine how hard it was raining. It had to be some kind of nervous irritation because the windscreen was an opaque torrent of streaming rainwater completely obscuring the view ahead.

"A stroll's out," he said, turning back to me and smiling. "You won't see anything anyway unless you take your glasses off. We'll have to sit here for another few minutes then I'll take you back unless you want to go somewhere else."

"What can you tell me about The Green Man?" I said, prepared to risk another outburst.

"It was once the best hotel in the village by miles," he replied, more calmly than I expected. "It's been going down the nick for a while though. It needs modernising to bring it screaming into the twenty first century. I bet they still haven't got satellite TV or Wi-Fi, have they? All the other big hotels have. The Deans aren't reinvesting the profits to smarten it up or bring it up to date, that is, if they make any money. Their father, God rest his soul, must be spinning in his grave."

"Is it haunted?" I said, pressing on with my plan.

"That's a good one," he chuckled. "I've not heard that one before. If it is, it'll be their father moaning about how they've let all his good work go to the dogs. Why? Have you seen a ghost?"

"No, I heard noises in the night."

"What sort of noises?"

"Howling."

"Howling?"

"Like a wounded, wild animal."

"Are you sure you weren't dreaming…"

"I was wide awake. Last night something scratched at my door and called me by my Christian name."

"Did anyone else hear the howlin' and a-scratchin', Mr Lockwood?"

"Douglas, please call me Douglas."

"Did anyone else hear the howlin' and a-scratchin', *Douglas*?"

"You're not taking this seriously, are you?"

"Sorry, did anyone else hear anything?"

"No, no one heard anything. On the first night, Tuesday, the hotel was empty except for me. Last night there were four other people further down the corridor, but I didn't want to ask them. If they had heard anything, they would have come out of their rooms like I did."

"Have you reported it to Jane?"

"I mentioned the howling to Agnes. She said no one else heard anything unusual. I thought it might be Nadia, the waitress who's a refugee from Kosovo, having a flashback to the war but Agnes said it wasn't."

Derek scratched his head and looked confused. He tried to speak several times but decided not to on each occasion. Eventually he shook his head and settled for staring at me open-mouthed. Clearly he thought I had hallucinated everything and did not want to upset me by insisting that there could be no other explanation.

"What can you tell me about Jane and Agnes?" I asked rather than pressing him further.

"Not much really," he replied, sounding relieved that he had not hurt my feelings. "There's a lot of gossip in the village about Jane, because she never leaves the hotel. I'm one of the select few who's ever clapped eyes on her, because of my taxi business. We don't get on, as I said before. Agnes is very different. She's a bumbling, eccentric old dear, who could talk the back legs off a donkey, whereas Jane's the organised one but much more unforthcoming. When she does deign to speak, she's the most eloquent person I've ever met. Beautiful, it is. I could listen to her for hours."

"I've had that pleasure," I said disdainfully. "It's not as pleasurable as you think."

"Agnes has a weird dress sense, hasn't she?" he said, visibly amused by my aside. "Clashing pastel shades and long, dangly necklaces. I occasionally give her a ride down to Boughton, because they don't own a car. They're a throwback to another age."

"What about Nadia?"

"I'd recognise her if I came across her. Other than that, nothing. I wasn't even aware she was a foreigner."

"Have you met their sister Violet?"

"Now I *can* help you here," he exclaimed, becoming more animated. "When my father-in-law was in his late teens, he used to fancy her like mad. She was very good-looking and more sociable than her sisters. He doesn't remember seeing anything of Jane and Agnes so they must have been away at college or working somewhere else. She used to chat him up like he was her boyfriend and he was very flattered – until he found out that she did it to all the young lads. She was an unashamed flirt and broke a few prepubescent hearts, he said, because she had a steady boyfriend. The lucky guy didn't live round here. He always came by car. A big, flashy one it was, a Jag or a Merc. Then she disappeared. Everyone assumed she'd got married but it transpired that she'd had a breakdown and gone into a mental home near Sleighton. As far as I know she's still there."

"She's living at The Green Man again," I said. "Agnes sort of introduced us last night. She's heavily sedated and confined to her room."

"You what?" he yelled. "I'll have to tell the wife's father. Does she look old?"

"I haven't seen her face," I replied. "She was asleep with her back to me."

Derek looked at his watch and frowned. I passed him his photograph folder and he threw it behind him towards the back seat. It bounced off one of my crutches and its contents spilled out onto the floor.

"I've got to go," he announced abruptly. "Have I answered all your questions?"

"More or less," I said huffily. "One final thing. I can't access the Internet on my phone at the hotel. Which is the best Wi-Fi café in Watholme?"

"Just use your data. You don't need Wi-Fi."

"What's my 'data'?" I said, narrowing my eyes.

"Look it up on the Internet," he grinned as he started the engine.

The rain had turned to hail by the time he dropped me outside The Green Man. I did not have my umbrella with me and I was peppered from head to foot by a fierce bombardment of icy pellets from an angry sky as I struggled inside. The foyer was deserted but this was not uncommon, since there were no other guests living in. It was, however, an alarming lapse in security and another example of slack management. What was to stop anyone walking in and doing what they pleased, unless Jane was keeping an eye out in a room somewhere via a close circuit TV system? There was little likelihood of that judging by the absence of any other up-to-the-minute technological devices that I had come across during my stay. Was this how the spook that was keeping me awake at night had got into the hotel? Was it some roguish youths who had hidden themselves in the vacant attics and were playing an infantile game of cat and mouse to scare me for a cheap laugh at my expense? Although a long shot, this was the most plausible solution to the dilemma that I had so far been able to come up with. Yet they could not possibly have remained silent while they waited for the precise moment that I fell asleep unless they had an accomplice... this was becoming too complex a line of reasoning and I abandoned it immediately because it was, frankly, ludicrous, a sign that I was slowly but surely losing my marbles. I had been stuck in this hotel for nearly five days and my personality was changing rapidly. I was becoming a bag of nerves, a miserable, harmless fly trapped by two crackpot sisters in a sticky web of near insanity that I had stumbled into quite literally *by accident*. Those Belgians would not remember their stopover like this. They checked in, went out for the day, chatted jovially to their host for an hour in the bar on their return, and slipped off to bed. The next morning they had breakfast and set out on the next stage of their journey. It was part of their holiday, a part that contained a few good memories of Watholme, not recollections of the half told story of a nonentity and a fallacious hypothesis about intrigue and deception that not even an idiot would accept as tenable.

I sat myself down on the nearest chair and rested my chin on my forearms which were propped up by my crutches. I was weighing up whether I should take the plunge and return home by public transport immediately after lunch when Jane marched into the reception area. She was dressed in a pink jumper and blue, casual trousers, which I interpreted as signifying that she was off duty.

"Did you enjoy your trip out to Porterfield Nature Park?" she enquired, sounding as though she were genuinely interested, when I knew it was nothing more than affected courtesy. "It's changed a lot over the last sixty years."

"I couldn't see much of it because of the weather but Derek told me about how it's been tidied up and rebadged as a picnic area," I replied solemnly. "He doesn't approve. He preferred it as it was, wild and dangerous."

"I'm certainly with him there!" she remarked. "I haven't been up to inspect it yet. It's not worth the effort. I want to remember it as it was."

"It's ironical that I found it wild and dangerous last Sunday afternoon, isn't it?" I grinned, unable to stop myself from carrying on a conversation I had absolutely no desire to contribute to.

"Yes, it is," she muttered, not realising that I was making a joke.

"I'll be going then," I said. "Lunch at…"

"I'm glad I've run into you," she interrupted, raising her voice. "It's my day off and you're on your own again today, so I may as well finish my story. Does two o'clock suit?"

I nodded my agreement without showing any enthusiasm which she did not appear to notice, and we left at it that. I hauled myself up and prepared to make my get away while she was busying herself behind the reception counter.

"Agnes told me about your bad dream," she said as I passed. "It's probably the result of feeling insecure because there was no one else in this part of the hotel. You're our only guest again tonight, I'm afraid, but don't worry, all the doors will be locked except for the fire escape. There's a bar on the door at the bottom of the stairs; push it down and, hey presto, the door opens. You come out at the rear. If you need a member of staff we're in the chalets across the courtyard."

I was fuming when I reached my room. Not only had Jane made light of the midnight prowler, she now had the nerve to organise my calendar again, and that left me with three hours to kill until the appointed post-lunch ordeal. When I had calmed down, however, it struck me that I had not yet located a café or a pub with Wi-Fi. I thumbed through the brochures I had piled up on my bed-side table until I came upon three relevant leaflets that I had taken from the rack in the foyer. From the rough sketches of maps on each of them, I chose what appeared to be the nearest one, in the shopping square at the top of High Street. It would be a two-fold mission, for I intended to risk walking there and back without the aid of my crutches.

To raise my spirits even higher, it had stopped raining, and a weak, watery sun was shining through ever-thinning clouds. Was it a sign that the merciless rain gods were relenting at last? This welcome sight gave me another idea: I could use my umbrella as a walking stick. There may even be a shop near the café where I could purchase a proper one. I left the hotel that morning in an extremely bright mood, and, if I had been wearing a hat, I would have doffed it in true Victorian style to every person who crossed my path and wished them a very good day! As it was, I was limping along very slowly with a pained expression on my face.

The Wi-Fi café was precisely what I wanted, more like what used to be termed, I believe, an *Internet café* except that it served neither snacks nor drinks. It would probably close down soon, especially as there were only eight unoccupied computer stations placed along two of the walls and a counter at the far end, behind which sat a long-haired, hippy-type dressed in a grey shirt and trousers with his back to me reading a magazine. For a few startling seconds I thought I'd at last come across the young man who saved me when I slipped on the moors, but when he turned round he had a long straggly, black beard. Above him, on the wall, was a large, professionally-printed price list. When I calmed down, I chose the hourly rental option and handed over ten pounds, unaware whether this was cheap or expensive. I received my log-in and password and took a seat in the shop window, in front of a flat-screened pc much to the relief of my ankle which had started to throb. The first port of call was a biography of the Ayres.

The Wikipedia webpages contained roughly the same information that I had received from the young woman in the Ayre Centre, but with one or two significant additions and it helpfully provided links to their better known novels. The sisters were, it stated, regarded as minor authors, except in the Home Counties, until their premature deaths when their works were re-evaluated, leading to a sudden surge in sales throughout the British Isles. Their major contribution to contemporary literature was seen as the championing of equal rights from a feminist perspective, particularly highlighting the draconian laws imposed on married women, subsequently alleviated in the Married Women's Property Act of 1870. I printed out the synopsis of the plot of 'The Stone Seat' (at a further cost of one pound per sheet of paper) which I have reproduced, as follows:

> *'The novel begins as Edgar Millward, a widower and a once wealthy man who has fallen on hard times, is making his way with his sixteen year old daughter Isabella to a moorland village in the wilds of West Yorkshire, where he's rented a cottage. Constantly troubled by his lost prosperity, he descends into drunkenness and neglects the blossoming Isabella, who spends most of her time wandering on the*

moors, imagining she's queen of a vast, unspoilt kingdom in northern France, inhabited by friendly, hard-working peasants, handsome princes and fire-breathing dragons. However she soon becomes bored with the hardships of rural life and longs constantly to meet one of her handsome princes and be transported away to his castle and a life of easy luxury. One Sunday she meets John, a tousle-haired, young farm hand, and they strike up a friendship which is to last for the next three years. They become inseparable, sharing their love of the rugged terrain and eventually each other until, without explanation, she fails to turn up on four consecutive evenings. Confounded and worried, John goes to her cottage and, to his dismay, he observes her talking and laughing with Arthur, the suave, well-educated son of Edgar's former business partner, Samuel Matthews. Samuel had arrived four days previously to inform Edgar that he wished to resurrect their partnership. Edgar is only too happy to agree especially as it means that he will be able to return to Liverpool and make arrangements for Isabella to finish her education and find a rich husband. When John appears unexpectedly, Isabella ridicules his coarse, farmworker ways in front of Arthur, and he runs off in tears and spends the rest of the night sleeping rough on the moors. She meets John one more time to tell him that she is leaving the area and that she will be staying with the Matthews family in Liverpool for the foreseeable future. She says she will write to him occasionally and hopes he will write to her. Once again he runs away from her utterly distraught, resolving to have nothing to do with her. Things get worse for him some months later when he receives a letter in which she tells him she has married Arthur, and he now realises that he has lost her forever. Soon afterwards John becomes a wealthy man himself when his father dies and leaves him his farm. He boasts about this in his only letter to Isabella, which is intended as a parting shot. In true melodramatic fashion, another two years speed by until the melancholy, and as yet unattached John receives another letter from Isabella. She has been mistreated by Arthur who has turned out to be a villainous scoundrel, an inveterate gambler and an unashamed womaniser. She begs John's forgiveness and tells him that she has always loved him. She says that by the time he receives her letter she will be travelling back to the village with her six month old son and will arrive that very evening on the coach from Liverpool. John is infuriated that she has not had the courtesy of giving him the opportunity to reply, especially as he is unwilling to involve himself with another man's wife and child, despite harbouring strong affections for her. As bad luck would have it, the coach is caught in a violent storm as it traverses the moors in the dark. The coachman loses sight of the cart track which serves as a road and the horses run headlong into a swamp, sucked down in seconds by quicksand along with all the passengers. Meanwhile John is waiting patiently in the village when he hears shouting and joins a crowd of men who go looking for the now long-overdue coach. They comb the roadside without success, hampered by the tempestuous weather, and it is not until the following day that debris is seen floating on the surface of what is known locally as 'the bottomless bog'. John refuses to believe that Isabella is dead and goes off to find her on the moors. He is never seen again. Finally Edgar has a stone bench erected at the site of the accident to commemorate his daughter and grandson, giving the novel its title. The story ends with the assertion that whenever the wind blows the cries of John can be heard as he roams the moors searching for his lost sweetheart.'

The novel received a lukewarm reception at first, according to the web entry. It was regarded by some critics as the quintessential tragic romance, by others as over-sentimentalised pap, until a deeper interpretation was provided by a group of artists and poets called the Pre-Raphaelites in the early 1860s. They viewed the novel as both an affirmation that women are superior emotionally and intellectually to men, and a denunciation of the marriage laws as they applied to women in a patriarchal society, where a wife was a husband's property, tied to him until his death. The heroine Isabella not only leaves her cruel husband, she is portrayed throughout as a strong-minded, independent woman, who is briefly swept of her feet by a man she likens to one of the handsome princes she has previously daydreamed about. In the early part of the story, she is able to dominate the naïve, young farmer's boy at will, and his devotion to her means nothing when she has the chance to leave him to fulfil her destiny and her father's ambitions for her. Her attempt to return to her former lover is not merely the desperation of a damsel in distress fleeing towards a virtuous man whom she hopes will protect her, it is a cynical act. She is clearly making use of the now well-to-do John as a form of maintaining the affluent lifestyle she has become accustomed to. Moreover, her terrible death is not simply divine justice for breaking one of the Ten Commandments, but a suggestion to the reader to perceive the character of Isabella as the calculating instigator of her own misfortune rather than as a somewhat blemished victim. John, on the other hand, is a new breed of man, who is not afraid to show *unmanly* emotions. Nor is he, as appears on the surface, a simple peasant who cannot compete for the affections of an impressionable young woman with a more sophisticated gallant who is stereotypically a rogue. He is a poor unfortunate who has fallen helplessly in love and does not know what to do when faced with the awful realisation that his love is not reciprocated. In short, he wants to reject Isabella, not because he no longer loves her, but because he does not feel inclined to interfere with another man's 'chattels', thus emphasising the novel's key message.

This was a far more complex understanding of the implicit themes in the novel than the one I had received as a schoolboy and my impression, until now, had been entirely superficial. Perhaps I – and Jane, and Derek too – had failed to grasp that there was more to this multi-layered novel than 'over-sentimentalised pap', a self-fulfilling conclusion we had each reached independently. I have to admit that I had remembered Isabella as a selfish, scheming, young vixen who gets what she deserves, and John as a weak and emotional adolescent who does not stand up for himself. The underlying idea to me then, was that women are inherently stronger than men, a simple reversal of contemporary Victorian thinking, and I blushed at my complete ignorance. The critique also pointed out a serious error in the story, namely that a coach from Liverpool was unlikely to choose a route that was no more than a cart track across hostile moorland to a small, isolated village. Rather, Isabella would have had to make the final stage of her journey in the back of a wagon! As I stood by the printer, waiting for the above commentary to emerge, the young man put down his magazine and rummaged in a drawer under the counter.

"You don't need to print anything if you've got of these," he said smugly, holding up a pen drive. "Paste your text into a Word document and save it onto this. It'll save you a lot of time and money in the long run. I can let you have one for fifteen quid."

"Thank you," I replied unsmilingly. "As you can probably deduce from my being in your shop, I don't have either an iPad or a laptop at the moment. I want to refer to these résumés later today which is why I'm printing them out. Anyhow, you're too late because I've nearly finished."

Undeterred by the insolence of youth I pressed on with my research, which had to be to find a similar dissection of Catherine Ayre's 'The Governess'. The following is a summary of the storyline, again provided by Wikipedia:

'James Ryder, an affluent banker from the fictitious northern town of Queensbridge, is killed in a train crash returning from a visit to his company's headquarters in London. To compound this tragedy, his wife Anne and his twenty year old daughter Emily discover that he had invested his fortune in a failed diamond mine in Sierra Leone, leaving them almost penniless. When Anne has settled their debts, they are forced to move out of their comfortable house in the suburbs and take lodgings in one of the poorer parts of the town. This becomes too much for the frail, heart-broken widow and within six months she too is dead,

leaving a now destitute Emily to fend for herself. Taking advantage of her background and education she manages to find a post as a governess to the two children of the handsome Sir Alfred Spencer, a wealthy factory-owning squire in South Yorkshire. Alfred is himself recently bereaved but this does not prevent him from holding regular, riotous soirées and having affairs with a succession of lovers. On several occasions he arrogantly attempts to seduce the straight-laced Emily but every time she succeeds in fending him off. Finally he settles for using her as a confidante to help him deal with the various complications arising from his drunken promises of marriage to two of his mistresses, neither of whom is aware of the other. He is secretly very impressed with Emily's cool-headedness in helping him to overcome his problems and her talents as a tutor to his young son and daughter who adore her. He views her at first as a valuable asset, but gradually he comes to rely on her for help and advice. He is, however, rarely sober and often given to fits of rage-filled violence against his servants, which appals her. As time passes, the servants themselves also begin to look up to her, complaining bitterly about Alfred's cruelty. They maintain that they are trapped in a form of legitimised feudalism because they will not be able to find alternative employment should they decide leave the squire's service without his permission. Things come to a head when, in front of the whole household, Alfred, much the worse for wear, horse-whips a feckless groom for failing to prevent him stepping in a puddle when dismounting from his horse. Emily has seen enough. She organises a strike, stating that she will act as a negotiator on the servant's behalf and take their grievances to Alfred. At first they unanimously support her but when they come face to face with their master, they back down. Emily is dismissed summarily and returns to Queensbridge, finding temporary accommodation with an old school friend. She is unable to obtain a new post without references and has to settle for an unskilled job in a woollen mill so that she has money with which to survive. A year later she is surprised by a visit from Alfred. It is mid-December and he is heavily wrapped up in a thick overcoat with a scarf across the lower part of his face. He tells her that his life is in turmoil. The west wing of his magnificent palace has been damaged by a fire when, in a drunken stupor, he accidentally knocked over a candelabra that had ignited some curtains. To add insult to injury, he has been named as correspondent in a forthcoming divorce and he is angrily being pursued by creditors for unpaid bills. His children have rejected three governesses since Emily's dismissal and they are running around out of control. He is at his wit's end, he declares, and begs her to return to his country seat, not as a governess but as his wife. When she prevaricates, he slowly removes his scarf to reveal his badly disfigured mouth, the result of a vicious assault by the self-same groom he had brutally whipped. He swears on his wife's grave that he is a reformed man insisting that his disfigurement signifies his punishment for his previous wanton, debauched lifestyle. Emily reluctantly agrees to marry him on condition that he gives her total control of all financial and domestic arrangements and legal guardianship of his children. He acquiesces to all her demands unconditionally in spite of his not being able to arrange this legally. The story ends with the servants at the manor welcoming her back with open arms after which she promises them that, from then on, a new spirit of mutual respect will replace their earlier shackles of oppression.'

I did not include the discussion about this novel since its *explicit* meaning concerning the contrasting natures of the respective genders seems fairly self-explanatory to me, very much in keeping with that expressed in 'The Stone Seat'. Emily is strong, compassionate and altruistic whereas Alfred is weak, brutal and egotistical, seeking only to salvage his self-respect after deformity forces him back onto the straight and narrow. The Ayre sisters were clearly singing from the same hymn sheet, except with one essential difference: Emily enters a loveless marriage intentionally to change the working conditions of the servants and to rescue the children from delinquency – not simply to improve her own life. It goes without saying that the novel, the last one that Catherine Ayre wrote, was regarded as groundbreaking in some quarters when it was published in 1861, as Emily's prenuptial demands foreshadowed the Property Act nine years later and the rights bestowed on married women therein. I could, however, see no connection in either novel to the saga of Christopher Heath, although there was a minor similarity to the lives of the Ayres in both novels, namely that one of the heroine's parents is widowed and both are financially destitute and have to move house by the end of the first chapter. 'The Stone Seat' is also transparently set in Watholme.

As I ate my lunch back at The Green Man, I reflected on what I had been doing so far on the fifth day of my holiday. Instead of spending a leisurely hour or two walking down the disused railway trackbed to Boughton, as per my prearranged timetable, I had been mentally compiling a picture of the lives and works of the Ayre sisters – something I had deliberately set out *not* to do! Indeed I had been doing this ever since Agnes had decided to let me in on her conspiracy theories about their untimely deaths, when no one else in the entire world of letters had ever suspected that they could have been caused by anything other than typhoid. At the risk of repeating myself, there was a typhoid epidemic, Elizabeth and Amy caught it, and they died, simple as that. Even Jane, her sister and closest friend, had dismissed her allegations as nonsense. I had therefore to ask myself why I had been acting like a zealous student, spending half the morning mugging up on two famous masterpieces. Was it because I was seeking more evidence to discredit Agnes? Or was it, perversely, that I wanted to believe her?

Then there was Jane's half-finished account of the life and loves of young Christopher. Why was she so adamant that I should hear it to the end? Did this not signify that there would be a conclusion of some kind to come that afternoon, when all my as yet unanswered questions would finally be resolved? What I had learned from my trip out to the Wi-Fi café was that each of the Ayres' novels drew a great deal on the environment in which they had lived and contained many esoteric messages beneath the surface story. Was I expected to interpret Jane's shaggy-dog tale in the same way? For instance, is Christopher's distant grandfather, Amos Heath, the key to unravelling the mystery of the identity of the man who rescued me after my fall? Does this mean that both Jane and Agnes are telling me in a roundabout way that he is related to Christopher and hence to the Ayres, those women who made Watholme the village what it is today, and I am staying in the hotel that was built on the site of their burnt out cottage? If this is the case, why could she simply not have boasted on Sunday evening that I was not merely a lucky man, I was a privileged one to boot. The clouds inside my head were beginning to dissolve, as their meteorological equivalents had done two hours earlier, and I was now one hundred per cent convinced that she and Agnes had successfully kept their disabled guest both intellectually occupied and distractingly amused for the past five days. That was their purpose as Agnes had conceded. All that remained for me to discover was the identity of the shadowy prowler, and perhaps even this was part of an elaborate game they were playing.

CHAPTER ELEVEN

Thursday Afternoon

At quarter past two Jane had still not turned up. She had not kept me waiting without an explanation before and I began to suspect that something was wrong. The hotel had become eerily silent; I could hear no noise of any kind, such as the clattering of plates or muffled voices emanating from the kitchen. There was no point in sitting around and my time would be better spent finding out what was amiss. I dragged myself up and shuffled off to investigate. The rhythmical tapping of my new walking stick on the quarry tiled floor in the foyer was intensified by the lack of other background sounds, illustrating the unnatural stillness. The front door was locked but not bolted, signifying that a guest could not come back in without a key. It had, I assumed, been closed whilst I was having lunch.

I made my way through the silent dining room to the kitchen which was also deserted. It was surprisingly more spacious in broad daylight than it looked in the dark, resembling how I imagined it would have appeared on one of those quasi-historical TV programmes where a family of four has to cope with outdated household appliances and cooking equipment. In this case it would have been the nineteen sixties, and they would have had not one but two huge, heavy-looking cookers, two stainless-steel sinks and an abundance of painted, metal cabinets and other units at their disposal. Everything was coloured light blue. I observed in passing that my plates and cutlery were piled up in the smaller sink waiting to be washed since there was no dishwasher after all. The door leading out to the chalets had been left slightly ajar, and when I came out into the fresh air, I was greeted by the discordant twittering of blackbirds squabbling somewhere above me – which was disturbingly sinister, considering the time of year. As I stood in the doorway and cautiously glanced around, Agnes appeared from across the courtyard, hurrying towards me with a baleful look on her face. She was wearing a grey dressing gown which was also very strange, I reflected, as she drew nearer. There was something about this situation that disturbed me.

"What are you doing here?" she barked as if to a miscreant who was trespassing. "Is something the matter?"

"I was worried that you'd gone out and left me on my own," I replied, thinking quickly. "The front door's locked and there's no one in the main building."

"I'm sorry, Mr Lockwood," she said, noticeably changing her tune. "Please forgive my silly outburst. I'm a bit stressed because Violet's having one of her turns and we're having a spot of bother calming her down."

"Is there anything I can do?" I said, using the standard formula for situations such as this.

"No, thank you very much," she said, forcing a smile. "The best thing you can do is to go back to the lounge or your room and wait there."

"Is Jane in with Violet?" I persisted, making her look even more annoyed.

"Yes, and so is Nadia before you ask," she spat back.

"When you've sorted everything about, please tell her I'll be in my room," I said courteously, concealing my consternation at her uncharacteristic rudeness.

Judging by Agnes's aggressive behaviour, I was without a shred of doubt interrupting something that she did not wish me to witness – and who could blame her? It had to be an extremely complicated balancing act nursing an invalid whilst attempting to run a hotel, albeit an almost empty one. Yet Jane and Agnes had brought it on themselves by insisting that their sister lived in with them. In mitigation, had I been ambulant I would have been down in Boughton for the day, and they would have been able to deal with Violet without anyone being the wiser. It might have been interesting, to say the least, to learn what happened if the same situation arose in two weeks' time when the hotel was scheduled to be fully occupied by a group of boisterous schoolteachers.

Upon reaching my room, I stretched out on the bed and closed my eyes to determine how to make use of the remainder of the afternoon. A nap first, I thought, after which I would compile a short list of questions for Jane if she ever continued the adventures of the sexually maturing, working class schoolboy with a chip on his shoulder about backyard lavatories. I had already made a few rough notes after the first instalment on Sunday evening which would form the basis of an inventory to which I would add a few other items that were still puzzling me from later episodes. I was, however, rather hoping that I had escaped another boring session or two with her, since, as I have repeated ad nauseam, I could not fathom how her longwinded tale was connected to me. I was not being brashly conceited, I hasten to add. It is that I do not value social interaction with unfamiliar people who shamelessly patronise me, even if they have my best interests at heart. The majority of my queries appertained to Jane's endeavours to create an elaborate smokescreen to keep me guessing how the various fine points of her chronicle fitted together, such as the incredible amount of detail she had amassed to establish Christopher's working class roots, and the exhaustive descriptions of the areas and houses in which he had lived. It seemed to me that she had cleverly developed the story as a blow by blow account of a young man's transition from infancy to adulthood and how his schooldays were both shaping and altering his personality as he journeyed through the early stages of his life.

Boosted by the expert analyses of the 'The Stone Seat' and 'The Governess' that I had read at the W-Fi café, I could now declare with the utmost confidence that my gut feelings about this picaresque romp with its smutty, sexual undertones had been correct. It was a piece of fiction, nothing more than the product of her oft-stated fixation with the nineteen sixties, when working class heroes and heroines dominated the arts world, in the cinema and in the theatre. There were also two other key issues to get to the bottom of: why she had not yet disclosed the identity of the young man who had rescued me, and how she had so much intimate knowledge of Christopher's life, if she had not made most of it up.

Satisfied that I had seen through her well-intentioned deception, I lay back and shut my eyes. I could now relax and look forward to the moment when she finally revealed the end of her mock epic. I had no need to ask Agnes for further clarification of her contribution to my entertainment since we had well and truly exhausted our debate about the Ayres' renunciation of belles-lettres and their regeneration as small-town pillars of society in Bronte in Sicily. Her current belligerence towards me was, I am quite certain, caused by my criticisms of the flimsy evidence that she had gathered to accuse the Ayres of the swindle of the century.

I was woken from my impromptu siesta by a knock at the door. It was almost five o'clock and a squally rain shower was hammering on my window. As I struggled to find the switch to my bedside light, I remembered that I had asked Agnes to inform Jane that I was going up to my room. Regrettably she had interpreted my statement as meaning that I wanted Jane to come to see me.

"I'm making another theatrical entrance," Jane gabbled as she came in. "Shall I draw your curtains to shut out the storm or would you prefer them to be left open to heighten the effect."

She waltzed across to the other side of the room without pausing for my answer, closed the curtains, and sat herself down in the armchair by the window. She crossed her legs and clasped her knees, straightening her back in an effort to appear focused. She was wearing her black uniform again and her professional smile, indicating that this might not be a purely social call.

"I hate winter," she went on. "It's been a rotten week, hasn't it? But by no means the worst time to injure your leg. You wouldn't have had much fun walking around in this weather."

"How's Violet?" I asked groggily. "I trust she's back to normal, whatever that is?"

Her demeanour changed instantly. Her body stiffened and her eyes opened wide. The artificial smile vanished to be replaced by what I can only describe as a frozen, horror-struck expression. She looked like a little girl who had just been told that her pet kitten had died.

"How do you know about Violet?" she stammered. "Who told you? Was it Agnes?"

"I met her last night, when you were chatting to the Belgians," I explained. "Well, not exactly 'met'. Perhaps 'looked in on' is a better way of putting it. She was asleep and Agnes only allowed me to stay for a few seconds."

"Agnes is a foolish, old woman," she groaned. "I can't leave her for five minutes before she's giving guided tours of our quarters. What else did you two get up to?"

"She showed me her research into how the Ayres faked their deaths," I replied. "Remember, you laughed about it last night."

"Of course I remember," she retorted, clearly having forgotten. "Why did the silly bitch need to show you Violet to do that?"

"To prove that I'd had a nightmare. I suspected that someone who was mentally ill was living in the hotel and that it was this person who was responsible for the howling I heard on Tuesday night. I assume Agnes told you about it. We'd already ruled out Nadia and she was demonstrating that it couldn't possibly be Violet. Ergo I must have had a bad dream."

"And did you believe her?"

"Yes I did," I fibbed. "And I'm now convinced I dreamed the whole incident."

"Then no harm's been done."

"No, no harm's been done," I echoed, in an attempt to reduce the tension. "Look at it another way. You've taken care of me right royally this week and I'm beginning to feel like one of the family. So naturally I had to be introduced to my step sister!"

"That's very kind of you," she smiled icily. "Was there anything else that you wanted?"

"Ah yes, thank you for jogging my memory," I said, maintaining my pleasant tone. "We've missed our get-together this afternoon and I was wondering if you were going to have time to finish your story."

"We have over two days before you leave us," she said, appearing puzzled. "That's ample time, I should have thought. Are you getting bored, Mr Lockwood?"

"I'd also like you to do me a big favour," I announced, which startled her. "I'd like you to loosen the strapping around my ankle so that I can move it to drive my car."

I am still perplexed how this spontaneous request came to my lips and I was, without a shadow of a lie, nearly as stunned as Jane was. My only justification had to be my unconscious desire not to respond to her loaded question without first hearing the ending of Christopher's story.

"It's strapped up to help the healing process," she scowled. "Loosening the strapping too early will weaken the ligaments and there's a good chance that your foot will become numb without any warning. That's going to make it very risky for you to drive, and you'll be a danger not only to yourself but to other road users."

"It's not a very long journey back to Chester," I countered. "It's nearly all motorway and if there are no major holdups, it should take about two hours. If you did it for me tonight after dinner, it'd leave me over forty eight hours to get used to putting weight on the ankle joint and I'll be able to have a practice drive as well on Saturday."

"I'm not going to interfere in a medical procedure that I'm not sure about," she said firmly. "Why not go to A and E at the hospital tomorrow and see what they say?"

"It's a waste of time, because I know what the nurse will say," I frowned. "She'll say the strapping can't come off for another week at the earliest. That's why arrangements have been made for me to attend the Countess of Chester hospital in ten days' time."

"Well there's your answer," she laughed. "You'll have to be a patient patient!"

"But how am I going to get home on Sunday?" I said frantically.

"You'll have to do it the old-fashioned way by taxi and train or express coach," she insisted. "Your pal Derek might do you a deal and take you all the way."

"That means I'll have to abandon my car here for over a week and come back to collect it," I moaned. "Unless someone will drive it for me and return with Derek."

"That's more like it," she said, clapping her hands sarcastically. "One of Derek's taxi men might do it for you."

"That's given me three alternatives to choose from," I muttered. "It'll probably be cheaper to stay here for another week so that makes it four."

"We'll offer you a preferential rate if you opt to spend more time with us," she said as she stood up to leave. "Now, shall I continue telling you about Christopher this evening or will you be doing something else?"

"Will you be finishing it?" I asked, trying not to sound fraught.

"You'll have to wait and see," she replied impishly. "Shall we say nine o'clock in the lounge as usual?"

CHAPTER TWELVE

Thursday Evening

"Let's see if I can remember where we're up to," she said, as she smoothed her skirt across her thighs. "We've done those first few years in Watholme, we've done junior school but we left the grammar school in a bit of a mess, didn't we, Mr Lockwood?"

It was five past nine and Jane had just returned from the bar with a beer for me and a glass of red wine for herself. She was in her black uniform, yet another example of the over-formality and unnecessary fussiness of a medium-sized hotel which had seen better days and which was, for the present, conspicuously empty. Why she did not wear everyday clothes still escapes me. By the same token, however, I had on my sports coat, conforming to dining room etiquette that 'gentlemen should be attired in a jacket', which, surprisingly, was not a requirement at The Green Man.

"I'd started telling you about his lady friends, hadn't I?" she continued. "What I neglected to mention was how this new hobby of his began to dominate everything he did, and, in some cases, didn't do. He gave up sport and he gave up trainspotting, consigning both to the treasure chest of children's activities. He went out every night either with a girl, sometimes with a different one – two-timing isn't stressful, it's getting caught at it that is – or he went drinking with the boys. 'What's wrong with that?'

I hear you ask. Well, homework for starters. Then there were the nights out down the pub. Being boozed up isn't an aid to studying. And his best mates? They stayed in and read their books, did their sums or wrote their essays and only went out once during the week. Yes, Christopher was with a different set of people each evening. That's why he failed his Advanced levels whereas all his friends passed theirs. As I may have said before, there's always a price to pay. Success with the opposite sex led to disaster academically, but luckily he was young enough – he was still only sixteen – to be able to return to school the next year and retake his course. What he needed was a steady girlfriend, one who would encourage him to knuckle down and prioritise his studies, and, of course, someone to devote himself to."

"Where do you come into this?" I asked when she paused for a sip of her wine. "You weren't this steady girlfriend were you?"

"No, but you're quite warm," she frowned as she put down her glass. "On Sunday afternoons no matter what the weather, if he hadn't anything else to do, he'd catch a bus up to Watholme with anyone who'd accompany him and they'd go for a walk on the moors. Often he went alone. Occasionally his friend Steven would give him a lift in his dad's Morris Traveller shooting brake. That was when only Steven and Christopher remained in Boughton, as the others had left for pastures new after 'A' levels. Well, one particular Sunday afternoon at the end of May, when Christopher was seventeen, he and Steven went for a coffee in the café at the top of the High Street before they went back home. The café isn't there now. It's been replaced by a self-help bookshop that also sells scented candles, crystals and vegan health food. Anyhow, they were sitting sipping their coffees or whatever, when a large, well-built bloke leaned over from the next table and said in a loud voice: 'You're Christopher Heath, aren't you?' When Christopher appeared stumped by this straightforward question requiring a simple yes or no answer, the bloke added: 'Don't you recognise me? I'm Jimmy Hindley. I was in the dunce group in Miss Barfield's reading class at school.' Christopher's face lit up at once, not only because he did remember him, but because he was instantly reminded of when old Ada showed her one and only moment of compassion. Jimmy had fallen asleep whilst waiting for his table to be called, and she spotted him at the back of the classroom with his head on his desk. The class, to a child, shrank back in terror, expecting her to blow a fuse, but instead she smiled sweetly and whispered: 'He's so peaceful, bless him. Let the little lad get his rest.' That's what he told us after Jimmy had left. I was there too with Violet but annoyingly Christopher hadn't noticed me. I had my back to him, which gave him some sort of excuse."

She stopped speaking and sighed, a sigh that implied that her disappointment at being ignored forty years ago was still as intense as ever. She shook her head slowly and looked blankly down at her feet, until she had regained her poise, exactly as she had done two evenings previously, when she had been speaking of her affair with Brendon, Christopher's erstwhile best friend.

"Jimmy wasn't my boyfriend," she said, breaking into a smile. "His father owned the farm that Christopher once visited, the day he discovered the joys of the moors, if you recall what Agnes said on Monday afternoon. This chap and my father were bigwigs at the rotary club, and they'd been having an informal meeting at the hotel to discuss tactics for one of them to get elected president at the next AGM. It was Daddy who was voted in, so it must have been worthwhile. Jimmy had come along with his father, and I was ordered to take him out and keep him entertained for the afternoon. I think they wanted me to get off with him and perhaps one day marry him, bringing two of the wealthiest families together in a mediaeval-style power pact. There was absolutely no chance of that! He was quite good-looking but he was as thick as the proverbial animal excrement he walked about in on the farm. To ensure there'd be no monkey-business I took my little sister with me as a gooseberry. That wasn't Agnes, it was Violet, by the way. She was just turned sixteen and very, very pretty."

"How old were you then?" I cut in, risking a black look. "If Christopher was seventeen, you were what... nineteen?"

"Christopher was nearly eighteen and I was twenty," she replied. "Agnes was nineteen so she must have started university, which would explain why she wasn't there. I'd just finished my second year exams in Italian, my subsidiary subject, at Newcastle and I was waiting for my results. When it became obvious to Jimmy that he wasn't going to get anywhere with me or Violet, he decided to go to visit one of his buddies. That left a nice foursome, Steven and Christopher and Violet and me, all free agents in the courtship stakes. Brendon and I had split up when he went off to university and Violet was just embarking on her chosen career as a sex goddess."

She broke off again, only this time it was not because of some deep-seated frustration. It was as if two ideas had simultaneously entered her head and she was uncertain in which direction her story would proceed from there.

"I have a confession to make," she said, evidently having made a swift decision. "I'd always fancied Christopher ever since I looked after him when he started

Highton Junior School. Does that answer one of your umpteen questions satisfactorily? That's why I know so much about his childhood and his adolescent days. I followed his progress like a soppy girl who worships a pop star from afar. I was *besotted*, Mr Lockwood, and now I had him in my grasp for the first time. Well, after Jimmy had gone, I started chatting Christopher up in a rather forward way – okay, I was throwing myself at him – but he couldn't keep his eyes off Violet and he wasn't even listening to me half of the time. She kept on smiling at him, then looking down at her hands when she saw him gazing back at her, just like Princess Diana used to do. Heaven knows what Steven must have been thinking. You see, Christopher wasn't physically attracted to me because I was more like a big sister to him. I'd been a shoulder to cry on when he needed help through a difficult transition at Highton, and when I went off to the private school we only saw each other intermittently. I was never a potential girlfriend, I was always that rare specimen, a *female friend*, one he could have a laugh with and reminisce about the good old days."

"Wasn't there a bit of an age discrepancy between you and Christopher?" I said. "I mean, he was still a schoolboy and you were at university."

"I didn't want to marry him," she protested. "I wanted to have a fling and see what it was like. Besides Daddy wouldn't have approved – and not because I was older than Christopher. It was because of where he came from and what his dad did for a living. My infatuation with him started when my mother walked out on us. She moved in with a man half her age in his terraced house with a smelly, outside toilet in Oakgrove. I'd been going to see her after school before Christopher's family came to live there. It was an arrangement between my parents that Daddy would pick me up from her hovel at about five o'clock."

"Hold on, you weren't the girl on the roundabout, were you?" I gasped. "The one who showed..."

"Certainly not!" she roared back.

"Now I understand how you could describe Oakgrove so meticulously," I said, changing tack quickly.

"I told you my story was leading somewhere," she grinned, indicating that I had not upset her. "My mother didn't want custody of her three daughters, thank the Lord, and we didn't for a second wish to live in a grotty two-up, two-down with no bathroom. We went to visit as a threesome for an hour or two on Saturdays or Sundays and that suited all four of us, six if you count Daddy and Wilf the fancy man. In the end this arrangement only lasted a couple of years and we stopped going a few months before Christopher came to live there. Soon afterwards they emigrated to Canada and we never heard from her again. No one gave a monkey's either way."

At this juncture I remembered her berating Christopher for being a young man who was ashamed of his house with no bathroom and an outside lavatory. I smiled to myself that I now knew the probable source of his anxiety and ultimately his snobbery.

"Well, did you have that fling with him?" I ventured, growing in confidence that she trusted me enough to give me an honest answer.

"Who? Wilf the fancy man?"

"No, Christopher."

"What I'm about to say might explain why I never got the chance," she frowned.

"What I didn't see at first was what was going on between Christopher and Violet. It was a small café and we were sitting at separate tables, but close enough to carry on a conversation without raising our voices. When Jimmy had gone, Violet and I moved. I sat facing Steven with Christopher on my right and my sister sat opposite him. They were in their anoraks and Christopher was looking really handsome with his long, brown hair and sexy, skin-tight jeans. I was fairly scruffed up too but Violet had on her brand-new, leather miniskirt. She'd moved her chair back about a foot away from the table, and unbeknown to Steven and me, she was flashing her legs at Christopher. Not in a brazen, sluttish sort of way, just every now and then. Before you butt in, it was unambiguous what she was doing because of where he was staring."

"What did she look like when she was a teenager?" I said, ignoring her lack of refinement and trying to paint a more radiant picture of Violet, one which would replace the image of the grey-haired, old lady I had observed the evening before.

"She was slim and on the small side with long, black hair," she enthused. "She had a lovely face with large, green eyes, a bit like a younger version of Jean Shrimpton, I suppose."

"Why did she have to act so unsubtly, then?"

"She hadn't yet learned how to send out the appropriate signals," she laughed. "That's what the interpersonal communication experts would spout today. I bet you attended similar courses when you were a manager so that you could, quote, 'recognise and decode the non-verbal signals transmitted by your subordinates'. That was her Achilles heel. She wasn't very intelligent."

"That's not a very nice thing to say about your sister," I said pointedly. "Everyone's intelligent in different ways. You're contradicting yourself again. Academic achievements don't get you very far without other personal characteristics I believe you and Agnes were adamant about on Monday."

"My goodness you *have* been paying attention!" she exclaimed. "Yes, it is rather arrogant of me but she was never interested in school or learning. She lived in a dream world of her own creation when she was a child, and when her body started changing, she became convinced that a rich, young aristocrat would sweep her off her feet and take her away to his yacht in the Mediterranean. She used to go for long walks on the moors and fantasise that she was accompanied by this blue-blooded playboy who would change his nationality every week, depending on who or what she'd seen on television or at the pictures. When she was fifteen, however, she realised that she was unlikely to meet any multi-millionaires in this part of West Yorkshire but she was absolutely certain about one thing – that it would be her good-looks not her exam results that would be her passport out of bumpkin-land, as she called Watholme."

"I'd say that this showed a high degree of intelligence," I countered.

"It's a very risky strategy, especially if you're not brainy. She didn't want a reputation as a dumb blonde."

"Not if she had black hair..."

"Now you're teasing me," she grinned. "However you're right. It was her good-looks that attracted him, and the sexy leg performance was presenting him with an invitation to take things further."

Inadvertently I had allowed myself to be side-tracked once again, and I was not enjoying the hurly-burly of our sparring with each other about prurient matters. However it had not rained since late afternoon and the TV weatherman on the teatime news had forecast a mild and overcast Friday. Thus heartened and feeling more positive about my situation for the first time that week, I reconciled myself to being led to wherever she and her interminable odyssey would take me.

"How did it pan out for them?" I continued, in an effort to prevent her from continuing in the same vein. "We've been side-tracked by arguing about what constituted sex appeal among nineteen sixties teenagers."

"Very well," she said, licking her lips theatrically. "About fifteen minutes went by until Steven announced that he had to go home. It was half past four and he was probably wanting his tea after a couple of hours of slogging uphill and down dale on the moors. We left the café arm in arm, all four of us linked up across the pavement in a line. Steven was on the inside, then me, then Christopher with Violet nearest the road. We'd only gone a few yards when Christopher pulled himself away and moved to the outside, presumably to assume the gentleman's position for Violet's benefit. He could also have been deliberately separating himself from me, and I felt jealous of my sister for the second time that afternoon. It became worse when she told me later on that she and Christopher had a date the following Sunday. They couldn't meet during the week because he still had a couple of exams to swot for, and they couldn't go out together before then because Daddy didn't allow her to travel down to Boughton on her own. She didn't want to go out in Watholme because all the pub landlords knew she was under age. They settled for a day on the moors since both of them loved it there and they could wander unwatched and undisturbed. They did this for the whole summer, every Sunday come rain or shine. As their relationship flourished, they met up secretly during the week down in Boughton, usually somewhere indoors like a coffee bar. Significantly he never let her come near his home in Oakgrove. That arch conspirator Agnes went with her and spent a couple of hours in the library doing her university coursework. It lasted until August when Daddy found out. Violet had been spotted in a pub by one of his friends and all hell broke loose the next day. She was banned from going anywhere without a chaperone which had to be me as Agnes was also in the doghouse. It was a ludicrous situation, if you think about it, because both Agnes and I went off to our respective universities in September, leaving poor, little Violet grounded, without a hope of ever being able to go anywhere unless Daddy trusted the company she was keeping. He even insisted on giving her a lift if he allowed her out, with a strict, early pick-up appointment to make sure she wasn't up to any mischief. To add insult to injury, he didn't approve of Christopher who was immediately excluded. She had to tell him that their affair was over. Christopher was working class and he came from Oakgrove, where my mother had run off to live with her greaseball of a lover. That's what Daddy called him. He wanted Violet to marry someone who was sophisticated and wealthy, that is middle class, preferably upper class if she had the opportunity. It didn't matter that Christopher was bright and had prospects. What mattered was that he came from the wrong side of town, where he lived in a small, terraced house with an outside loo. Daddy had drummed this into her after he realised that she wasn't going to get any letters after her name, and the best she could hope for was a job in an office."

"What did they get up to on the moors?" I asked when she paused for a moment. "Did they just talk or did they do something else?"

"The former," she said, shaking her head. "Christopher was too decent a guy to do the anything else bit. They had their favourite spot, a huge piece of black, rectangular rock named The Devil's Fingernail, which they climbed to the top of and sat in their own cloud kingdom."

"Did they miss each other when they were forced to split up?"

"I know Violet did. She missed his good looks, his sense of decorum and their weekend walks. All of her next few boyfriends had one thing only on their minds, to get their hands on her body. I only saw him once more to ask him how he was feeling. It was the last time we met and he was very nasty to me. He was finishing off his gap year job in a supermarket in Sleighton and about to go to Manchester University. He'd passed four 'A' levels with good grades the year before and he chose to earn some money instead of being the youngest undergraduate in his department. When I said hello to him at a party, he screamed he was done with the Deans and told me to eff off. He was drunk and making a general fool of himself, the ungrateful so and so. Two years later I got my degree and went off to Belgium to teach English."

"Is that the end of the story?" I said, clapping my hands slowly. "If so, who's the young man who helped me last Sunday?"

"There's one last chapter," she murmured looking down at her feet. "But before I carry on, I need another drink."

When she stood up I observed that she had tears in her eyes, and she took out a white, embroidered handkerchief from her sleeve and blew her nose. I felt my lips tighten at this sudden swing in her mood, and I anticipated that the dénouement I had craved for so long was going to be a tragic one, accompanied, no doubt, by a roll of thunder from outside.

"I've brought us both a stiff one," she said considerately as she returned from the bar. "Buckle your seat belt because here we go."

She sat down and went through the routine of smoothing her skirt in an effort, I assumed, to collect herself.

"Nearly three years had passed since the time they met in the coffee bar in Watholme when they bumped into each other again – literally. He'd just finished his second year in Manchester and Daddy had given Violet a job in our hotel working on reception. They were both in a pub in the centre of Boughton when they walked into each other as they came out of their respective toilets. If there's such a thing as love at second sight, this was it. Unfortunately she had a steady boyfriend but she was out with the girls that evening, and he was out with Brendon and Philip who were celebrating their success in their final examinations at university. They sat together and chatted for about an hour before he plucked up courage and asked her to come back with him to Philip's house for a nightcap. He promised he'd get her a taxi as she'd miss the last bus, but she turned him down. She couldn't be unfaithful to her boyfriend, she said feigning a frown, because he was loaded and drove an expensive Mercedes sports car. She did say, however, that if the offer was still open, she would be free on one evening the next week. Regrettably he was due in Manchester flat hunting, he said, but he told her he would write to her and send her his address."

"Hang on," I intervened. "How do you know what happened if you weren't in contact with him any longer?"

"Violet was my little sister," she said, raising her index finger in admonishment. "She couldn't wait to write to me when she got back home later that night."

"I'm sorry," I replied shamefacedly. "Please go on."

"They must have corresponded regularly for the next few months," she continued. "The rest is a huge mystery but I assume they must have got it together during the summer holidays. I'd just come back home from Belgium, when one evening at the beginning of November he turned up at the hotel at about eight in the evening. I wasn't there, by the way. I was at the cinema. He told Daddy that Violet had agreed to go to Manchester with him in his old banger of a car, a cream and green Austin A55 it was, which his father had bought him for his twenty first birthday. He asked where she was and if she was ready. All I know was that earlier that evening she'd received a message from him calling the whole thing off, and she'd gone out with her ex-boyfriend with the Mercedes as a kind of revenge. He was called Edward Lister incidentally. That's when Daddy got angry. He threw Christopher out physically and warned him to stay away from his daughter or there'd be trouble. She already had a boyfriend, he thundered, and she was out with him for the evening. Christopher must have felt betrayed and belittled by Violet's duplicity, and no doubt jealous of Edward, who he now saw as his rival. He stormed out of the hotel trembling with rage and headed for Manchester. It was a filthy night and he must have lost the road over the moors…"

She jumped up from her chair and burst into tears, desperately clutching at her sleeve for her handkerchief. I sat back in helpless astonishment as she struggled to retrieve it.

"They never found his car, let alone his body," she sobbed, pointing to the window. "Somehow he must have skidded into the bog on the hairpin bend below Wildheath Crags. His beloved moor had taken him selfishly away from us and it has steadfastly refused to give us any part of him in return."

"Derek told me about the accident the other day but he didn't know it was Christopher," I said quietly. "I guess Violet took it badly, didn't she?"

"She'd fallen head over heels in love with him, from what I could gather, when I introduced her to him and Steven in the café," she went on. "I believe he fell in love with her then too. So when they met each other for the second time she tried to make sure that it was for keeps. When she got the message that he'd ditched her for good, she was at first distraught, then angry. She arranged to meet Edward in a fit of pique to show Christopher that she had other admirers and make him green with envy. When she found out later that week what had really happened, she blamed herself for his dreadful death, repeating over and over that if she'd stayed in and watched TV or something, any misunderstanding would have been cleared up. She broke down completely shortly afterwards and she's never recovered."

"So who was the young man who rescued me?" I said, rather too forcefully it transpired.

"Oh him," she snapped. "I never saw him, did I? It was probably James Snowden. He's a keen jogger. He's a chartered accountant and lives at the other end of the village. Please excuse me, I have to look in on Violet before I go to bed."

She hurried away, abandoning me once again to reflect on yet another eerie coincidence. I already knew the grisly details of a young man's 'death by accident', without being aware of his identity. Somehow everything in this neck of the woods seemed to be connected. I was however too drained to sit alone in the deserted hotel lounge and mull over the how and the why. Besides I could hear rain drops stealthily spattering the windows and gradually getting heavier. Despite what the TV weatherman had said, a storm was brewing. I left the half empty glasses where they were and hobbled off to the warmth of my bed.

CHAPTER THIRTEEN

Friday

For the first time for nearly a week I woke up the next morning in the certain knowledge that I would have the day to myself. Both Jane and Agnes had finished their respective works of fiction, and, unless Nadia somehow managed to find the English to regale me with horror stories from the Kosovo War, there was absolutely no reason why they should insist that I sat down and listened patiently to any of them ever again. Furthermore I had finally discovered the identity of my rescuer, anticlimactic as it was. I needed his address to send him a card to thank him, or, better still, to visit him if he lived nearby. His telephone number would suffice. Yet, other than that, what was there to do for a man who could neither walk nor drive? I had succeeded in ambling short distances without my crutches but a hike of any description was out of the question. It did not matter, however, because it was, as usual, teeming down outside. The weather forecasters were way off the mark again. That left me with two alternatives. I could mooch about in my room or I could loosen the bandages around my ankle and see if I could drive. This was, as Jane had warned me, fraught with danger, and I would need another person with me who could take over behind the wheel in case it became too painful for me to operate the accelerator and brake pedals. That person had to be Derek. I telephoned him whilst I was eating my breakfast without telling him the real purpose behind my requesting his services for an hour. He was available at ten thirty, which left me roughly an hour and a half in which to get to work on the strapping. If I made a mess of things, I would be able to ask him to whisk me off to the hospital to have the dressing repaired.

There was, however, one other thing I could not stop thinking about. I may have been too hasty in condemning the soap opera entitled 'Christopher Heath'. It could not simply be a wishy-washy, shaggy dog story for my amusement; it had to be much more complex than that. There was the perplexing matter of the extremely truncated ending for a start. Was this because Jane had talked herself out? The last few years of Christopher's life at university were missing because, of course, she would not have known anything about them. It also seemed odd that the distressing ending was as much about Violet as it was about Christopher. As it happens neither of them was a very remarkable character; he was a working class boy who went to university after a grammar school education and therefore had some potential. Yet he was not as 'clever' as Jane and Agnes had made out and he did not have the opportunity to develop his abilities, since his life was cut short in his early twenties. Furthermore, the character of Violet never progressed much further than an attractive, young woman who, predictably, only seemed interested in romance.

Undeniably it was a tragic love story on the surface, but on another level was it intended to be a poignant testament to the class struggle which continues to prevail in this country, despite political leaders of both parties attempting over the years to convince the electorate that it was a thing of the past? This would explain why she had made Christopher the main character. Somehow I could not help comparing Jane's carefully constructed story with the Wikipedia synopsis of 'The Stone Seat' I had read in the Wi-Fi café. There were several similarities. For instance, a wifeless father has an important part to play, and both storylines feature a young, middle-class woman who wanders on the moors daydreaming about magic kingdoms and handsome princes. The love element centres on her virtuous relationship with a young man who is ostensibly working class, and the heart-rending finales involve the death of one of the protagonists in the bottomless bog. Was the unearthly howling that had made my hair stand on end in the hotel yet another parallel? The fictional John vanished without trace on the moors, forever crying out in vain for his beloved Isabella. I had Derek to thank for providing me with the old wives' tale about the man killed in the road accident who was rumoured to haunt the moors and wail like a wounded animal, the man I now recognised as Christopher Heath. What puzzled me was why Jane had not completed her epic with this chilling payoff, which would have provided a fittingly macabre climax. Perhaps she omitted it deliberately because of what I had heard three nights ago or perhaps she was not aware of the local legend. If it were the former she may have feared that I would dismiss the rest of her marathon fable as nothing more than a gruesome ghost story. It did occur to me as I contemplated these new challenges that she may even have used the real Christopher's premature death and the aforementioned similarities to 'The Stone Seat' as the basis of her narrative, to produce an oral novel as it were. Was it real life imitating art or vice-versa? Moreover there may also a number of similarities between Jane's early life as a teacher and the heroine of 'The Governess' but is this not stretching things too far? In the end I concluded that

I had been influenced far too much by my research at the Wi-Fi café, and that I was deceiving myself into thinking that I had become a literary critic overnight. I had more pressing tasks to get on with and I went off to find my toilet bag, a roll of sticking plaster and a pair of sharp scissors.

* * *

"You're not only endangering yourself and others on the road, you're putting my life at risk as well," said Derek heatedly after I asked him to sit in the passenger seat of my car and supervise my attempt to drive. "That's why I'm categorically refusing to cut your bandages."

We were standing in the hotel lounge and he was wagging an admonishing finger at me.

"I can't bend forward far enough to do it myself because my stomach gets in the way," I replied in frustration. "I've put on weight after a week of sitting around, eating a lot and doing nothing. All you have to do is sever the pieces that cross over the front of the ankle joint and that should release the support provided by the heel lock."

"You're getting too technical," he frowned. "What happens if it goes wrong? How do I put it all back together again?"

"With the sticking plaster, dear Liza, dear Liza," I grinned. "With the sticking plaster."

"Why didn't you ask Agnes or Jane to do the honours for you," he said, still not smiling.

"I did and they refused."

"I prefer your other suggestion," he said assuming a more business-like tone. "If I charge you one pound a mile, that's about a hundred and fifty quid there and back for me and the bloke who drives your car. I'll throw him in for free because he'll be using your petrol on the way there, and we'll be coming back together. Alternatively, the train fare from Boughton will be about sixty quid plus a fiver at least for a taxi to the railway station. You'll have to change twice, at Leeds and Manchester, and when you get to Chester you'll need another taxi to get home. It'll take you twice as long."

"I thought you'd choose that one," I sighed. "That leaves me with only one other realistic alternative, which is to go home on the bus and leave my car here until the ligaments have healed. That would be very inconvenient and cost me two bus and four taxi fares plus a flat battery into the bargain, which corresponds to the hundred and fifty pounds on the same basis as taking me home. So that's out as well."

"You could stop here another week," he proposed. "I'm sure the old ladies will give you a discount."

"I'm not staying a minute longer than I have to," I scowled. "If you won't cut the strapping then I'll have to use you and your employee. When are you available?"

"Let me see," he said, inhaling deeply. "Your room's booked till Sunday morning. How about eleven thirty?"

"Haven't you got any slots tomorrow?" I said despairingly.

"Saturday's our busiest period," he returned. "It's shoppers during the day, and nights out later on. We'll be at it till the crack of dawn."

"You'd better be wide awake when you pick me up," I said brusquely but with a twinkle in my eye. "Otherwise you're not only endangering yourself and others on the road, you're putting my life at risk as well."

"Ouch!" he snorted, offering me his right hand. "Don't worry, Ellis will be driving your car and he's not working on Saturday night. I'll knock off early to get some kip."

We shook hands warmly and, with our business completed, he made for the doorway, where he suddenly turned round.

"Before I forget," he said dramatically, "the name of the chap who crashed into the bottomless bog was Christopher Heath, so the wife says. According to her, he lived in Boughton although he'd grown up in Watholme. Apparently he'd been intending to elope that night with Violet Dean, Jane's and Agnes's sister. He arrived here at the hotel unexpectedly only to find Violet out on a date with the posh boy, the one with the flash car. Christopher became so angry that he had to be thrown off the premises by Violet's father. He drove away in a blazing temper and a few minutes later crashed into the bottomless bog. He was on his way to Manchester where he was a student, and he must have taken the road across the moors as a short cut to the main drag to Lancashire. The whole thing was observed by a courting couple who were parked up just about where we were sitting yesterday. The police had to assume it was young Christopher from the couple's description of the car and his parents reporting him missing a few days later. His mum and dad were devastated when they learned what'd taken place, made a lot worse when they found out about Violet. They didn't even know about her because he'd never talked about her, and anyway he'd never brought his girlfriends back to their house, they said. At the inquest it transpired that Violet hadn't shown any interest in Christopher. Her father stated that posh boy was her longstanding boyfriend, and it was Christopher who was continually harassing her. He'd turned up out of the blue and started shouting. Her father said he would have set the dogs on him, if he'd had any. They couldn't verify this account because Violet had had her nervous breakdown by then and she didn't give evidence. Posh boy didn't testify because he said he hadn't a clue what was going on other than he'd received a phone call from Violet earlier that afternoon asking him to take her out. So the father was the only actual witness as to what went on at the hotel. Agnes lived somewhere down south at the time and Jane, not long back from working abroad, hadn't been present during the incident. The coroner's verdict was death by misadventure because of Christopher's alleged speed in the stormy weather, and the case was closed, but he recommended that the concrete barrier we now call 'the stone seat' be erected to prevent further casualties in future. As I said yesterday, according to local superstition, Christopher can sometimes be heard howling with rage at the deceitfulness of his one true love, and like the banshee, it means that something horrible is about to happen – in most cases round here gale-force winds and heavy rain."

He was laughing as he spoke about the howling but I could not reciprocate. I had not yet fully recovered from what I had heard three nights previously. Nevertheless he pressed home his point with the subtlety of a lump hammer.

"Didn't you say that you'd heard the howling *inside* the hotel, Douglas?" he went on. "That's another reason not to drive, isn't it? Christopher's ghost is warning you… whooooo!"

"Jane told me that the man who brought me down from the moors was a Watholme man called James Snowden," I said dismissing his pathetic attempt at humour with a withering look. "Do you know him?"

"That's Jogger Jim," he replied, still adopting his comical tone. "He's a fanatic. He runs around the village at least twice a day, at breakfast time and last thing at night. Nice bloke though. Married, two kids."

"Does he live in Watholme?" I said, seizing my opportunity to obtain his address.

"At the opposite end of the village," he replied. "About fifteen minutes' walk from here. I don't know exactly where. Why not ring the place he works? It's Currer and Bell, Sleighton Boulevard, down in Boughton. They're a firm of accountants."

Those were annoyingly his last words on the subject. One glance at his watch informed him that he was already going to be late for his next booking. He tapped me lightly on the shoulder, nodded his farewell and rushed off, forgetting to charge me for the half hour he had spent with me. Needless to say, I did not remind him.

I was about to return to my room when a well-dressed, late middle aged man carrying an unfurled umbrella came into the hotel. He was wearing a mushroom-coloured, belted greatcoat and a grey, tweed trilby. He looked, to say the least, wet and windswept.

"Excuse me," he said politely when he saw me. "Do you work here?"

"No, I'm a guest," I replied. "You need the receptionist."

"Yes I do, I suppose," he sighed, wiping his dripping nose with his finger. "I've been sent to enquire about a couple of rooms for the night. I'm the advance party. There are four of us. What's it like here?"

"It's very nice. The double rooms are very comfortable and the food's excellent."

"We only want half board. We're off to the Dales tomorrow."

"It's probably best if you ring the bell on the counter then," I smiled, pointing to my right. "The receptionist will be out back or in the kitchen."

"Thanks a lot," he said timorously. "I'm sorry to sound a bit like a lost child. We didn't expect to be spending the night in Watholme. Our car developed a fault on the road up from Boughton. I coaxed it to the garage down by the old railway station but the mechanic says it won't be ready until tomorrow lunchtime. It's a Nissan and he doesn't appear to like Japanese cars. We're booked in at the George and Dragon in Sleighton so I'll have to ring them to tell them we won't be coming today. My wife and her two companions are having a coffee at the moment, and the waitress in the café recommended this place. I've been sent here to check it out."

"Best of luck," I said as I moved off to leave. "I'll no doubt see you around."

Poor chap, I thought. He's ripe for plucking if Jane gets the chance to corner him tonight.

This rather comical encounter made me forget for a moment how annoyed I was by Derek's attitude towards me. Not only had he refused to help me with my bandages, he had profited to the tune of a hundred and fifty pounds by doing so! Yet there was one thing in his favour: it had taken him a mere five minutes to recount the tragedy of Christopher Heath whereas it had taken Jane five days – and he had provided a proper ending. Nevertheless there were discrepancies in the two accounts, mainly involving the nature of Christopher's relationship with Violet. In Jane's explanation they were long-standing, star-struck lovers, but according to Derek, Violet already had a steady boyfriend, which he had alluded to when we were chatting by the Nature Park. In addition why had Jane not given evidence at the inquest? She might have been able to support Christopher's claim that Violet intended to go to Manchester with him on the night in question.

Perhaps she was prevented from doing so by her father. Or perhaps she had invented most of this episode in her account of Christopher's life, and Derek's version of Christopher as a trouble-maker was true. In due course I settled for the latter, since it covered all the knowns and left little or nothing to conjecture that Jane had made up most of her story.

All this analysis and weighing of evidence was making my brain hurt. I was grateful that Derek had provided me with a suitable – if not ideal – end point at which to forget Christopher Heath and Violet Dean. I needed a telephone directory and I knew someone who was bound to have the very thing. I looked over at the reception desk and observed that the newly arrived gentleman was hovering over the brass bell on the counter.

"Bash the button with the palm of your hand," I shouted. "That's what causes it to ring."

He turned round with a diffident expression on his face and looked at me appealingly.

"I don't like bashing buttons," he said nervously. "It's so rude and uncouth. I leave that sort of thing to my wife or one of her…"

"I'll do it for you then," I said as I shuffled closer. "I want Jane too and when I'm done, I'll introduce you to her."

"That's very kind of you," he said, now sounding more cheerful. "My name's Andrew Baxter. That's Andrew not Andy. My wife says that Andy is vulgar so I never use it."

"I'm Douglas Lockwood and I prefer Douglas, but I don't mind Doug."

"Pleased to meet you," he said cordially. "I'm from Sheffield."

I rang the bell and, to my obvious astonishment, Jane emerged immediately out of the dining room.

"I heard you two talking," she smiled. "I was coming anyway."

"Do you have such a thing as a telephone directory?" I asked without any preliminaries. "I want to ring Currer and Bell, the accountants in Boughton. You don't happen to have their number, do you by any chance?"

"No, I don't have the number to hand," she said brusquely, as though she felt somehow annoyed by my request. "I'll lend you our directory but please return it as soon as you've finished with it."

She went round behind the counter, bent sideways and squinted at the shelf underneath. A few seconds later she produced a slim, pristine booklet and passed it on to me.

"They're a lot smaller and thinner these days," she went on. "That's because hardly anyone has a landline and there isn't yet, to my knowledge anyway, a directory of mobile phone numbers."

"Businesses should still have a proper telephone," I retorted. "It proves that they have a permanent office and are therefore legitimate. Never hire a workman you don't know if he's only got a mobile number."

"I'll bear that in mind the next time I need a plumber," she said sarcastically, shifting her gaze – and modifying her facial expression – towards Andrew Baxter. "Good morning sir, how may I help you?"

"This is Mr Baxter," I persisted, keeping my promise. "He wants to book a couple of rooms."

Andrew smiled politely at me and pushed himself forward. He had been standing behind me like a shy teenager whilst I chatted to Jane.

"I'd like to book two double rooms, if you have any available," I heard him say softly as I limped away. "Both with twin beds if that's possible."

"Would you like a view of the moors or the village?" Jane chanted, as she began her familiar routine.

"I hadn't foreseen that," came Andrew's reply. "I'd better take one of each providing that we can change our minds after I've consulted..."

I did not hear anything else as I slowly climbed the stairs to my room. Poor old Andrew, I mused. I was very much looking forward to meeting his wife and her two companions, as he put it. I was picturing them as large, stout ladies with rosy cheeks and booming voices like the ones depicted comically on those now frowned upon, seaside picture postcards.

I found the accountants' number straightaway, conveniently situated in the directory's business section. I entered the numbers on my mobile phone and the call was answered immediately by a human being no less. I asked for James Snowden and was put through without any fuss directly to his extension.

"My name is Douglas Lockwood," I began confidently. "I believe it was you who rescued me last Sunday afternoon after I'd slipped and fallen on the moors during a heavy shower."

"I think you've got wrong person," a low-pitched, disembodied voice replied after a brief period of silence. "It wasn't me. I was at home all day playing games with my children. Who gave you my name?"

"I'm staying at The Green Man," I explained. "One of the staff here thought it might have been you."

"Sorry, mate. It most definitely wasn't me."

"One other thing," I persisted. "Do you ever jog past the hotel late at night?"

"Sometimes but not lately. The weather's been too bad...."

I left it at that with, infuriatingly, two mysteries still to unravel again. Who was it who helped me on Sunday afternoon, and who was it who stared up at my bedroom window on Monday night?

After lunch, which, predictably, I ate alone, I parked myself in the lounge with the Daily Telegraph. I do not take this newspaper out of any particular political allegiance, but simply because it has at least two excellent crosswords and an absorbing puzzle page. However, my main aim in sitting there was to inform Jane that the man she had named as my knight in shining armour was not the one she had supposed him to be. When I first told her about him, she said she had an idea who the unidentified man might be, but it wasn't until the very end of her story that she gave me James Snowden's name, almost as an afterthought as I recall. Since I was in shock and in no small measure of pain at the time of my accident, I did not make any effort to scrutinise the young man who helped me stagger back to the edge of the village through the freezing wind and the stinging rain. In addition my spectacle lenses were wet through and I would not have been able to see him clearly in any case. From what I remember he had shoulder-length, lank, dark hair, and he was dressed predominantly in grey. As I tried to visualise him more clearly, it occurred me that he had not spoken. He had merely picked me up, put my arm around his shoulder and kept me upright as I struggled down the treacherous slopes back to safety. The whole encounter seemed only to have lasted a few painful, exhausting minutes.

The opportunity to ask her further questions came about ten minutes after I sat down with the arrival of Andrew Baxter's party. His three female companions were not at all as I had imagined them. To begin with, they were small, slim and, for their ages, extremely striking with the same chestnut brown, page boy hairstyles. They were clearly sisters. His wife, who looked the oldest, probably in her early fifties, was wearing a white raincoat and a purple silk scarf under which she sported light-coloured corduroy trousers and brown loafers. The other two wore matching blue cagoules, denim jeans and green, leather bootees. When I saw their faces, I noticed that their features were so similar that they had to be identical twins. Jane exuded a charm that I had not seen before as she painstakingly dealt with their requirements and allocated them the rooms she had recommended. Andrew and his wife, Jennifer (not Jenny presumably), chose a room overlooking the village and her sisters settled for a view of the moors; they were the ones recently vacated by the Belgians at the far end of the corridor from me. They had no luggage with them. The man from the garage had agreed to bring their suitcases as soon as they rang him with the location of their overnight accommodation.

"What thoroughly nice people," Jane remarked as she ambled towards me. "They're staying for one night with an option on two. Their car's broken down…but I suppose you know that already."

"Yes I do," I replied. "I had a chat with him when he first came in. However, on another matter, I phoned James Snowden a couple of hours ago and he said he wasn't the chap who helped me off the moors last Sunday."

"I thought it might have been him," she said without a moment's hesitation. "But then again he doesn't have 'long, dark hair'…isn't that how you described him?"

"So who was it?" I cried in exasperation. "I saw him again, you know, from my bedroom window. He was looking up at me from across the road."

"I wish you'd told me that earlier," she gasped. "Now, please excuse me I have work to do. I'm expecting a very busy weekend."

She hurried off in the direction of the kitchen and abandoned me without an answer to my sixty four thousand dollar question. I resigned myself to the probability that I would never discover his identity but I was no longer overly concerned. I had just about survived my ordeal in Watholme, and I was going home in less than forty eight hours' time.

The rest of the afternoon passed without incident, other than the arrival of several more guests, probably weekenders. In addition to Andrew Baxter and his wife and her twin sisters, I saw three more couples. From their appearance I assumed they were walkers – hikers or ramblers, whatever the correct term is – and they were all in their twenties.

After dinner at half past eight they went directly to the lounge where Jane served them regularly with beer, wine and spirits for about an hour, after which they said their good nights and went off to their rooms for an early night. I had been sitting well out of their way under the window in semi-darkness trying to read with little success because of their raucously childish behaviour. They were playing drinking games, which are popular among young people these days, but I found them too complicated to follow and hence irritatingly distracting. A few minutes after they had gone and a more peaceful, soothing silence was restored, Andrew crept into the lounge without spotting me and went over to the bar counter. He was sporting a garish, pink sweater and loose-fitting, fawn trousers. He scratched his head, just like Stan Laurel used to do, because he did not know how to summon Jane who had left the serving area when the revellers had gone. 'Ring the bloody bell', I screamed silently to myself, 'That's what it's there for'. Fortunately for him, she magically appeared from the dining room carrying freshly washed glasses.

"Good evening, Mr Baxter," she said jovially, flashing her professional smile again. "Are you having a drink or do you want to see me?"

"I'll have a small sherry," he whispered. "My wife and her sisters have gone to bed and they think I've come down to browse through those leaflets. They don't like me drinking, but to tell you the truth, I could do with something stronger than tea to calm my nerves. I've had a trying day what with the car breaking down and having to walk everywhere in the bad weather."

"Do you mind if I join you?" she beamed. "I've had a long day too."

"Not at all," he replied in a surprisingly assured voice. "I was hoping to find Mr Lockwood after dinner but he must have already retired for the night. Let me treat you. What are you having?"

"I'll have a whisky and dry ginger," she said. "It's just a nightcap to wet my whistle, mind you," she said with that very familiar wry smile of hers. "I'm not an alcoholic, you know."

"In that case I'll have a pint of best bitter and a vodka chaser," he said more solemnly. "I might as well be hanged for a sheep as a lamb."

They continued to stand at the counter while she poured their drinks and I took this opportunity to sneak past them. Incredibly Jane, who was facing me, did not seem to notice as I crept by. Perhaps she had deliberately ignored me. I did not however go straight upstairs but I hovered out of sight in the hallway next to the bar.

"Shall we get more comfortable?" said Jane almost immediately. "I have a story you might find interesting if you can stay for a few minutes."

I heard them move their chairs as they sat down and the clink of their glasses as they placed them on a table.

"Christopher's house had an outside toilet," she began after a deep breath. "It was one of the reasons why he started smoking..."

"He'll be in for it when he gets back to his wife," I said out loud to myself as I let myself into my room and switched on the light. "I hope the booze knocks him out or he'll be awake half the night wondering what on earth Jane's been talking about."

I was still smiling when I went to close the curtains. The weather was changing for the worse again and I could hear a gusty wind getting up. As I approached the window it began to rain, so rapidly and violently it was if someone was throwing buckets of water against the pane. I saw my own reflection distort itself out of all recognition as the torrent battered the glass to be replaced in a flash by the drenched and contorted face of the young man who had carried me off the moors in a similar downpour. I blinked my eyes and looked again but there was only a misshapen version of my own, bespectacled features staring blankly back at me against the blackness.

Seeing the artificial creation of my brain in the window and listening to Jane astutely foist herself onto Andrew, made me contemplate again what had been happening to me all week. Her sheer artistry as a story-teller had conceivably awakened in me a long-dormant inquisitiveness and an equally latent belief in the supernatural, fuelled by the power of suggestion to make me hallucinate events and remember them as real.

It must be something similar to incorporating things into my dreams that are happening in programmes if I fall asleep with the television on. Did I therefore in similar vein dream the howling in the hotel and the scratching at my door as a result of Derek's so called old wives tail? In spite of all these new uncertainties, thanks to Andrew my mood had changed to one of devil-may-care amusement, and I could not be bothered to rack my brains about these things any longer. I slept well that night. I finished the bottle of wine I had opened the previous evening, I watched an hour's TV, and I read more of '*The Master and Margarita*' before I turned in. I woke once only to go to the lavatory and, even half-conscious, I could not stop myself giggling as I heard the wind wailing in the distance as it blew across the hills. Or was it the ghost of Christopher Heath on the prowl again?

CHAPTER FOURTEEN

Saturday Morning

I felt much the same at breakfast the following morning, the beginning of my last full day in Watholme. There were eleven guests, including me, in the dining room and Nadia was having difficulty trying to keep pace with the different demands and preferences of each diner. It must have been infuriating for the chef to have to deal with us all at once at around eight thirty, especially as he would have nothing to do for the last hour or so of the allotted meal time. He would not have fried enough bacon, sausages and eggs in advance – and whatever it was that the two finicky vegetarians among the young couples were demanding loudly. It was at least a quarter of an hour before Nadia even noticed me, but I had my newspaper and that meant I had a crossword to solve. Soon enough there were only Andrew and Jennifer and their companions, the twin sisters, left in the dining room. As I was finishing my sixth full English of the week, without any kind of acknowledgment Andrew came and sat opposite me. He was dressed in a fawn cardigan and matching slacks and he looked like a badly frightened rabbit.

"Will you do me a favour, Douglas?" he whispered, leaning forwards over the table. "If Jennifer asks you about last night, tell her you enjoyed our little chat over a couple of drinks."

"Certainly," I grunted, swallowing a mouthful of food. "What did we chat about?"

"Football," came his swift reply. "Sheffield United, not Wednesday, and their chances of promotion this season. Jennifer doesn't like sport of any kind so she'll leave it at that."

I did not have the heart to tell him that I am not the slightest bit interested in football either.

"What did you do really?" I asked mischievously, knowing full well what had happened.

"Jane told me a remarkable story," he enthused with an extraordinarily bemused look in his eyes. "It was the life history of a fascinating young chap who used to live in these parts. It might have been a funny way of pointing out various landmarks to me, you know, like the moors and such. Whatever it was, she's a wonderful raconteur with an amazing eye for detail. I could have listened to her for hours."

"Why did she tell you about this particular young man?"

"I don't know really. I'm not sure what we would have talked about otherwise. I let her get on with it as I had nothing better to do."

"What time did you get to bed?"

"Some time after eleven. I woke Jennifer up and she wasn't best pleased. She'd be even more furious if she found out I'd been drinking with a woman. That's why you've got to cover for me."

I told him his secret was safe and he looked very relieved. As he stood up to leave, he bent down again and murmured in my ear.

"I'm going to the garage in a few minutes to see about my car. If it's not ready today, we'll be here for the weekend. Jane says she'll tell me another story tonight if that's the case, so can I count on you again to say I was with you?"

"Enjoy the next instalment of '*whatever it was*'," I said genially. "If you do discover what it's about, please tell me tomorrow at breakfast."

Back in my bedroom, I lay back on the bed with my hands clasped behind my head. I could not stop myself laughing again for Andrew had innocently exposed Jane for what she was. She was a storyteller and she had one favourite subject: Christopher Heath. It had nothing to do with me, despite Agnes insisting that it was the first time her sister had recounted his short life history. The mystery of the identity of the young man who had brought me down from the moors was merely the excuse she needed to launch into the full-length tearjerker. Andrew was lucky because his version was much shorter with a happy ending: Christopher must have got the girl and fulfilled his potential.

What I had been listening to for most of the week contained characters based on real people skilfully interwoven with incidents from the past, the car crash for instance, to produce a modernised version of 'The Stone Seat'. Agnes had done something similar with her nonsensical tale about the Ayres. They were both crazy but harmlessly so, nothing more than elderly cranks attempting to justify their existence in a failing hotel. I was in good spirits again because I was no longer burdened with trying to figure everything out. Moreover my ankle was less painful, and I was now able to move about without using either my crutches or my walking stick. With a little patience I should easily make it to High Street and back and I resolved to test this out after my breakfast had settled. If I succeeded I would then see if I could drive my car during the afternoon. It was not raining and a sickly sun was forcing its way half-heartedly through thinning sheets of unbroken, grey cloud high in the sky. It was perfect weather for a stroll, a coffee and perhaps a couple of souvenirs. I had not got much further with my planning when I heard someone tapping on my door.

"Who is it?" I called out, as I heaved myself upright.

"It's Shirley," a resonantly pleasant voice responded. "May I come in?"

I gave my consent without a moment's hesitation, assuming that it was one of the female guests, perhaps one of the twin sisters, but it was someone I had not seen before. It was a middle-aged woman and she was stunningly attractive. The very first sight of her left a lasting impression etched deeply into my memory. She was dressed in a black, two-piece suit, with an immaculate, white shirt, complemented by flesh coloured tights and smart, purple leather court shoes. Her hair was jet black with grey highlights here and there, pulled loosely from her forehead and gathered into a neat bun at the back. Her face radiated beauty from any angle, her sparkling turquoise eyes the main focus of attention. She was carrying an expensive-looking, purple handbag. Had I passed her in the corridor, I would have assumed that she was a businesswoman, perhaps even a hotel inspector, since it seemed somehow incongruous that anyone else would choose such a formal outfit on a weekend. When I invited her to sit down on the armchair by the window, she smiled so graciously that I almost bowed. As she walked past me I noticed a strong smell of expensive perfume and she was wearing subtle, brown eyeshadow and tasteful, pink lipstick. She was the only woman I had seen in makeup that week. Was it going out of fashion?

"I'm Jane's and Agnes's cousin," she said when she had settled herself. "I live near Sleighton. My husband's a great intellectual, Professor of English Literature at

Leeds University. Please don't think I'm boasting. His nickname's 'Prof' and that's what I call him at home. We often receive Christmas cards addressed to the Professor and Shirley. Sometimes it's the other way round, depending on who sent them."

I stood spellbound, hardly taking in what she said. She was a picture of elegance, sitting attentively upright with one leg crossed over the other and her handbag on her lap. Her voice was soft and bewitching, like Circe's was to Odysseus, her occasional pure vowels the only indicator of a West Yorkshire accent.

"I'm here for the morning," she went on after a short pause. "I wanted to meet you before I go back home."

"What's so special about me?" I asked with genuine curiosity, although I must have sounded quite boorish.

"They've spoken a great deal about you," she replied. "You've caused quite a kerfuffle and I had to come to see you for myself. Jane, Nadia and Joseph are busy clearing up after breakfast and Agnes is out in the village. I'm at a bit of a loose end so I'm having a snoop round."

"Who's Joseph?"

"He's the head chef."

"I've never seen him."

"He doesn't live in and he's not very sociable. He spends all his time in the kitchen and doesn't fraternise with the guests."

"Is there anyone else who works here that I haven't seen? Does anyone live in the attics, for instance?"

"I don't think so. Jane and Agnes would have told me. They do sometimes take in strays like Nadia. I went up there earlier this morning and there's no sign of bags or cases or anything out of the ordinary. The rooms are still habitable but the beds have been stripped and the mattresses are rolled up. Why do you ask?"

"I thought I heard strange noises up there the other night, but it doesn't matter. You said I've caused a kerfuffle. What do you mean by that?"

"Well, you've upset Agnes for starters and that's bad news for Jane. She'll have to put up with Agnes's whining and whinging for weeks after you've gone."

"I didn't mean to but I admit I could have handled things better."

There was a short, embarrassed silence and I wanted to change the subject. However Shirley beat me to it.

"What do you think of the hotel?" she said touching her bottom lip with one of her fingers. "Actually I'm part-owner, another reason why I'm here. I like to speak to guests and get some feedback on how it's doing. I've heard about your accident. Have you been looked after properly?"

"Yes, everything's fine on that score," I returned. "This room's very cosy and the food here is first class. Joseph's a fine chef."

"We should have a stair lift for people with disabilities. Has this been a cause for concern, Mr Lockwood?"

"It was difficult at first climbing one slow step after another. I soon got the hang of it, but, yes, a stair lift would solve a lot of problems, not least any legal ones. And please call me Douglas."

She smiled at my attempt to reduce the stiffness of our conversation. I was still standing in the doorway and I decided it would put things on a more relaxed footing if I sat down on the as yet unmade bed.

"Their father would have had one installed immediately," she went on. "It's typical of Jane and Agnes to neglect their responsibilities and try to muddle on. When he died, this place was the best hotel in Watholme. It's still very much like it was then, regrettably, because they haven't done anything to it. It should be closed for the winter and redecorated throughout. Better still, all the furniture in the lounge and that awful kitchen should be thrown out and burned. The second floor – what you call the attics – ought to be updated and opened up again."

"You said you part-own the hotel. Jane never revealed that. I thought Violet might be the other co-owner…"

"Violet's become a vegetable, Douglas, I'm sorry to say. I usurped her role quite recently but I don't come round here often enough. Today, before I disappear again, I'm going to have it out with them."

I was dismayed by her sudden change of tone and the intensity of her lack of sympathy for the unfortunate Violet. Her face was contorted with resentment and her hands were quivering; her negative feelings were clearly rooted in her inability to change the status quo because of the lackadaisical attitudes of her cousins. Then as though nothing had happened, she became calm again and resumed her even-tempered manner.

"Has Jane been telling you the life story of Christopher Heath?" she continued. "Agnes will have been boring you to tears too with fairy tales about the Ayre sisters."

"Yes, they have," I grimaced. "For most of the week. I've heard the full stories from both of them."

"In that case, let me tell you a few things about *them* which I hope will amuse you," she said light-heartedly. "They're both a bit barmy but they weren't always like that. Jane's the eldest. She was her father's favourite. He wanted her to become a 'lady' by which he meant he would do everything in his power to give her the chance to marry a wealthy man, preferably one with a title and a stately home. When she was eight he had her transferred from Watholme Primary School to a posher one in Boughton. After she passed her scholarship – they all did at that school – he paid for her to go to a private school near Sleighton. Then she went to Newcastle University and got a first class degree in French and Italian. She's very intelligent. Her father was disappointed she didn't make Oxbridge but she didn't want to go to either place. She wanted to live in a big, Northern city. After she graduated she got herself a job in Belgium teaching English. That's when things started going pear-shaped. Being a staunch socialist she tried to organise a trade union among the teachers and other staff. No one was interested really and it sort of petered out. However, to everyone's surprise she was having an affair with the head teacher, who was married, and she became pregnant. To save her face and his marriage she resigned her post and came back to Watholme to have the baby. A few weeks later, about the same time that Violet was taken ill, she had a miscarriage. It was probably due to the stress of being cut adrift by the ghastly Belgian, Violet's breakdown, the death of Violet's lovely boyfriend in that awful car accident – and, to cap it all, her father's reaction when he found out the truth about why she'd come home so unexpectedly. She's been here ever since and she never goes out. I'm not exaggerating. She hasn't left this hotel since Violet first went into hospital."

"My God!" I interrupted. "That must be well over forty years ago. But hold on a minute, according to the local taxi driver, the coroner's report on Christopher's death stated that a young man called Edward Lister was Violet's steady boyfriend. According to her father, Christopher had been harassing her."

"How on earth do you know that?" she replied adamantly. "It's incorrect, anyway. It was only because of what Violet's father said at the inquest. Edward was quite charming and he had pots of money but he was a drip, a classic upper-class twit and, if anything, Violet used him."

"How are you so sure of your facts?" I contended. "Jane's told me the life story of Christopher and never once mentioned you."

"I'm the same age as Violet. I used to come here as a child and we played together on the moors. When I got older I tried to avoid coming here altogether and I kept well away from the ugly sisters. Violet and I went around the pubs and clubs at weekends but if she clicked with a bloke, I backed off and left her to it. She did the same for me."

"What about Agnes then? She was also a schoolteacher, wasn't she?"

"Agnes grew up in Jane's shadow. She stayed at Watholme Primary School and then went to the local girls' grammar school. She spent most of her time reading and had a thing for Victorian authors. As you're well aware, she's obsessed with the Ayres, and, lo and behold, she read English Literature at Hull University. She didn't have any kind of social life there, so university hardly touched her. It was the natural conclusion to her journey on the qualifications' conveyor belt that she dropped off the end straight into teaching. She taught English in Nottingham but when her father became ill, he sent for her to take over the hotel. Spoilt, darling Jane was recovering from her miscarriage and Violet was in a psychiatric hospital. She's such a sweet person that she's never complained that she had to leave the job she loved or that a potentially brilliant career had been ruined. All she has left is her loony ideas about the Ayres. Did she tell you that she's had some essays published? She contributed to a book on the real-life contexts of nineteenth century novels. She identified every one of the locations around these parts in 'The Stone Seat' and the places in South Yorkshire where Catherine Ayre set 'The Governess'. This last one involved a lot of travel on public transport in order to research where the author herself had worked near Doncaster. I suppose she's bored you to tears with her theory that the Ayres faked their deaths. She's been at it since she was a sixth former at school when she began to question how they could have died so young, two of them almost simultaneously. She reckons they skedaddled to Italy but she refuses to go to wherever it is their graves are supposed to be in order to prove that the sisters are buried there."

"Do you mean to say that she's made that bit up?"

"Not entirely. She honestly believes that the dedication from someone or other she found in the front of an old book is the key to the whole deception. There's also a letter. What would you think if I told you that Jane forged them both?"

"I'd think that was despicable!" I gasped. "What a horrible..."

"Well, she did," she interrupted. "I'm staggered that Agnes hasn't twigged it being a schoolteacher. She must have asked her kids to design and make a historical manuscript. You get a piece of plain paper, write your message on it, then you tear it here and there. Apply lemon juice liberally and stick it in the oven for ten minutes. Bob's your uncle – an aged and authentic looking document."

"That's a horrible thing to do to your sister! My God, she's allowed Agnes to waste half of her life...not to mention that she's making a fool of herself."

"Jane's always been *very* untrustworthy. She's oh-so-articulate and that makes her sound very credible. She even invented the family tree that suggests Christopher had an ancestor called Amos! It's correct for three or four generations but that's as far as it goes. You can see why Agnes fell for it hook, line and sinker."

I was becoming shell-shocked by the amount of new and contradictory information from yet another of the Dean clan. It must be a family trait, I thought, bombarding people with extracts from their family history that they would rather not listen to. I needed to take a time-out.

"Would you like a cup of tea or coffee and a biscuit?" I asked.

"No thank you," she replied. "They don't agree with my stomach. I only drink water and sometimes a little cordial."

I went into the en-suite bathroom and filled up the white, plastic kettle. As I busied myself with a cup and a teabag she stood up and looked out of the window.

"You have a wonderful view," she went on. "I love those moors more than anything in the world. Have you managed to get up to Wildheath Crags yet? They're so savage and yet so romantic…"

Why did she refer to the Nature Park by its obsolete name, I wondered? Was it force of habit or typical Yorkshire stubbornness – or was she, like Derek and Jane, showing her disapproval of the sterile refurbishment and the change of name to one more innocuous?

"Yes, I've been there – but mainly as a spectator," I said, shaking my head in the hope that she would recognise my reciprocal disgust. "There isn't much to see, is there? It didn't help that it was chucking it down. I sat in a taxi and stared at what looked like gently undulating sand dunes at the seaside through a waterlogged windscreen. I did try to experience the moors at first hand, but it ended in disaster and spoiled my holiday, as you can see."

When I had made my drink, she retook her seat, resuming her attentive posture and, beguilingly, she kept on smiling at me. I straightened my duvet more as a displacement activity than a necessity and when I sat down I did so carefully, keeping a firm grip on my cup and saucer.

"How does Christopher Heath fit into this dysfunctional family?" I asked, to break the silence. "Jane's told me a lot about his short life but I'm not sure how much of it's true."

"I'll answer that in a minute," she said somewhat impatiently. "I have to tell you about Violet. They say in Yorkshire that the first born child is spoilt rotten because it's lavished with attention by neurotically careful parents. The second child isn't such a novelty, but it's looked after expertly because now they know how to go about things. And the third child feeds itself and changes its own nappies...that's Jane, Agnes and Violet in a nutshell. Violet was left much to her own devices, especially after her mother walked out on the family and moved in with a toy boy. No doubt Jane's told you that she, that's Violet, spent a great deal of her childhood wandering about on the moors. Her father was too busy to notice, running a popular hotel on his own and making sure Jane got a good education. No one, least of all Violet, thought it was dangerous, but these days she'd probably have been taken into care. She lived in a fantasy world of her own creation and she didn't let a soul into it until she met Christopher."

"Not even you?"

"Of course! I was always there with her in spirit."

"Jane said her father kept a very close eye on her."

"That was when she reached the age when she started to get interested in boys. I'm well aware of what Jane said, by the way. She's written it all down as a novel and I've read her manuscript."

"I was right!" I said excitedly. "That's confirmed something that's been bothering me all week – and it explains why she sounds so eloquent."

"Yes, it should do. She's bored enough people with extracts from it. She tells them that she's never told anyone about Christopher before and swears them to secrecy. It is a secret, I suppose, but only between her and her listeners. You must be the only person who's been given the full version because of the length of your holiday and you're on your own. But I have to warn you that although the bare bones of her account are accurate, there are quite a few factual errors and she's invented a great deal. Before you ask, I used to know Christopher quite well, much better than she did. At the beginning she calls him a snob because he's ashamed of his outside loo. She's made that bit up. He wasn't at all like that. He may have been worried about his pals at the grammar school or his tribe of girlfriends finding out about it, because he was a sensitive lad. It was Jane who was the snooty one, and she's projected onto him her own snobbishness about the scruffy house in Oakgrove where her mother went to live with her boyfriend. It had a very smelly, outside toilet that was dirty, full of spiders and creepy-crawlies, freezing in winter and she – an eleven year old, public school girl – loathed using it. The other two hated it just as much as she did though, and it wasn't very long – a couple of years at most – before they refused to go for their Sunday visits. They didn't see much more of their mother after that."

"Agnes said there were other versions of Christopher's story. Was she referring to yours or Violet's?"

"She probably meant Jane's variations of the biography."

"You mean there's more than one version?"

"She has at least two more. They're much shorter and she adapts them according to the amount of time her listeners have at their disposal. You see, Douglas, Jane was obsessed with Christopher. She was crazy about him for many years before he met Violet. She was always going on about this pretty little-boy-lost after he started at the same junior school as her when he moved down to Boughton. She kept tabs on him at the boys' grammar school and, as soon as he was old enough, she even tried to get off with him. She didn't know that she was regarded as a cradle-snatcher, and a friend of Christopher's only went out with her to gain some brownie points for dating an older woman. She became insanely jealous when Christopher became involved with Violet. She made up all sorts of lies about him, like the one about the outside toilet. I assume she's told you all about Christopher's and Violet's on-off relationship."

"Yes she has, in some detail."

"Although Violet didn't know at the time, Jane was responsible for their first break-up. She told her father, who by then had banned Violet from having anything to do with Christopher, that they were still seeing each other surreptitiously. Violet wasn't allowed to go out for months afterwards and she was very upset – not because she had to stay in but because, as an impressionable teenager, she'd fallen head over heels in love. Christopher was very much cut up too."

"Where does Edward Lister fit into this?"

"He was the son of one of her father's rich acquaintances. He lived in a grand house in its own grounds in a well-to-do part of Boughton. Her father encouraged her to go steady with him, because he wanted her off his hands as quickly and as profitably as possible. She didn't pass her scholarship and went to the secondary modern school. He regarded her as a failure, a mindless dimwit who wouldn't make anything of herself unless through a lucrative marriage. He didn't give a damn about her true feelings. She only wanted one man and that man was Christopher."

"Yes, Jane said that Mr Dean didn't think Christopher was good enough for her."

She swallowed hard and stopped speaking. I was sure I saw tears forming in her eyes but she recovered after a few seconds and smiled at me as she continued.

"Christopher was from Oakgrove, remember, and Mr Dean's wife had run off to live there with another man who was a labourer at the nearby mill. It wasn't a rough area by any means but it wasn't affluent either. Christopher didn't stand a chance. Violet was ever so happy whenever she was with him, but when she told him her father had forbidden her to see him ever again, he thought she was finishing with him by passing the buck. He said it was a pathetic excuse. What hurt her most was that he started playing the field again, and then he went off to university. She was sure she'd lost him forever. She had some compensation though. Shortly afterwards Jane got her comeuppance. Christopher told her to her face that she was a meddling bitch and that he was sick of the sight of her."

"That's funny. I got the impression that she still regards him with a great deal of affection but I do remember her referring to him as an arrogant prat but I can't remember why."

"Of course she does, Douglas. She resents him because she couldn't possess him but she never hated him. It was

218

Violet she disliked, simply because he chose her. She'd been in love with him for many a year, and when he matured into a handsome, young man, she assumed the ever so grateful, little boy friend would become her *boyfriend*. But she underestimated the shallowness of youth. He'd become a male, chauvinistic pig, I believe the contemporary term was. He saw women primarily as sex objects and not to be trusted…well…he did until he got to know Violet better. He said he couldn't help it. He'd spent his formative years almost exclusively in the company of women, first his mother, then his primary school teachers. They were responsible for programming his attitudes. What was it he always used to recite? Ah yes: '*Girls are made of sugar and spice and all things nice, but boys are made of slugs and snails and puppy dogs' tails*'."

"There was more to it than that, wasn't there?" I said confidently. "It implies that, in those days men and women were seen as different species and women were in some ways better than men. Nothing could have been further from the truth. I was taught that *a woman's place is in the home* and other such stupid phrases. In films and on TV men were portrayed as superior. They were workers, breadwinners, calm and rational. Women were housewives, cooks and cleaners, flighty and illogical and obsessed with their appearance. They did as they were told. They had babies and they took care of children. That was their job. Domestic violence wasn't frowned on. It was OK to beat your wife, but not to hit any other woman. Sorry to go on, but that's how I was brought up. It's one of the reasons why I never got married. I couldn't have lived with that type of woman, and, while we're at it, the twenty first century kind either."

For a few seconds, Shirley seemed astounded at my diatribe. She jerked her head back and shut her eyes, and then, in contrast, she stared vacantly right through me, her mouth wide open.

"I'm very sorry if I've upset you," I said feebly. "A lot of men of my age are regarded as institutionally sexist and racist but it was the world we grew up in. The whole of society was responsible. I know how to act in public – I went on enough courses at work, but deep down inside... I'm terribly sorry. I'm spoiling your explanation."

"Goodness me, Douglas, you are a strange man," she laughed. "I was simply telling you what Christopher said, not making a political statement. It may sound odd but I agree with you. Their mother left their father because he used to hit her. He could be a very violent man when he was that side out. He had a filthy temper. He once struck Violet..."

She twitched again as if reliving the incident vicariously. Then, like Jane and Agnes had done many times in the lounge, she put her handbag on the carpet, uncrossed her legs and leaned forwards.

"Christopher became different the more he fell in love with Violet," she continued, lowering her voice. "It helped immensely that they had one thing in common. They both loved the moors. They spent hours there walking or sometimes just sitting together talking and smoking. Everyone smoked then, Douglas, as you'll doubtless remember. They made a pact that when they died, they would have their *ashes* scattered there... that was their joke. They were happy days. He was the perfect gentleman. He wasn't arrogant or bossy, he was very respectful considering he was older than her, and he didn't try to touch her up...they were passionately in love with each other."

"Did Christopher ever go jogging?" I broke in yet again. "Jogging on the moors...?

A speech is structured and coherent, a conversation is not. The first is a monologue which demands a silent audience. The other involves two people, alternately speaking and listening, their minds working in tandem unless they are arguing. Our conversation was becoming very disjointed because it was not meant to be a discussion. It had slowly dawned on me that Shirley had come to see me with a purpose. She was setting the record straight. It was a clarification, and I was spoiling her flow by constantly butting in. It was evident that I was unsettling her the more I cut in on her, but it was my final opportunity to have some of my questions answered, the ones I had listed from Jane's account, questions which Jane had carefully deflected. I would have to bide my time and be patient.

"You were describing Christopher," I said apologetically in familiar fashion. "Please continue. I'm finding your, er, explanation, as you term it, extremely enlightening."

"On the one hand he was very intelligent and witty," she continued with a wave of her hand. "He was always polite, gentle and kind to Violet, but, on the other hand, he wasn't as clever as Jane makes him out to be. He was in some respects a typically working class man and, no, I don't recall that he ever went out *jogging*, as you put it. Rather he assumed he had the right to go boozing with the lads during the week, and he went to the rugby on Saturdays if Boughton were at home. He couldn't cook and he couldn't sew and he didn't like shopping unless it involved clothes or records. His mother did his washing and ironed his shirts. He had no social pretensions so he had absolutely no idea what sort of job he wanted to do.

He worked on a Saturday for his dad who by now was running a second hand car showroom, and he received twenty shillings a day out of the till for his pains. That meant he had money in his pocket, not bad then for a seventeen year old schoolboy. What separated him from the crowd was his insecurity, his shyness and his respect for young Violet, despite his chauvinistic attitudes. His mother had knocked some of the rough edges off him and taught him good manners. I'm not making myself very clear here because he was more complex than your average young male. That's what Violet liked most about him. He wasn't a stereotype."

She stopped and sat back, like Jane and Agnes had done several times, to await my reaction. Her face was strained and expectant as if she was demanding a response. I chose another burning question.

"So why does Jane emphasise his lower-class background so frequently? She goes into immense detail about the cheap and cheerful types of houses he lived in."

"It could be to do with her ambition to have a novel published. I've overheard her debating it with Agnes. No one writes about the working class these days, she maintains. They're old hat, she says. Perhaps differences in class are no longer of much interest to those who read books. They're certainly not to the expensively educated, liberally minded intellectuals who put pen to paper or make films about their middle class preoccupations. Their main characters are pure bourgeois, they're socialist professionals, they live in bijou cottages or expensive city flats, they drink wine and eat tofu and quinoa, and they know the names of wild flowers...are you getting the picture? Working class characters are seen as sexist, homophobic, stupid and surly or comical at best, or they're portrayed as fascists, racists, drug addicts, criminals and mindless chavs. It's always been like that. That's why Agnes prefers the Ayres, Dickens and Hardy to Jane Austen and the rest, especially modern day authors. The working classes are generally treated more respectfully, she says. In the nineteen fifties and sixties there emerged a whole load of angry, young men from blue-collar backgrounds. It was a cultural revolution..."

She stopped in mid-sentence. She had been speaking very quickly and gasping for air as she reeled off her invective in a curious, flat monotone that sounded like a religious chant. I noticed also that she was beginning to look exhausted by the physical exertion of forcing the words out. Had she, like Jane, learned her impassioned tirade off by heart?

"That's what Jane says, anyway," she said, breathing more deeply. "Between you and me, Mr Lockwood, she's stuck in a time warp, the nineteen sixties or thereabouts. What does she know? She doesn't read novels, she doesn't watch much TV and she hasn't been to the pictures since the night Christopher died. You should read 'The Governess' if you want to know who Jane would like to have been!"

"I hadn't thought of that. I suppose aspects of her early life do resemble the plot of 'The Governess'.

"But I didn't come here to rant on about literature and social issues," she smiled. "That's for Jane and Agnes to do. I came to see how *you* are, and, if you're willing, I'd love to hear about your rescue."

I outlined what had happened without revealing my misgivings. She listened carefully, sitting up straight again with her hands on her lap and her head cocked to one side spoiling the symmetry.

"Would it shock you if I told you that Jane is certain that the man who rescued you was Christopher?" she murmured as soon as I had finished. "She believes his spirit lives on, wandering the moors and now he's come back to her..."

"Hold on!" I said a tad too aggressively. "That also sounds like the ending of 'The Stone Seat' by Elizabeth Ayre. John, the hero, disappears, presumed dead, but his ghost lives on searching for Isabella who drowned in the bottomless bog."

"Jane's right," she laughed. "You are quick on the uptake. That's why Agnes gave you a copy of the novel. Did you read it? "

"How did you know that?"

She did not answer immediately. It was if she was silently provoking me to challenge her again.

"Nothing is as it appears in these parts," she said enigmatically. "Agnes was warning you about Jane. She wanted you to recognise that she was a charlatan."

"I did connect the two briefly but I didn't think it important," I went on. "I never believed her story was absolutely true anyway. There was too much mindboggling detail."

"You asked me earlier why she's made such a fuss of you. She believes Christopher saved you for a purpose and she hopes it's a good omen. She told me about the howling and the scratching at your door. Maybe you didn't dream it. She's convinced you have second sight and brought him back to the hotel for some reason. She desperately wants to see him again, but she's scared that he's come back to expose what really happened on the night of the accident and why it doesn't tally with the coroner's report. She's got a lot to hide. Let me tell you what actually occurred, and then perhaps you'll understand why I'm here. I ought to have made myself clearer earlier, but I was enjoying our little chat so much that I forgot."

She waited to see if I had any impulsive comment to make. I shrugged my shoulders and opened my eyes expectantly.

"I still don't know how you know all these things," I sighed. "I've spent the entire week trying to work out why she's never left me alone – and that applies to Agnes as well. All I've done is go around in circles until this morning when I thought I'd cracked it. So please, put me out of my misery!"

"Here goes, then," she grinned, pretending to take a deep breath. "Violet met Christopher again when he was home from university towards the end of his second year. To cut a long story short he asked her to write to him at first, but when he came home in summer they started getting it together again. By this time Christopher had a car so they could get away from Boughton if they wanted. Whenever her father asked where she was going, she lied and said she was going out with Edward. Eventually Christopher asked her to go to Manchester to live with him and Violet said yes straightaway. She was desperate to leave Watholme and her boring job at this hotel, but more than anything she wanted to get away from her father. Now here's the unpleasant bit. By this time Jane had returned from Belgium with a bun in the oven, no job, precious little money and no home of her own. She couldn't accept that her future would include being a mother, and like Violet, she didn't relish that future under the same roof as her father. When Violet told her she was eloping with Christopher, her whole world caved in. Not only was her silly, little sister escaping, she was running away with the man that she loved, irrational as that may seem to a logical mind like yours. On the day that they'd chosen, Christopher phoned the hotel to let Violet know that his car had broken down. His father was mending it as he spoke so he wouldn't be coming to pick her up until later that evening. It was Jane who took the call. Christopher thought he could trust her not to betray them. She did more than that. She told Violet, who was packing, that Christopher had had second thoughts about taking her to Manchester and that he didn't want to go out with her anymore. She suggested that her sister, who by now was sobbing her eyes out, should ring ever-reliable Edward and go out for a drink with him instead – and Violet did just that for some reason that still mystifies her. So Christopher turns up at eight o'clock that night to be met by her father. You've heard the rest, I assume. A glittering future wasted. Jane had conveniently gone to the pictures...that's why she didn't give evidence at the inquest. She wasn't there when Christopher arrived."

"I assume that Violet was very upset when she found out that Christopher had drowned and that led to her nervous breakdown."

"Yes, but that wasn't the root cause. It was when Jane confessed to Violet that she'd lied. In an attempt to make amends, Jane vowed she'd never leave this hotel until Christopher's body was found and they could be certain that he was dead. Violet went berserk and tried to kill her with a bread knife. Luckily, for both of them I suppose, she collapsed before anything horrific happened. Two days later she was admitted to hospital. She's rarely spoken about it much since then as she's nothing to say. Occasionally she appears to snap out of her psychosis and act normally, and you'd never guess that she'd relapse again a few hours later. She's been like that for over forty years."

I was about to thank her for sparing me the torment of further speculation about what had got under my skin for the best part of a week, and I felt as if I had finally been given the full picture. The most significant new features concerned Jane, not only for the despicable things she had done to both her sisters and Christopher, but also her present alarm about Christopher returning from the grave. Did it mean that she believed she was now free of her vow and able to leave the confines of the hotel, or was she afraid that he was coming for her bent on revenge?

I had to probe Shirley further but I was too late. Her face had glazed over and she was staring straight past me at an old painting of Wildheath Crags on the wall next to the door. Slowly she stood up, her face now completely expressionless. She was holding her handbag under her left arm. It fell to the floor as both her arms simultaneously slid down her sides, hanging limply below her waist. She remained totally still.

"Do you want me to show you my knickers," she said in a little girl's voice. "Give me sixpence and I'll pull them down."

Her facial expression did not change. Without looking at me she calmly lifted her skirt to reveal that she was wearing tights. She raised it up higher and there, astonishingly, were white panties. Persil white panties.

CHAPTER FIFTEEN

Saturday Afternoon

It was Agnes who came to my rescue. She had just arrived from the village where she had been doing some shopping, and she heard me mindlessly shouting for help at the head of the staircase to an otherwise empty hotel. Shirley had informed me earlier that Jane, Nadia and Joseph, the chef, were out of earshot tidying up in the kitchen. Andrew and his party were probably at the garage enquiring about the state of their car, and the other guests must have either departed or gone walking for the day. Agnes dropped her bags by the reception desk and, belying her age, she galloped frantically up the stairs like a cavalry charger. I reached my room ahead of her where I hovered outside, uncertain whether or not it was judicious to go back in. The door was open and Shirley was still standing catatonically holding up her skirt. Mercifully her grip on the hem had slackened and only her lower thighs and knees were visible.

"There, there now," cooed Agnes soothingly as she pushed herself past me. "Everything's going to be fine and dandy."

She took hold of Shirley gently by her arms and directed me to pick up her handbag. Slowly she manoeuvred her patient skilfully away from the armchair and past the foot of the bed. '*What's Violet doing here?*' she mouthed to me reproachfully as they passed. I followed them down the corridor where I gave her the handbag since I thought it wisest to go no further. When they reached the communal bathroom, Violet turned round and gazed at me without showing any sign of recognition.

There is a song written by an American Blues singer which contains the line *'If I didn't have bad luck, I wouldn't have any luck at all'*. At that juncture it applied to me perfectly. Just when I had thought that my dealings with this outlandish family were done and dealt with, along came another staggering episode and much more to mull over. How many times that week had I supposed erroneously that I could finally unwind and get what I could out of what was left of a ruined holiday? I did not stay long in my room. I needed some air. I would take the stroll I had promised myself earlier and I put on my raincoat and grabbed my umbrella. I made my way gingerly downstairs to find the main door was locked and bolted. I groaned out loud and I probably swore because this time without a shadow of a doubt I was being discouraged from leaving the building. I might be able to go out but would I be able to get back in? What about Andrew and his wife and the others? They were shut out too. I had had quite enough of this madhouse – for that is what it was with its three doolally sisters – and I finally lost my temper. I threw the umbrella into the lounge and flung my arms into the air.

"Be careful you don't break anything," shouted Agnes from behind me as she came out of the dining room. "Enough damage has been done this morning in one way or another."

She was dressed in a bright yellow jumper and navy blue slacks. They were creased and shabby as well as, for her, uncharacteristically grubby. She had had a full-length, fawn greatcoat on earlier which had hidden her clothes from view.

"I'm coming to open the front door," she said as she passed by. "I closed it up so I could get Violet back to her chalet without any embarrassment. She's asleep now and we're back to normal again, at least on the surface. Jane's on her way here. We'd like a word with you before you go wherever it is you're going."

When Jane arrived she too was dressed bizarrely; she was wearing Agnes's orange, floral-patterned housecoat over her black suit. Imperiously she motioned us to sit down at the nearest table. It would have been wiser to move elsewhere, to the dining room for example, but she firmly insisted that we were to stay where we were. The two women placed themselves next to each other facing me and I had my back to the foyer, in keeping with what had become their preferred arrangement.

The sun was shining brightly outside and the dazzling beams of light streaming in through the windows had trapped tiny specks of dust floating in the air making everything look worn out and dingy. I observed that the dark green upholstery on the chairs was soiled here and there with a greyish film of dirt now depressingly discernible. On each of the tables there were numerous scratch marks and circular glass stains. The sunshine had drawn my attention to the neglected state of this part of the hotel for the very first time. I had not registered any of this before because I had spent the majority of my time there in artificial light with my eyes directed firmly elsewhere. Violet in her incarnation as Shirley had hit a large, rusty nail on the head. The entire lot needed throwing out or, even better, burning.

"We're very sorry that you had to endure that," said Jane, unbuttoning her housecoat. "We were so busy with the breakfasts that we completely forgot about her. I presume you're okay."

"It was another illuminating experience," I said, tickled inwardly at my apposite choice of words in view of my current musings on my surroundings. "She seemed quite normal. I'd no reason to suspect that she wasn't who she said she was. Shirley, that's the name she gave me by the way. She didn't mention her surname but she referred to her husband as the Professor. She answered most of my questions quite plausibly but I smelled a rat when she talked about the past. It seemed that she was speaking from Violet's perspective too often. I also thought it was strange when she didn't seem to be aware that Wildheath Crags had been transformed into Porterfield Nature Park."

"Violet was having one of her lucid periods when she's in full possession of her faculties," Jane continued. "Earlier this morning she announced that she was going to have a bath and do something with her hair while we were in the kitchen, so we deemed it safe to leave her to it. She had the radio on and was listening to Radio 6...or was it Radio 2? No matter. She must have gone through her wardrobe deciding on suitable clothes but we've no idea why she chose that outfit..."

Agnes, who until then had been staring at the floor with her legs spread and her hands clasped together between her knees, raised her head and looked daggers at her older sister.

"Get to the point, Jane," she scolded. "Mr Lockwood isn't the slightest bit interested in what she was wearing. He's probably more interested in finding out how she managed to stroll past you, Nadia and Joseph and get up to his room."

She turned to me and forced a smile so artificial it was almost comical. Jane shook her head vigorously from side to side and for once seemed lost for words.

"Shirley is the name of her imaginary cousin," Agnes added, while Jane's was still fuming. "She's not a dual personality. Violet invented her as a sort of companion when she was a youngster. I suppose it was someone to talk to when she was out on the moors. She spent hours up there on her own, you see. The Professor is Christopher, or rather what she envisages he would have become if he hadn't died and they'd got married. He's Professor of English at Leeds University. She's built a new world around him. She can even describe his modern-day appearance. He's still handsome of course and looks distinguished, with long brown hair swept back and greying at the temples. She burbles on and on about where they go for holidays, which restaurants they frequent and their favourite programmes on TV. It's her way of coping and it's been like this ever since she was sectioned. She cries a lot and she'll never recover. She's never aggressive or anything like that. Sometimes she sits in a chair with her head on one side, away with fairies. That's when we have to put her to bed."

"What's she been telling you?" asked Jane vehemently, taking over. "She eavesdrops on our conversations. We never know when she's listening or how much she takes in if she is. *And*, despite what Agnes just said, why *had* she chosen that particular suit and, I despair, why did she lift up her skirt?"

"She said she was called Shirley, your cousin and joint-owner of the hotel," I repeated quite calmly. "She said she was here for the day, and she asked if I had been made comfortable after my mishap, and if I was enjoying my holiday."

"I hope you answered 'yes' to both questions," muttered Jane, who was becoming increasingly more fractious.

"Indeed I did," I nodded. "She also told me about you two and Violet..."

"Just what precisely?" snorted Jane indignantly.

"Shut up, Jane!" barked Agnes. "Shut up and let him speak..."

"Among other things about your job in Belgium," I continued. "And that Agnes had contributed to a book on the Ayres..."

"Was there anything else, anything nasty?" Jane broke in again.

"He won't tell us if there was," squawked Agnes. "Use your common sense, woman. Anyway, if there was, remember it came from the mouth of a long-term, psychiatric patient."

"In the persona of Shirley she explained that she had been a close friend of Violet's," I went on before Jane could protest again. "She was so credible and self-possessed, I had no reason to doubt her. Like you two she's very articulate with a broad range of knowledge. She also told me a lot about herself, that is, Violet, in the third person. She brought up the subject of her affair with young Christopher and, before you ask, it didn't differ much from your account, except for the ending... the night he died."

I sat back and folded my arms like an inscrutable interrogator. I had deliberately paused before I delivered the last few words so that I could study their faces. The two sisters remained expressionless and motionless, like statues, as if they had been magically transmuted into stone.

"Go on," said Agnes, suddenly blinking and coming back to life. "You can't leave it there."

"She's made it up," screamed Jane without moving.

"Whatever she said, she's made it all up. She's been telling lies."

"You could be right, Jane," I said sardonically. "She's by no means a reliable source of information, is she? But she also told me that you're writing a novel about Christopher from a working class angle, and she suggested that you'd subconsciously based it on 'The Stone Seat' with the genders of the two main characters who died in the bottomless bog reversed..."

"Nonsense!" Jane sneered. "It's a true story not a novel. Violet's not going to rush out impulsively and start looking for Christopher. She won't end up dying and wandering out there forever..."

"No, but you might..."

"What? Why should I...?"

"Because of your promise..."

"Stop it you two," Agnes bellowed with more than a note of reproach in her voice. "Mr Lockwood clearly knows a lot more than he's letting on. I think we should ask him politely to begin at the beginning."

I sensed that for the first time that week I had gained the upper hand, and I was tired of the obstructive tactics that Jane was intent on using. She had blown hot and cold ever since Agnes came on the scene on Monday afternoon, and I wondered if there was a competitive element between them for my attention – indeed between her and anyone.

"I don't want to meddle in family matters," I said impassively. "Nevertheless you've forced me to become a compliant participant in something that's mushroomed out of all proportion. If I hadn't sprained my ankle last week, would you have even forced yourselves to talk to me? I doubt it but that's irrelevant now. The fact is, without my knowledge, something highly significant had happened to me which affected you. Although I can't prove it – to myself, not just to you two – I appear to have run into a ghost, or at least, that's what you really think, isn't it? And you couldn't believe your luck, could you? I was a captive audience, wasn't I? At first I was delighted that you were providing me with some entertainment and an intellectual challenge or two to make my enforced confinement in the hotel into some kind of pleasant break. I was also flattered, Agnes, that you'd decided to use me as sounding board to test out your thesis on the Ayres when, according to Violet, you were already well aware that most of it didn't hold water. We discussed it the other night and you conceded I was right in my criticism."

Agnes looked away and stared down at her feet again. I turned my attention to Jane who was glaring ferociously at me.

"The most sinister aspect is why you chose to spin out the tragically short biography of a nondescript young man for absolutely no reasons other than those of your own. It was obvious from the word go that someone born over sixty years ago couldn't be the man who brought me down from the moors – but you kept me on tenterhooks right up to the end when you rather stupidly gave me the name of a local jogger. Didn't you guess I'd contact him? You believe it was Christopher, don't you? When I heard the howling, and the next night the scratching, you convinced yourself that I was here as some sort of go-between...between you, Violet and the spirit of Christopher...didn't you? Unless you rigged it..."

"I assume that it's Violet we have to thank for your sudden change of attitude," Jane growled. "How could I have rigged it?"

"The howling on the first night was easy. I was the only person in the building. You were in bed in the chalets and conveniently didn't hear anything. But the scratching would have been more difficult. Whoever did it had to make a quick getaway and the easiest place to hide was upstairs in the attics."

"May I remind you I'm nearly seventy?" Jane scoffed. "I'm also fairly broad in the beam with a large bust, so I'm not very mobile. That goes for Agnes as well."

"I'm not accusing anyone in particular. If I were to, I have to start with Nadia...on both occasions."

The two sisters looked at each other and started giggling. Had I been less well-mannered I would have described it as witchlike cackling.

"That's utter rubbish," said Jane clearing her throat. "It's so far from the truth, it's ridiculous. She's perfectly harmless. She wouldn't dare come into the hotel in the dark on her own..."

"Then it must have been Violet."

"She's out for the count at night," protested Agnes. "You saw for yourself the state she was in on Wednesday night."

"So who does that leave?"

The two sisters, who had been staring at me intently, looked at each other again. Then in one swift movement they moved their heads in concert and switched their attention back towards me.

"Christopher!" they cried in unison and burst out laughing again.

"I'm afraid I regard *that* as '*utter rubbish*', as you put it," I countered. "We're getting nowhere with this argument so let's leave it at that."

"I'm going then," announced Jane, manifestly affronted. "We've lots to do, Agnes. Rooms to tidy, beds to make and we have to help Joseph with lunch."

"I'll be along in a minute," said Agnes wearily. "I have a couple more questions for Mr Lockwood."

We sat in silence contemplating our respective navels until Jane had disappeared into the dining room. As soon as the coast was clear Agnes promptly perked up.

"Correct me if I'm mistaken but Violet's acquainted you with what really happened on that fateful Monday night in November 1971, hasn't she?"

I nodded.

"She *is* telling the truth actually. Jane did something despicable but it was also partly her own fault. You see, Violet had misled father into believing that Edward Lister was her boyfriend when really it was Christopher. She did it to gain his approval and to get him off her back. The last person Daddy expected to turn up at the hotel was the unfortunate, young Christopher and there were no other witnesses to what happened then. Four days later when Christopher's officially declared missing believed drowned, a hysterical Violet attacked Jane frenziedly with a carving knife in the kitchen. She was disarmed by the chef before she could do any serious damage but Jane miscarried an hour afterwards, and Violet collapsed in a heap, never to recover. A week later I got a phone call from Daddy saying he couldn't cope with dealing with his two ailing daughters and running a hotel. He had more staff than we do, but the miserable, old reprobate didn't trust any of them. He was a hands-on manager and he wanted to keep things in the family. He begged me to come home to take care of my sisters. I agreed wholeheartedly, of course, but unfortunately my school didn't. The headmistress gave me a choice in the form of an ultimatum: a week's compassionate leave, no more than that. I resigned on the spot. And before you give me a grilling because I wasn't here when it all took place, it

237

was Daddy who gave me a blow by blow account and I'd no reason to disbelieve him. He wasn't to know that Jane had lied to Violet. That's why he gave the coroner the *facts* but only from his distorted point of view."

A black cloud must have been passing across the sun because little by little the room darkened. Agnes must be about to reveal something portentous, I thought, and I prepared myself for yet another unexpected shock.

"So there you have it, warts and all," she said, holding her arms out with her palms outstretched. "The upshot is that both Jane and Violet want Christopher to have resurrected himself through you. In fact Violet is expecting him to come back at any time. That's the main reason why she left the hospital and came back to live here. You're his messenger. Jane will be able to leave the hotel again, and as for Violet...who knows what will happen?"

"I've got the complete picture now, thank God" I said. "That leaves one final query about this morning's most embarrassing episode. Do you know if Jane's account of the incident on the roundabout when Christopher was a youngster actually took place, and, if so was Violet the little girl involved? That would explain why she lifted up her skirt in my room."

"If you're referring to the bit in Jane's tale where she describes Christopher's first visit to the play area in Oakgrove, well no, it wasn't her. It wasn't Jane either. To my eternal shame, Mr Lockwood..."

The sentence remained unfinished. In one swift movement Agnes pushed back her chair and rushed out of the room.

CHAPTER SIXTEEN

Saturday Afternoon and Evening

In spite of the perturbing drama of my last full morning in Watholme, I was still determined to spend part of the afternoon in the village. After I had recovered from the shock of Agnes's staggering confession and the speed of her hasty exit from the lounge, I returned to my room to find that it had been tidied and the bed had been made. Nadia was cleaning the mirror in the en-suite bathroom. She was humming to herself, and I coughed and tapped on the door gently so that I did not startle her. She had however already seen my reflection and she gave me a delightful smile.

"Hello Nadia," I said slowly, as one tends to do to foreigners. "Please tell Jane that I won't be down for lunch."

She nodded her head rapidly to show that she had understood.

"You go anywhere nice?" she responded.

"Hopefully," I said. "I'll be back for dinner."

A few minutes later she gathered her paraphernalia together and waved goodbye. She had laid out a fresh supply of teabags and sachets of coffee and I was tempted to make myself a drink. I glanced at my alarm clock and it was nearly midday, so I decided against it. The teashops would be filling up by now with weekend tourists and I grabbed my coat and my brolly. It had clouded over when

I got outside and a chill wind was blowing, indicating that winter was arriving early in Watholme. If Derek's cynical joke proved to be based in reality, there would be snow by evening. I made it eventually to the top of High Street and quietly surveyed the scene.

There were lots of small shops and one-room cafés, almost certainly converted from houses in the past fifty years. Every one, except the post office, seemed to have an annoyingly quaint name based on the novels of the Ayres, as I have observed before, but today it seemed that they were more mawkish than ever. I bought half a dozen postcards illustrating various parts of the area, including an old monochrome one of Wildheath Crags which Derek would have approved of. Perhaps it had been taken by his father?

I ate lunch in an old-style bistro. I had toad-in-the-hole followed by rice pudding. It was an excellent meal, spoiled somewhat by an over-fussy proprietor. She spoke with a south-eastern accent and asked where I came from. I told her I had been born and brought up in Watholme and I was making a nostalgic journey from my home in Cheshire. She did not pester me again. It struck me as I strolled back to The Green Man in mid-afternoon that the Dean sisters and a local taxi driver had affected me more than I realised.

When I entered the hotel Andrew was sitting in the lounge reading a magazine. He was wearing the same fawn cardigan he had on at breakfast, but since then he had put on a pair of ill-fitting, shapeless jeans. It seemed that he liked to change his outfits regularly. Three matching maroon suitcases were standing next to his table.

"Is your car fixed?" I shouted across to him as I passed through.

"Yes, thank goodness," he said. "We're off to Sleighton as soon as the ladies are ready. They've nipped out to the shops for some last-minute souvenirs."

"Oh dear, you won't be able to hear the end of Jane's story," I laughed.

He put down his magazine and stood up.

"She *did* finish it last night," he said as he walked towards me. "You asked me to tell you if I understood it. Well, it was straightforward enough but I take your point. It sounded very wordy, like she was reading a short story from an autocue. It was about a working class boy from round these parts who got to the top of his profession. He became Professor of English at Leeds University. He married his childhood sweetheart which happens to be her sister Violet. They visit the hotel regularly. Apparently they were here this morning. We were out so we must have missed them."

I did not comment on his statement or reveal that I had seen Violet. What was the point? We were not going to meet again. It did not occur to me, however, to ask him how he had found out about her social call.

"Thanks for covering for me last night," he went on. "Can I buy you a drink or something as a token of my gratitude."

"It's a bit early for me," I replied. "I didn't have to do anything anyway."

"You gave me peace of mind," he said. "That's worth its weight in gold. How about a bottle of something to have with your dinner?"

I declined his kind offer and we shook hands. We stood silently for a few seconds, as strangers do in these circumstances, since neither of us had anything further to contribute to what was to be our parting conversation. In the end I opted for a well-worn cliché.

"Have a safe journey and enjoy the rest of your holiday," I said as I turned to leave.

"You too," he smiled. "I hope your ankle gets better soon."

I spent the remainder of the afternoon in my room, watching TV and listening to the wind whipping off the hillside. Every now and then a billion and one hailstones crashed against the window. The gods in this corner of West Yorkshire must be easily offended. After a bland dinner (grilled fish and chips with no starter or dessert – I was too full after my huge lunch to eat anything else), I went and sat in the lounge, hoping that I could have a final word with Jane. She did not disappoint me. About a quarter of an hour after I left the dining room she hove into view as if I had summoned her. I could not be sure which direction she came from because I was reading. She was wearing a thick, Arran sweater and black, corduroy trousers which had seen better days; she was carrying a dark blue raincoat over her arm and a folded umbrella.

"I hoped I'd find you here," she said warmly as she pulled up a chair and placed her belongings on the table between us. "I owe you an explanation...no, it's more than that. I owe you a justification for my behaviour over the past week. I don't need to ask you what you must think of me and my sisters, nor how what we've been doing has affected your vacation. We, that's Agnes and me, apologise unreservedly, and we would be very grateful if you'd take those awkward few minutes with Violet no further."

"That's very nice of you," I replied. "I had no intention of doing anything actually. I'm not that sort of bloke. Who would I tell in any case and what would I say?"

She stared at me as if she was expecting me to answer my own question but I merely raised my eyebrows (it was becoming a habit) and smiled.

"I decided to tell you a story to entertain you, as you've quite rightly said," she pressed on determinedly. "However, there was more to it than that. I *am* writing a novel about a working class boy, and I wanted to run a version past you to get your opinion on whether it's good enough for publication. By now you don't need reminding that it's founded in fact. Write what you know about, that's what the experts advise. There's no better place than the wilds of Watholme to set a tragedy, is there? The Ayres did it highly successfully so I followed suit. I've worked out three possible endings which affects the shape of each narrative. You know one of them and we'll call that the tragedy. The second one's a soppy love story in which the hero and heroine end up getting married and live happily ever after. I'm still working on the last one which revolves around a love triangle. It's a mystery thriller in which the jilted lover dies but the police can't work out whether it was suicide or murder."

"Andrew, the guest who left this evening, enjoyed what you told him last night. He was very impressed. That's a vote for the second alternative already."

"That's good to hear but how do you rate the tragedy of Christopher Heath?"

I exhaled sharply and looked away. It was something that had by turns engrossed and infuriated me. How was I to respond without hurting her feelings?

"I'd prefer not to discuss it further," I sighed. "But since you insist, I have a few questions before I can give a verdict."

"Go ahead."

"Who was the little girl on the roundabout who showed Christopher her underwear? Agnes confessed this morning that it was her. Was it her?"

"She was a peculiar, little girl, a blatant exhibitionist. It was her way of competing with me for father's attention. I suppose she also enjoyed frightening little boys by threatening to tell her mother. It backfired on her though. She mistook a short-haired girl for a gullible, fresh-faced boy, and this wee lad-lass reported the incident to *her* mother. Agnes got into trouble and she was smacked by her step-father. We stopped going to Oakgrove after that."

"Did she grow out of it?"

"Yes, as I told you. It put her off boys for life, it seems, and women with short, brown hair who wear trousers."

"Are you being facetious?"

She grinned and rocked her head vigorously from side to side.

"It's pointless carrying on if you're not taking me seriously."

"Don't you think it's funny?" she said, stifling her laughter. "Straight-laced, old Agnes being a flasher! It was she who mentioned women's knickers when you met her for the first time on Monday afternoon. Now you know why!"

"Why did Violet choose to copy her and lift up her skirt in front of me?"

"She's sixpence to the shilling. Perhaps it floated into her mind as she drifted off back into dementia. What's your next question?"

"Okay. Is the ending of your story is based on actual events? I've heard two different versions. Which one is true?"

"Truth is a subjective concept. Therefore the one I told you is true."

"So why did Violet attack you? It wasn't an unprovoked assault, was it?"

"Memory gets distorted and people remember what they choose not to forget," she said evasively, her face contorted as if she was in pain. "Only my father knows what took place when Christopher turned up unexpectedly and he's dead. As for the attack, well, Violet had become unhinged with guilt and sorrow. I bet Agnes told you about the breadknife, didn't she? She's always been jealous of me. I tolerate her because I'm streets ahead of her. I've always kept myself in check. She wouldn't recognise me if I revealed my real self."

"Why did you lie to Violet?"

"About what?"

"Don't play games with me, Jane. You're well aware of what I mean. Why did you lie about Christopher's phone call?"

"I told you a story, Mr Lockwood, to entertain you. I assume Violet and Agnes have concocted some extra details. The fact is it was my father who stopped her going to Manchester, wasn't it? It wasn't me. I was at the cinema. He did it to protect her. How would she have fitted into student society in a decadent, dangerous city?"

I was becoming utterly exasperated by her diversionary tactics. Yet she was quite within her rights to use them. I reminded myself that whatever had happened here all those years ago was, I repeat, none of my business. Yet she owed me some kind of explanation for creating this web of intrigue and drawing me into it. I decided therefore to change my approach.

"Is it true that you never leave this hotel?" I asked less harshly.

"I have to be here twenty four seven," she replied equally cheerfully. "Anyway I've always been something of a recluse, ever since I came back from Belgium. You may have noticed, however, that I'm carrying my mackintosh."

"Have you never been on holiday?"

"I can't leave Agnes in charge and I don't want to go anywhere on my own."

"You could close the hotel and go off together."

"And leave Violet and Nadia? Who would take care of them?"

Yet again she had demonstrated her skill at evading a direct answer and my stomach churned.

"I have one final question," I said resignedly.

"Good, I want to go for my walk before it starts raining again."

"Do you believe that Christopher's spirit has come back to haunt you?"

"It's not me he appears to be haunting, is it?" she declared triumphantly. "It's you. You've seen him. Violet's been waiting for him to come back every day since she came home. That's the major symptom of her present condition. I reckon that's why she went to visit you. She believes it's a sign that he saved you and so you must be some sort of intermediary. He's reaching out to her through you. She believes he's coming back to take her away."

Before I could respond, the room was invaded by the three boisterous, young couples. Jane got up immediately and went over to the bar.

"If you want any more drinks," she said to their ringleader as she filled six pint glasses with lager. "Please ring the bell on the reception desk and my sister will serve you."

In due course she returned to my table and picked up her things.

"Now, you promised me a verdict on my story," she said.

"It's brilliant," I declared enthusiastically, although I was obviously lying.

"Thank you," she beamed. "I knew you'd like it. I'm going out now. I've enjoyed chatting to you this week. It's been good to meet you."

As she paused in the doorway to put on her raincoat, I sat back and asked myself why I could not have been more like Andrew and swallowed everything whole. Regrettably I am not that type of person and, if I were, she might not have gone to the length of giving me the complete picture of her baleful, family tragedy. In essence, her obsession with her so-called novel was to her an act of self-justification, when it could be interpreted more accurately as the manifestation of a guilty conscience and injudicious denial.

"We're all a bit mad round here, aren't we?" she shouted to me as she disappeared into the night.

CHAPTER SEVENTEEN

Sunday

I woke up early on Sunday morning with an aching head. The six young revellers had invited me to join them for what they designated 'a Saturday night drinking session' and the unfamiliar amount of alcohol had dehydrated me. They were third year English Literature students from, of all places, Manchester University, studying a module on nineteenth century female authors. During the summer they had made similar weekend visits to Foleshill, near Coventry, the home of a young George Eliot, and to Steventon in Hampshire, where Jane Austen had spent her early life. They were here to soak up the 'Ayre atmosphere': a tour of the village and an expedition to the moors with a half hour put aside to inspect the bottomless bog. Everything of note had been dutifully recorded on their mobile phones. I did not attempt to keep up with them, but I noted that they had not mentioned Mrs Gaskell, and I wondered if, in their modularised lives, they knew about her, since she was living, so to speak, on their doorsteps. She had been a good friend of Catherine Ayres and she might have been complicit in her disappearance if I were to believe Agnes's version of events. I decided quickly however, not to mention this to either the students or Agnes for obvious reasons: they might have believed her. The cat would have been out of the bag and I would have been responsible.

After a couple of rounds I bought them all a farewell drink and went off to bed. Irreverently they had christened me 'top man' and asked me what I'd done with my life. It was then that I realised that I did not have much to tell that might have been of interest to them. I had worked for fifty years in the engineering industry. I have not married, I have no children and I have never been to any exotic destinations in Africa, South America or the Far East. I was amazed at how dreary my existence has been compared to what they had already accomplished by the age of twenty one. Was this why my week at The Green Man had so captivated me?

Throughout the night the wind had wailed louder than ever before, sending plastic bags and all kinds of lightweight litter cartwheeling down the street below. According to Derek it heralded some imminent disaster. Fortunately I was not staying in this neck of the woods to find out what it might be.

After my final breakfast, I packed what few personal effects I had brought with me and at half past ten I vacated my room and went down to the lobby. It was empty. By the sound of things earlier the students had already checked out, and fittingly I would be the last person to leave. I was determined to savour the moment. I went outside and stood on the pavement. The overnight hurricane had blown itself out and there was a sinister silence pervading the immediate vicinity. There were no people or cars in sight, other than my stationary Honda. Nor were there any stray cats or dogs roaming the street in either direction as I looked to my left and then to my right, and no birds flying around when I carefully focused my attention upwards to survey the bright blue sky. The wispy strands of the cirrus clouds high above indicated that the weather had taken a turn for the better;

something or someone had at last appeased the spiteful weather gods. I closed my eyes and basked in the cool, morning stillness. I was totally alone. Soon Derek's taxi would appear from around the corner and normality would be restored.

I went back inside to be greeted by Agnes, standing behind the reception desk sifting through a stack of typewritten sheets of paper. She was dressed in a sober, grey frock and a purple cardigan and she was wearing rectangular, rimless spectacles. A string of artificial pearls hung around her neck. She was playing hotel manager.

"I'll be with you in a jiffy," she said cheerily. "I'm checking this week's invoices."

I took off my car coat and placed it on top of my suitcase.

"I'll have one last look around then," I said, knowing full well that I did not need to; the features of the each part of the hotel would remain indelibly imprinted on my brain.

Eventually she finished whatever it was she was doing and she coughed politely to attract my attention.

"It's Jane's day off today," she announced. "I haven't seen her since last night so she's probably having a lie-in."

"We said our farewells after dinner," I responded. "I haven't seen her since then either."

She obviously did not know that Jane had gone out for a walk for the first time since Christopher had died, and I did not tell her as I did not want to prolong a now meaningless conversation for both of us.

"This is what you've been waiting for," she said handing me my bill. "We're only to charge you for drinks according to Jane. Will you be settling up with cash or by credit card?"

"Please say goodbye to Violet and Nadia for me," I said as I took out my wallet. "And give my compliments to Joseph. He's a fantastic chef."

"We trust you've enjoyed your stay at The Green Man," she said in a surprisingly formal manner. "We'll miss our little chats of an evening. We'd be very grateful if you'd recommend us to your friends and acquaintances and, if you're ever in Watholme, don't hesitate to pop in and say hello. We would also like to think that you'll stay here again. We hope your ankle mends soon and best of luck at the hospital."

When I had settled my account and she had given me a receipt, she came out from behind the desk and shook my hand.

"Goodbye, Mr Lockwood," she murmured. "Have a pleasant journey home."

I have to admit that I was dumbfounded by Agnes's lukewarm behaviour. It was if she had forgotten the events of the preceding few days or perhaps she was trying deliberately to erase them. I could sense that the implicit message in her detached attitude towards me was the fervent desire never to clap eyes on me again. She had made me responsible for her recent disappointment, when it was she who had forced me into becoming an unwilling, if not entirely innocent, evaluator of her obsession with the Ayres. The fact that things had got out of hand because I had taken her seriously was a gross miscalculation on her part. I did not return her good wishes nor did I express the usual valedictory platitudes. I simply raised my hand and waved at her good-naturedly. Without further ado I put on my coat, picked up my suitcase, my crutches, my walking stick and my umbrella and limped histrionically out of the hotel, fully determined never to return. My car was outside and, after I had stowed my luggage, I sat in the front passenger seat to wait for Derek and his extra driver, Ellis.

The trip home went smoothly and largely uneventfully. Derek took the wheel of my car. We joined the M62 south of Halifax after which it was plain sailing, motorway all the way until the outskirts of Chester. I was worried that we might lose Ellis if we found ourselves in heavy traffic, but Derek reassured me that the escort car, his silver Toyota, had satnav on board.

"You look knackered," he joked as we left Watholme at the beginning of the journey. "Celebratory last night booze-up, was it?"

"Some students invited me to join them," I yawned. "If I had been celebrating, it would've been because I'm leaving."

"You're not impressed with our famous, little village, I take it?"

"There's nothing wrong with the village. It's those bloody women who run the Yorkshire museum of horrors. They've both got a screw loose."

"That's very funny, Douglas. I'll add it to my patter for the tourists."

"I did manage to meet Violet. You were right about her. She's still very good-looking. She must be at least sixty but she looks twenty years younger. And do you know what? She's the sanest of the three! By the way, I saw Jane leave the hotel last night. She was going out for a walk."

It was slow going as the road climbed steadily towards Halifax. The desolate moorland gradually receded when we reached the summit, to be replaced by green fields divided into smaller units by mile after mile of drystone walls. The route took us through several picturesque villages that, like Oakgrove I presume, had sprung up to serve the long demolished woollen mills and factories that had come into existence in the nineteenth and early twentieth centuries. These days they have probably become the homes of people who can afford to commute to Boughton, Halifax or further afield. Derek once again provided the background information. He reeled off fact after fact about each chocolate box lid settlement until we passed through Halifax and I noted, without a word from my chauffeur, that it resembled Boughton and Watholme. The town itself had most likely been established at the bottom of yet another glacial valley and had expanded on all sides to the surrounding hillsides.

When we hit the motorway the steady speed of the car and the rhythmical note of the engine began to make me feel drowsy.

"Get your head down if you want," said Derek sympathetically. "I'll wake you when we reach Chester."

It was my good fortune that Derek had made all the conversation. This meant that I did not need to fill the silences with any of my depressing experiences at The Green Man. Actually I was dreading it. How could I justify to such a down-to-earth fellow what I had allowed to happen to me? I had decided that, if pressed, I would only include a varnished account of Christopher Heath's life and how his death had affected the Dean family. This would have given him a clearer understanding of why Jane had become a recluse and brought him up to date about Violet's fragile state of health. I would also have mentioned that Agnes was doing a project on the Ayres without revealing any details, and how her research was being hindered by having to travel everywhere by public transport. If he had asked about what he had flippantly referred to as the *howlin' and a-scratchin'*, I would have conceded that he had been correct in his inference that I had been dreaming. That would, without a shadow of a doubt, have more than satisfied him.

My moderately-sized, semi-detached house was cold after a week without central heating but it seemed like a castle compared to the restricted space of a hotel room. I did not have much in the way of food in the refrigerator since I had planned to go shopping when I returned from my holiday. I had not foreseen that I might be unable to walk far or drive! I made myself a bowl of tinned soup as a late lunch and ate it standing up in the kitchen so that I could survey the back garden. There were leaves to clear up from the surrounding trees, mainly blown in from other people's gardens, dead flowers to cut down, and bushes to prune ready for winter. It is not a large garden but it is filled with many different kinds of perennial plants and a variety of established shrubs.

Derek and Ellis had not stayed long. Derek complained that he was losing business with two drivers out of action. Had he forgotten that I was about to give him a cheque for a hundred and fifty pounds? I offered them a cup of coffee but they politely refused, although they both went to the bathroom before they left. Surprisingly neither of them commented on my house, as newcomers are inclined to do on first entering. It is very tastefully decorated and chock-full of pictures and objets d'art. My elderly neighbours have often said that it explains why I have not married: there is no need of a woman's touch. I could have made a friend of Derek; he was 'my kind of guy' (to borrow a phrase that those 'with it' students had used). He was forthright, he had a dry sense of humour and, over time, I might be able to talk about myself without embarrassment, which I have rarely before been inclined to do. I shall miss him.

As the day wore on and I sat in the dark in my living room, my mind drifted back to that week with Deans and the alarming and confusing things that had happened. Yet in the familiarity of my castle I was no longer concerned about ghosts, bumps in the night or mentally scarred women. From a familiar vantage point I did not regard it as a precious week wasted, nor did I begrudge the large amount of money I had spent in taxi fares. Rather it had served to fill, albeit temporarily, an ever-expanding hole in my life. I felt suddenly empty inside because I had nothing to occupy my thoughts any longer. I had developed new interests whilst arguing with Agnes, and I had found myself doing extensive literary research which I never had had cause to concern myself with previously. How I envied those young students. In similar vein, Jane had taught me to listen carefully and to question the minutest inconsistency whenever I detected one. 'Detected', yes, that was the word I sought. I had become a literary detective and I had solved my first case by forcing Jane and Agnes to face hard facts. When I went upstairs to unpack my suitcase and go to bed, I found the copy of 'The Stone Seat' which Agnes had given me. It was then that I made the first decision of a new era. I would resume my sparring with the Ayre sisters and read it from cover to cover. It would afford me the opportunity to study for myself how much Jane had used it as the basis for her account of the life of the unfortunate Christopher Heath.

CHAPTER EIGHTEEN

Some Weeks Later

My euphoria did not last long. When I read the first few pages of 'The Stone Seat', I recalled why I had rejected it as a schoolboy. It was awash with obscure Yorkshire dialect which was almost impossible to decipher, and one whole page was in Latin. Scholars and Ayre aficionados alike must have infinite amounts of patience and stamina to endure sentence after sentence constructed in turgid, Victorian English. I regret I possessed neither. I gave up half way through the fourth chapter. It had ruined my appetite for trying any of their other novels, especially 'The Governess' because of its resemblance to Jane Dean's early life.

I had my bandages removed at the hospital a few days after I came home. It was not easy to walk again straightaway since my ankle muscles had weakened considerably but, after a few days of steady progress, I was moving normally. I was soon able to revert to my previous, lethargic lifestyle, gardening notwithstanding, and the memory of the Ayres and even the Deans receded steadily as each day went by. Then came the bolt from the blue. Four weeks after I said farewell to Watholme I received a telephone call from Derek. It was Tuesday.

"I hope you don't mind me ringing you," he said falteringly. "Have you read this morning's paper?"

"It's only twenty past eight," I replied. "I've not got round to it. Why, what's up?"

"Oh dear," he went on dolefully. "I have some bad news. I'm aware that you don't regard it as anything to do with you but after your, er, weird experiences last month, I thought you might like to know that The Green Man burnt down after something exploded on Sunday night, or to be more accurate, the early hours of yesterday morning. It's been on TV and on the radio over here, and in all the local newspapers. Maybe it's not been reported nationally."

"Christ almighty," I yelled in consternation. "Were there any casualties?"

"It's not believed that there were any guests staying there because there were no cars outside, but some of the people who lived in are still missing..."

"You mean Jane and Agnes and Violet, don't you... and dear little Nadia?"

"Agnes has survived..."

We both fell silent. I could hear him breathing heavily. He was probably nervous about disturbing me at such an early hour and unsure how I would react. He might also have been in two minds about ringing me in the first place.

"Thank you for informing me," I reassured him. "Any idea what caused the fire?"

"According to the authorities it's too early to tell but it appears it might have been started deliberately. Agnes has been taken to hospital after inhaling smoke. The paramedics said she kept mumbling something like 'Oh no, what have they done?' Anyway that's the source of the rumour."

"What a bloody tragedy. What a way to go. What a horrible way to die. I hope they were killed by the explosion rather than slowly and painfully by the flames... As if that family hasn't been through enough...and Nadia survives the Kosovo massacres and then gets herself burnt to death. What a bloody tragedy."

"My sentiments exactly, Douglas. I'm sorry you had to find out about it from me, but it'll be less of a bombshell than reading it in the papers or seeing it on TV. And I didn't want you to miss it altogether. Now I come to think of it, would it have been better if I hadn't contacted you?"

"You did the right thing, Derek. Thank you for ringing. I'm glad I gave you my number. I'll keep in touch with events via the media and the Boughton Gazette on the internet. If I don't sound very upset it's because it hasn't sunk in properly yet."

"Life must go on. I'll keep you updated, if that's okay, especially if I hear anything off the record."

It took me a while to absorb fully the harsh reality of what had happened. Two women who I had had intimate dealings with, in the sense that they had taken me into their confidence, were dead, along with an innocent young woman who had sought sanctuary from evil, mass murderers. My memories of sitting and talking with them, no matter how jaundiced, had now become much less tarnished. When I opened my newspaper I ran across the article almost immediately. It was on page five, a short, factual report with an untypical comment by the Watholme Parish Council. It was presented as a straightforward news item rather than a disastrous event, with the emphasis on the damaging effect it would have on tourism.

As more information became available from the press, radio and television, I learned that the blaze had been caused by '*a gas leak ignition*' in the hotel kitchen, which could equally well have been accidental as deliberate.

It had been preceded, a female neighbour stated, by '*a dreadful wailing*' which had woken her up just before one in the morning. She had rushed to her bedroom window to '*ascertain the cause*' and had seen a '*long-haired youth*' running away in the direction of the moors. '*He looked like Jesus*', she said. Another witness, a middle-aged man, did not confirm any of this. He said that that a strong wind had intensified to gale force shortly after midnight and this would have produced the '*screaming noise*' as it roared across the neighbouring moors. It was this man who had summoned the emergency services. Both concurred, however, that a huge explosion had caused the fire, which, fanned by the blustery weather, had quickly caught hold and spread to the outbuildings. A group of ghoulish onlookers had soon gathered to watch '*the conflagration*'. Two people had been seen running into '*the inferno*', after which the roof had caved in and it would have been '*totally impossible for them to survive or to effect a rescue*'. Neither body had yet been found, hence the two people, '*thought to be women*', could not be identified. It was being assumed that it was Jane and Nadia. Agnes, '*the third person who was known to be living there*', had not gone into the blazing building. She had returned to her sleeping quarters to salvage '*some important documents*'. I had no need to guess what they were. It was '*this woman*' who gave the name of a probable further fatality, her younger sister Violet.

The articles were accompanied at first by harrowing photographs of the blazing hotel, which were soon replaced by less dramatic pictures of the smoking rubble. Five days after the disaster the stories petered out altogether. No one, apart from Agnes and me, could possibly have realised the significance of two related elements. The hotel burnt down on the first of November, the exact anniversary of the drowning of Christopher Heath, plus the unsubstantiated sighting of a '*long-haired, youth running away*' from the hotel after the '*wailing*' but before the explosion.

It came as a shock when Derek telephoned me again. It was ten days after the fire.

"There's something else which is going to alarm you," he said after we had exchanged pleasantries. "Do you remember telling me on the journey to Chester that Jane Dean had gone out for a walk on the night before you left? Well, she went AWOL. She didn't go back to the hotel for two days. The police found her wandering on the moors and she wouldn't tell anyone what she'd been doing."

"Or seeing...."

"She never uttered a word about it to anyone, so I'm told. Do you think it had something to do with the fire?"

"I was going to ask you the same question. Do you believe in the long-haired man?" I asked suspiciously.

"I might do but the fire was nearly a month afterwards. If I did believe the rumours, why should the long-haired man tell Jane he was going to start a fire then?"

"Perhaps he told *her* to do it. Have you spoken to Agnes?"

"Agnes is leaving Watholme. The last I heard was that she's going to rent a cottage up in the Dales. She asked the coroner's office to excavate the foundations of the hotel because she was looking for something or other, but they turned her down flat. So she's buggering off. I'm sorry to keep on ringing but the whole village is buzzing. There are at least a hundred and one theories about how and why the fire was started. The big money's on an insurance fraud that went tragically wrong, possibly involving the mysterious young man. As you spent a week getting close to them, I wondered if you'd any suggestions."

"It was actually the other way round, if you recall. No, Derek, I don't have any ideas and I don't wish to speculate. I'm not being bloody-minded but I washed my hands of them when I checked out. I'll notify you if anything occurs to me. If I was a betting man I'd put my money on an accident."

"What about the loony sister?"

"It could be but she's got no form. None of them has, although Violet and Agnes were smokers. It was probably an accident. An oven was left on, the kitchen filled with gas, someone switched the light on or lit a fag. Boom!"

He has not rung me since. Perhaps he thought I was being uncooperative, but I had not lied to him. I spent a miserable week in The Green Man agonising about why Jane was disclosing to me something appalling that had befallen her family, and I have already concluded that I believed it was some form of expiation for what she had done to her friend Christopher Heath and her sister Violet. Why she had chosen me as a confidant is still a bone of contention but she did, and, in the words of Agnes, '*it doesn't matter what you think because it happened*'. The very second I stopped reading 'The Stone Seat' I promised myself that it marked the close of a short and painful period in my life. I was back home, I could walk freely again, and I had returned to my old routine. There were no further reports in the national media, and I did not keep an eye out for the outcome of the inquest. I was reasonably happy and a sense of joyous calm was coming back into in my life. I was sleeping well again at night. I was no longer haunted.

A few days later, shortly before Christmas, my peace of mind was shattered once again by one of the Deans with the arrival of a letter from Agnes. How she managed to obtain my address escapes me, unless she had copied it weeks ago out of the hotel register. It read:

'*Dear Mr Lockwood*

I wish to inform you that I hold you to blame, but not directly responsible, for the deaths of my sisters and the loss of my hotel. This is not casuistry. If you had never set foot in The Green Man they would still be alive. When you told her about the young man who helped you down from the moors, Jane was certain it was the ghost of Christopher Heath that had rescued you. In short, she assumed that he had finally returned from the grave and supposed, quite illogically, that he was reaching out to her through you. This is why she decided to tell you his life story, a story she had written down in the form of a novel. She made a terrible mistake, however. She told Violet that Christopher had come back and Violet believed her every word.

You were doubtless amazed that Violet was living with us in such an unsuitable environment. This is because she had been displaying outstanding signs of improvement in her condition at the hospital over the last few years. She was showing interest in other people and had developed a curiosity for the world in general again. She was speaking fluently, she was reading a lot and taking part in educational activities. She even passed GCSEs in English Literature and Social History. However she was by no means cured. When we agreed to let her come home, we did so in the full knowledge that she had to take her medication regularly or she would rapidly revert to her previous comatose state. Unfortunately we kept her sedated for too long in the busy summer period. In this instance Jane and I were both responsible and to blame for her deterioration. When Jane told her that you had seen Christopher, she did so in good faith but it reopened deeply entrenched wounds. Violet began to brood again about that horrible day when he had his terrible accident and Jane's unforgivable lies.

After you left us we made an alarming discovery. Unbeknown to us, Violet used to wander around the hotel, especially when we were busy in the kitchen or cleaning rooms. She remembered that when we were younger our living quarters were in the attic, and she went up there intermittently. She rummaged around and came across a lot of her old clothes and other things neatly stacked in a trunk. On the morning she came to visit you in your room, she had taken advantage of the fact that we were run off our feet making everyone breakfast. She was so eager to meet you, the man who had resurrected her one and only love. She went to the attic and put on a smart suit deliberately to create a favourable impression, but she utterly failed on that score, as I have no need to remind you.

Moving on to later that day, Saturday night, Jane had decided, God knows why, to go out for the first time for many a year. Perhaps she was searching for the man that she had betrayed to seek his forgiveness. She was gone for two days and came back in an ambulance, suffering from exposure and mumbling incoherently about ingratitude. How Violet found out is still a mystery because we never mentioned anything about it to her. All the hate she had for her perfidious sister emerged in a torrent of verbal abuse and culminated in her accusing Jane of trying to take Christopher away from her for a third time.

This animosity must have festered for, on the eve of the anniversary of his death, she attacked Jane and tried to throttle her. Luckily there was no one staying at the hotel, and Jane was able to get Nadia and me to help calm her down and take her back to her flat. We thought we had sedated her but she mustn't have swallowed her pills. A few hours later, in the middle of the night, there was an explosion in the kitchen and a huge fire broke out. Jane and Nadia bravely tried to put out the flames but they were impeded by Violet, who was throwing things at them like the madwoman she was. She was screeching that Christopher wanted her to do it. I, in utter selfishness, tried to retrieve my research instead of helping them or calling the fire brigade. Although this may sound contradictory, in a way I'm glad Jane and Violet are both dead and I'm finally rid of that millstone of a hotel. I ran the place and did all the work along with Nadia, while Jane swanned around talking to customers and occasionally writing her magnum opus. She gave the impression that she was the brains behind everything but that was her, all talk and no action.

I intend to continue to try to prove beyond any doubt that the Ayre sisters and their father were fraudsters. You will remain sceptical of course, but experience has taught me to validate my evidence carefully, and that I must go to Sicily to find those graves and search through old church or civic records. I expect Violet in the persona of Shirley told you that Jane had forged various documents relating to Sicily such as the letter from 'Aunt Lisa'. Well, Violet told lies too. Whoppers.

And Jane staunchly denied all of them. Both of my sisters were liars, Mr Lockwood. Perhaps it will be the next owners of the land on which The Green Man stood who will excavate something valuable from the old foundations to assist me when they erect their new building. It's ironic, isn't it, that two buildings burnt down on the same site. I shall sell the land which, along with the insurance payout, should give me enough money to keep me in comfort for the rest of my days. It's a prime plot, isn't it, opposite the Ayre monument?

Finally, according to Joseph, our cook, who I touch base with occasionally, mournful wailing has once more returned to the moors after dark, and a mysterious, long-haired man has been spotted on several occasions prowling round the village. It is even alleged in some quarters that this stranger started the fire. Is this a publicity hoax, mass hysteria or does Christopher's ghost really exist? We never did uncover who helped you when you hurt your leg, or who was responsible for banging the dinner gong, howling like a wolf and scratching at your bedroom door, did we? Was it an evil spirit you encountered, a resentful demon who once was Christopher Heath, intent on destroying my hotel and taking revenge on the two women who had caused his untimely death? That's what Violet seemed to imply when she started the fire but we shall never know, shall we?

There will soon be the inquest to deal with. The content of this letter will not form any part of my testimony. Like my father did once, I will simply deal with facts of what happened on that dreadful night. I will not trouble you ever again unless it is to send you a copy of my published book on the Ayres.

Sincerely

Agnes Dean

The letter was undated and there was no return address. In any case I did not wish to contact her. It had, however, served its purpose. I did feel to some extent remorseful, but not because I might have brought about the deaths of three women by inadvertently causing two of them to believe that I had resurrected an evil spirit. It was because I persisted in trying to fathom out why Jane was so keen to tell me about a long-dead, young man, when the answer had been staring me in the face more or less from the outset. I had even guessed as much on the Monday afternoon, although I did not have enough information then on which to make a considered judgement. Instead of continuing on a misguided, egotistical quest to discover the truth, I should have politely declined to participate again or, failing that, at least listened patiently without comment or further exploration. By the same token, in taking Agnes seriously and showing her ill-conceived ideas to be little more than a series of highly implausible speculations, I made, as I predicted, a vindictive enemy. I had proved to her conclusively that her intuitive speculation was rooted in fantasy and forgery as Violet indicated, even if Jane said it was not. Whatever the truth is, Agnes should be eternally grateful that I have spared her from academic ignominy. It was crystal clear why she sent me the letter. She was punishing me to ensure that I have a price to pay for what I did to her during that wretched holiday in Watholme. She has made me a scapegoat for her failing project. If I were to feel ashamed of myself in this respect, it would only be because of the cynical stance I adopted.

On first reading, the letter made me see a few things more distinctly, and it confirmed what I had established before I checked out of the hotel. There was no Ayre conspiracy and there was no phantom, merely the deluded conceptions of two demented sisters. There has been, for many years, even centuries, a bogeyman legend in these parts (which Derek and even Jane alluded to) stemming from the superstitious misinterpretation of a fearsome wailing emanating from the moors whenever a strong wind blows. It is central to the final, horrifying chapter of Elizabeth Ayre's 'The Stone Seat'. In my case, there was only a young man who had fortuitously stumbled across me on the moors, a shy, young chap who clearly wished to remain anonymous. Perhaps he had something to hide. I must have been in shock after my fall which is why I cannot remember precisely how he brought me to safety outside The Green Man. I did see him once more from my bedroom window late on Monday night, and he was flesh and blood, not some shimmering, ethereal apparition. He was out jogging again. It was as simple as that, but Jane blew things out of all proportion because of an unfortunate coincidence. She had interpreted my description of his physical appearance to mean that my rescuer had to be the dead Christopher because of a remarkable resemblance.

As the week progressed and I started hearing things (or was I dreaming?), she erroneously attributed to me a sixth sense, and her conviction that I was some kind of psychic intermediary was utterly illogical. As a consequence she awoke virulent reminders of a twofold tragedy which happened many years ago for which she was culpable, and this affected Violet, whom she caused to visit me in the guise of Shirley, her make-believe cousin. In effect I may have unwittingly revived Jane's guilt fixation at destroying the lives of two ill-fated lovers, not to mention the death of her own unborn child. *She* was a murderer and she was in desperate need of atonement. That was why she was writing her so-called novel about Christopher Heath. It is her confession, even if she could not face the absolute truth that she had lied to Violet on that fatal evening, and as a consequence influenced her father and the official findings of the inquest.

The banging of the gong, the noises in the attic, the howling and the scratching had to be Violet's doing since, according to the letter, she was in the habit of wandering around the hotel unsupervised. It might even have been Jane but, as she said, her age and corpulence go against her. It had to be Violet who caused the fire whether by accident or deliberately on the anniversary of Christopher's death. That cannot have been another coincidence. She had hinted that the hotel needed refurbishing, and most of the furniture should be thrown out or burnt. Perhaps, in her madness, this is what she was trying to do. As for Agnes, she had no emotional investment in Christopher Heath, therefore Jane was ultimately to blame *and* responsible for everything and no one else. I was no more than an innocent catalyst as the unfortunate events began to unravel one by one, and I was miles away when they came to their inevitable, disastrous climax.

When I read the letter a second time, however, I was thrown by the penultimate paragraph and my previously held, rational conclusions evaporated. Why was she implying that Christopher's ghost might actually exist like both Jane and Violet did? Was this pure malice and intended to torment me? Was it to add further weight to her accusation that I had brought him back to life, and that I was ultimately to blame for the fire in which three women died? It was then that I began to revise my frame of reference, and I re-examined each separate, paranormal episode. It is a fact that some mysterious person helped me from the moors but it has never occurred to me until now how he knew that I was staying at The Green Man. I did not tell him. It is a fact that Jane went white as a sheet when I described him to her. This prompted her to tell me all about a man who had been dead for over forty years. Would she have done so otherwise? I saw him twice more, once in the street outside the hotel, and again when his face appeared in my bedroom window. That was uncanny. Was Agnes admitting that she had heard the gong and the howling when she had previously denied it? Was she lying to cover up for Violet's regular walkabouts or was it, as she was now indicating, the work of a malevolent phantom – or a poltergeist? What about the scratching at my bedroom door on the Wednesday night? There was no sign of the perpetrator when I opened my door, and I had seen for myself that Violet was asleep in her chalet. Lastly, the first news reports of the fire stated that a female eyewitness had caught sight of a long-haired man running away from the scene. Did he – Christopher – start the fire as an act of revenge against Jane, who had caused his death by lying? Now Agnes had supplied new elements to this bizarre occurrence, the multiple sightings. To add to this wealth of incidental evidence, I have to include Jane's unexplained disappearance on the moors. She had to have gone out in search of Christopher because she, like Violet, believed in ghosts. Millions of other people believe in the existence of ghosts, and I most definitely had undergone several baffling, if not supernatural encounters. Above all, the date of the fire is of paramount significance, the anniversary of Christopher's death. There is one other factor that also perplexes me: the similarity of the Ayre's stories 'The Stone Seat' to the life and death of Christopher Heath, and parts of 'The Governess' to the thwarted ambitions of Jane Dean. Are they somehow eerily connected?

I am therefore left with this puzzle. I am a man of science and I should not harbour these uncertainties. Ghosts are a human being's fear of the finality of death and a manifestation of the hope that the soul lives on forever. Christopher's spirit does not roam the moors, forever howling. His lifeless body lies at the bottom of a deep swamp as nothing more than a rotting skeleton. This is what common sense tells me, but not my gut feeling. Did I actually meet the ghost of Christopher Heath and did he vengefully burn down the hotel and murder Violet, Jane and Nadia?

Since I have no close friend to share my ambivalent thoughts, a good friend who will not laugh at my insecurity like Derek did, I have written down my account of the weeks up to the fire in an attempt to make sense of them. Sadly I have failed. That leaves me with but one course of action to put an end to my quandary: to return to Watholme and search for Christopher Heath just like they do in ghost hunting programmes on TV. I will choose a stormy day, one that is wet and above all very windy. I will take my waterproofs, my new walking stick and a torch with me. I will drive past the blackened remains of the Green Man and park my car opposite the bottomless bog and the stone barriers. From there I will work my way upwards to what is left of the intimidating Wildheath Crags, even if it means continuing after dark, until I have covered every square inch of that 'blasted heath'. I will take great care not to trip and fall. I will call out his name when the wind howls and summon him to appear. If he does not, I will have my answer...but what do I do if he does appear? The wind and the rain are not the ideal conditions in which to ask a malicious phantom about why he chose to help me in my hour of need and then went on to destroy without mercy those who loved him...

I am being absurd. Is this what Jane tried to do but obviously failed? Despite my attempt to rationalise these perplexing experiences, two crucial mysteries will always remain unexplained, which will forever form the source of my fraught, confused state of mind and determine how much of what I was told is true and how much is fiction, particularly as Jane and Violet Dean have accused each other of being inveterate liars.

First, who *was* the long-haired man? He is not known in the village but he has been seen by different people on a number of times since he came across me on the moors. If he is Christopher's ghost, why did he rescue me, or to put it more succinctly, why did he choose me in particular to intrude into the lives of the Deans? That is the biggest mystery unless it is that the Deans chose to believe, for some reasons only know to themselves, that I had indeed resurrected a former friend and lover, unaware that I might have unleashed a terrible monster. If so, by the same account, why did they choose me? What is so special about me?

I must accept that there is, as yet, no rational explanation beyond doubt for what took place during my week in Watholme. I have done all that I can by offering an alternative explanation for the mysterious deaths of three women, one which a coroner would not entertain. I am unable to go further because Jane and Violet Dean are dead. It has to be someone else's responsibility to separate the facts from fantasy about Christopher Heath's ghost, just as it will be if Agnes Dean ever publishes her foolish claims about the Ayres sisters. Or are they, I fear, one and the same thing?

Acknowledgements

Thanks to Gill Alderson, Pauline Cheetam, Brian Horton, Stuart Lund, Peter Snow and Georgina Wright for their invaluable support and advice in reading and editing parts of this novel.